T0408835

THE RIGHT PLAYER

Kandi Steiner

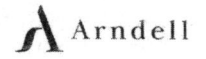 Arndell

Arndell

Keeperton Australia acknowledges that Aboriginal and Torres Strait Islander people are the Traditional Custodians and the first storytellers on the lands of which we live and work. We pay our respects to Elders past, present and emerging. We recognise their continuous connection to Country, water, skies and communities and honour more than 60,000 years of storytelling, culture and art.

ALSO BY KANDI STEINER

A Love Letter to Whiskey
(Coming Fall 2026)

Love of the Game series
The Wrong Game
The Right Player

CHAPTER 1

Belle

His face looked like a potato.

I never noticed before. Maybe it was because I wasn't used to seeing him in the morning light. Maybe it was because, under normal circumstances, he would pat my ass and kiss my cheek on his way out the door, and I'd roll over in bed and sleep for another thirty minutes before dragging myself out of the sheets that smelled like him. Maybe it was because *normally* when I kissed that dumb potato face, I was so distracted by his lips that I didn't care.

Maybe it was because for the last year and a half, Doctor Jordan and I had an understanding, and that was all that mattered.

He had a busy schedule as a pediatrician and wasn't looking for anything serious. *I* had sworn off anything resembling a relationship long, long ago. What we both *did* want was steady, reliable, mind-blowing sex.

And for those reasons, we were a match made in heaven.

I had a firm three-date rule — meaning, no guy made it past three dates with me. That was just enough time to have some fun without catching any serious feelings. But with Jordan, we'd had an understanding. We didn't *date*. We didn't have deep, long conversations. What we had was casual sex without anything more demanded of us.

Jordan was tall and lean, athletic, built like a golf pro. He always dressed like a doctor. You know what I mean — khakis, polos, long sleeves under a sweater vest, his golden hair always gelled and swooped to one side. He had what I liked to refer to as a news broadcaster smile, wide and bright with too many teeth, but I much preferred what that mouth did under my sheets. And he even wore these wire-framed glasses from time to time, mostly when he was reading something, that just topped off the whole look.

When it came to me and Jordan, I didn't need much.

I didn't need flowers. I didn't need Valentine's dinner dates. I didn't need to meet his family. I didn't need his time, or attention, or anything other than a great lay on a consistent basis.

And he never asked anything of me, either.

When we were together, we talked briefly, maybe ate a late-night dinner or had a bottle of wine while we joked around, ended our short time together with a romp in the sack, and then we went about our day to day without having to answer to anyone else.

It was perfect.

And now, the potato-headed motherfucker had a girlfriend.

He was ruining *everything*.

"I really am sorry," he said for the fortieth time that morning. It wasn't even seven yet and the jerk was dressed and ready for work, teeth brushed and breath minty-fresh, his white coat laying over the arm of my sofa and waiting to transform him from average good-looking guy to smokin' hot doctor.

I, on the other hand, still hadn't cleared the sleep from my eyes.

Jordan folded his hands between his knees, leaning closer to where I sat across from him. "I didn't expect it to

2

get serious with Ella. I mean, *neither* of us did. We met at the conference, and we both thought it would just be a little fun, but... I like her, Belle," he said, looking at me like the dog he was about to kick out of the house. "I really do. And she wants to take it to the next level."

"The next level," I deadpanned. "Meaning, the level where I get booted."

He grimaced. "Don't think of it like that."

"How else am I supposed to think?" I huffed, tossing my hands up in the air.

"I don't even know why you're upset," he said. "We've never been exclusive. We've never even gone on a proper *date*. Surely, you didn't think this would last forever."

I ground my teeth, but to his credit, he didn't say it with even a slight hint of annoyance or pity or arrogance. It was a genuine, accurate statement, as if he was reminding me that the shirt I was wearing was blue.

The fact of the matter was that had this been the version of me that existed even a few months ago, I wouldn't have batted an eye at him calling off our little arrangement. If anything, I'd known it was coming — eventually. He told me about Ella when he met her, and they'd been hanging out just as consistently as we had. It didn't bother me, and again, had this been a few months ago, I would have wished him luck with his new girlfriend, biting my tongue against telling him that he was likely going to end up with his heart broken, and then I would have saluted him on the way out the door and made a silent bet with myself as to when he'd walk back through it after he and his precious *Ella* broke up.

But the me who existed *now* had been slowly waking up over the past few months and realizing that everything around me was changing.

Except for me.

My best friend was getting married. My party friends were all settling down into relationships. The few single buddies I still had were dispersing, either moving to different cities or slipping into varying levels of alcoholism that I did not find cute or appealing. All my previous friends with benefits were locking themselves down, losing my number, politely asking me to take them off my *for a good time call* list.

And then, there was me.

Belle Monroe.

President of the Single Forever Club, and newly removed from my position of Hot Doctor Jordan's Favorite Fuck Buddy.

"I guess you just couldn't help yourself," I commented after a moment, meeting his gaze. "Had to get in one last round before you locked yourself down, huh?"

Jordan's neck turned red, and he cleared his throat, looking away from me ashamed. The motherfucker had called me at almost midnight last night. And normally, I wouldn't care.

But normally, he wouldn't be dumping me the very next morning before I even had the chance to make a cup of espresso.

I made a mental note, jotting this down as just another prime example of why the three-date rule is essential.

Jordan stood, grabbing his white coat off the arm of the couch. "I *am* sorry, Belle. You know I care about you."

I held up a hand, cutting him off before he could say another word. "Don't."

"Why does it make you so uncomfortable to hear that? We've been..." He paused, waving a hand between us. "Doing whatever *this* is for over a year now."

"*This* was a fun arrangement, one that mutually benefitted both parties."

Jordan heaved a sigh at that, looking out my floor-to-ceiling windows at the Chicago skyline being dusted with the morning sun. "Well, I guess it shouldn't hurt too bad to lose me, then."

My cold heart defrosted a bit at his words, and I met his disappointed gaze like a dog with her tail between her legs.

But I didn't have anything to say.

I'd shut out the possibility of *anything* resembling love a long, long time ago. Love, I'd learned, was a trap. It was a glitter-covered black hole that would swallow you up and spit you out and leave you shipwrecked and alone time and time again. The only way to avoid that kind of heartache was to not participate at all, to cut all strings before emotions had the chance to form.

That was how you kept yourself safe.

And no one could change my mind about that — not even hot, sensitive, caring Doctor Jordan.

Jordan watched me for a long moment, waiting, like he wondered if his words had struck some chord with me. He watched me like maybe this was the day I would confess all my feelings.

But I just sat silent.

Resignation found his features, and he nodded, something of a smirk on his lips as he leaned down long enough to press them to my forehead. "Goodbye, Belle," he whispered.

And when he was gone, I threw a pillow — a throw pillow, funny enough — at the door he'd walked through.

A growl ripped from my throat, and I ran my hands back through my long, strawberry blonde locks, tucking them behind my ears and grasping the back of my neck. I let my eyes close and attempted the stupid breathing technique Gemma had taught me for work-related stress situations, but after about sixty seconds, my annoyance grew to an unavoidable boiling point.

I jumped up from the couch, not even bothering to get dressed before I was in the elevator and on the way down to Gemma's.

Gemma was my best friend in the world, my life-keeper both at work and outside of it, too. Our mutual hate for algebra had brought us together in high school, and the mountains of shit we'd had to climb over together had bonded us for life. We'd been through more hell together than most married couples, including the death of her asshole cheating husband, and the metaphorical death of the man I always thought would be *my* husband — but that's a story for another time.

If *anyone* in this world was my soul mate — it was that girl.

She only lived a few floors below me in a skyrise downtown, a blessing I had been grateful for after her husband passed away. At first, I worried she'd move even farther out of town or, worse, stay in the three-bedroom suburbia hellhole of a house she'd lived in with Carlo.

But thankfully, she'd loved my idea of living in the same building. *It'll be just like college*, I'd told her, and that's exactly how it had been.

Having her just a few floors down meant I could bombard her every morning before work, or on any given evening when I wanted someone to watch trashy TV with or to go out on the town with. I was always there for her, and she was always there for me — only a few dings of an elevator separated us.

Of course, *now*, when I barged into my best friend's place, she wasn't the only one there.

Zach looked up from his tablet with a smirk when I blew through the front door of Gemma's condo, one that looked similar to mine, though hers was smaller, had less windows, and was peppered with little specks of proof that a man lived here with her, too. She'd let me decorate her new space when she moved in, which you would think would have been a given, since I was an interior designer, her best friend, *and* her boss. But Gemma was a list-making, highlighting, organizing, clean-until-the-knuckles-bleed kind of gal, and it was both a feat and a high honor getting her to give up control to me.

"Ah, good morning, Belle," Zach said when the door shut behind me, looking back to his tablet. "Coffee's hot."

"Where's Gemma?"

"Shower," he said, lifting a brow when I didn't immediately move for the coffee pot like usual. "Everything okay?"

"No," I said on a huff, flopping down at the kitchen island in the bar stool next to his.

I liked Zach. I had since the moment I met him. He was sexy in the ex-football player, self-made entrepreneur, boy-next-door kind of way. But right now, I was irritated with every man in the world.

I grabbed his tablet and tossed it across the room and onto the couch.

"Hey," he said, but it was on a chuckle and with his smile still in place.

"Jordan just dumped me."

Zach's brow rose again. "I didn't realize you were dating."

"We weren't."

"Oh."

I blinked.

Zach smiled uncomfortably.

And then I sighed, dragging a hand over my face. "You don't get it."

"Afraid not," he agreed on a laugh.

"What good are you, Zach?"

"Oh, he's completely useless," Gemma said, joining us from the bedroom. Her long, brunette hair was still wet from the shower, dripping water over her petite shoulders as she bent to press a kiss on Zach's cheek. "But I keep him around because he's kind of cute."

"Kind of?" Zach said, pinching her side. Gemma giggled and pretended like she wanted to get away, but in the end, she wound up wrapped up in his arms and leaning her hip against his thigh. She was a tiny little thing in his arms, and they might as well have had heart-eye emojis for faces in that moment with the way they looked at each other all gooey-ooey like.

I wanted to gag as much as I wanted to swoon. Those two were so cute together it made me nauseous.

Gemma had been through enough shit to last her a lifetime, and I truly believed Zach was her reward for never calling her ex out on his transgressions. The motherfucker *cheated on her* and then told her he had terminal cancer. She never even got to call him out on it. Or rather, she *chose* not to, deciding instead to stand by his side as he lived out the last months of his life.

The other woman showed up to the funeral, and Gemma didn't kill her.

File this under reasons Gemma is better than me.

It took a while for her to heal, but a couple years ago, I convinced her to get on a dating app. The premise was that she would take a new, different guy to each Chicago Bears home game. Gemma was a season ticket holder, and to be honest, I hated sports so much that this was partly to get her out and dating again, and partly to make sure it wasn't *me* who'd have to fill the seat next to her.

Zach was the lucky bartender who overheard me getting Gemma in the dating app scene, and he volunteered to be her practice round... but let's just say he wasn't satisfied with just one game.

And the rest was history.

Now, the lovebirds were just months away from their wedding, and as much as I missed my best friend having nothing but time for me, I loved Zach so much that I couldn't even be mad.

They were meant for each other.

"Why don't you have coffee in your hand?" Gemma asked me.

"Because I had a different wake-up call this morning. One in the form of Jordan dumping me."

Gemma frowned. "Wait, you guys were dating?"

I slapped my forehead. "Come on, bestie. You know more than anyone that I don't date."

"Right... so..." Gemma might as well have had smoke coming out of her ears as she tried to figure out my dilemma, and she and Zach shared confused looks.

I sighed. "We've just had an arrangement, that's all. For the last year and a half, we've been banging on a consistent basis. Do you know how hard it is to find an insanely hot guy who is also educated, professional, and single? And then, to find that kind of guy and him *not* be anxious to tie you down? He was perfect." I pouted, flopping back in my seat. "And then he went and got himself a girlfriend."

I mumbled under my breath, and Gemma quirked a brow. "What did you just say?"

"I said *stupid potato-headed motherfucker,*" I repeated.

Zach barked out a laugh. "Do all your exes get adorable pet names like that?"

"He's not my ex," I defended, crossing my arms. "And I didn't realize his head looked like a potato until he was breaking up with me."

"Convenient timing," Zach commented.

I flicked him off.

"Hey, I'm sorry," Gemma said sincerely, leaving Zach's arms to wrap hers around me, instead. She rested her chin on my head as I leaned into her. "Did you tell him you didn't want to split up?"

"No. What would the point be? He wants something serious."

"And you don't?" she asked. "Even after more than a year of being with him?"

"You already know the answer to that."

Gemma sighed softly, patting my arm. Not many people in my life knew the real reasons why I blew off any kind of relationship, but Gemma was one of them. The poor girl had known me and my college ex well. We'd always hung out with her and Carlo, a little foursome, double dating all the time and being all sorts of adorable.

Gemma and Carlo got engaged right after college, and I just *knew* that the ring from Nathan would come next.

Instead, he dumped me.

You're a good time, Belle, but you're not exactly the girl you take home to Mom, if you know what I mean...

And I did. I knew exactly what he meant.

I was good for sex, for fun, for spring break and frat parties and wearing his jersey number while I screamed like a little fan girl in the stands at every single game he played. And that's where the road ended for me.

It was a moment in my life that could have destroyed me. And, though I'd deny this to anyone who ever asked, other than Gemma — it *did* break me. For months, I wallowed and felt sorry for myself and tortured myself replaying every minute of my and Nathan's relationship. I was searching for clues, for the errors I made, for what I did that was so bad that he had filed me into a category where a ring and a wedding and a little house full of babies was off the table.

But then, I had an epiphany.

What if that *wasn't* the life I was supposed to live?

What if, for me, my work was my husband? What if I could have all the fun that goes along with being in a relationship — the laughter, the butterflies, the excitement of kissing for the first time, the knock-your-socks-off sex — and then... because the shoe fits... I take myself out of the picture, and continue living my kick ass life while the guy goes off and gets hitched, or whatever he decides to do?

Suddenly, being the *good time girl* didn't sound so bad.

At least, that's what I told myself.

From that moment on, I wore that badge of disgrace like it was a badge of honor, instead.

I wouldn't be just a good time, I would be the *best* damn time any guy I hooked up with would ever have.

And I'd never have to make them breakfast in the morning.

"It's his loss," Zach chimed in. "On to the next, right?"

"Damn straight. And," I added, holding up one finger. "I'm going to add doctors to my list of *Never Ever Ever Again Will You Ever Even Consider This Type of Man.* Right under football players."

Zach smirked at that. He was the only football player I tolerated, and it was probably because he didn't play anymore — except to toss the ball around with Gemma, which was actually quite adorable.

"Oh! What if..." Gemma framed my arms, and I knew before she said another word that I wouldn't agree with whatever she was about to propose. "What if we got *you* on a dating app."

"I'm already on them."

"I mean to actually *date* someone," she expanded. "I know you're El Presidente of the Single Forever Club, but what if you just *tried* it?" Her expression softened. "A lot has changed since college, Belle. You don't have to play this role forever."

"I like this role," I pointed out, tapping each finger. "Hot sex, no one telling me what to do or where to be, no one complaining that I work too much, no one to take care of when they're sick or just being a baby."

No one to take care of me, I thought, but I didn't say that one out loud.

"Maybe it's time for a change," Zach offered, and the word crawled over me like a dozen cockroaches, eliciting a shiver and grimace.

Change.

Why does everything have to change?

"It's fine," I said finally, hopping out of my seat. I grabbed a mug from the cabinet and filled it to the top with black coffee. "By the end of the week, I'll have a new, hotter, better player in rotation." I pointed at the two of them. "Just you wait and see."

Gemma offered a sad smile, she and Zach exchanging looks that told me more than their words ever could have.

I knew they wanted to see me happy, but what they didn't understand was that fairytales weren't for everyone.

Some of us got stuck with the kind of stories that made you cry, that made your heart ache, that made you hold your knees to your chest and rock in a corner, or drown your sorrows in a bottle of wine or two.

That was the kind of story I had the leading role in, and I'd accepted it long ago.

I just had to find the next chapter.

Makoa

For as long as I could remember, there had only been two things I ever wanted in my life.

Love, and football.

The latter was easier to admit, and, I found out early in life, far easier to accomplish, too. I started throwing a ball as soon as I could pick one up, and then my dad was tossing spirals to me in the backyard, teaching me how to catch and protect the ball while I ran. My parents put me in Pee Wee football as soon as they could, and from there, I was unstoppable.

I was picked out as a top receiver by my Pee Wee coach, played in the Pop Warner Super Bowl twice, and even received the MVP Award the second time around. I went on to play varsity all four years of high school, and then four years as a starting wide receiver for The University of Hawai'i at Mānoa. Being six foot five and two-hundred-and-twenty pounds made me one of the tallest and largest receivers in college, and that, combined with my record-breaking high-catch seasons, got me the national attention I needed.

At twenty-two years old, I was drafted to the San Francisco 49ers in the second round of the NFL draft. I mostly rode the bench in my time there, but I made the cut, made the *team* each and every time.

And now, five years later, I was moving into my new home, in my new city, and getting ready for my first season with my *new* team.

The Chicago Bears.

Not that my position was set in stone, yet. As a free agent, I was essentially guaranteed training camp and pre-season games, a tryout more than an official position.

But I wouldn't accept anything less than a spot on that team.

I was manifesting it in every way I could — by wearing the team colors, practicing every day in the "off" season, running drills and watching tape, getting close with the players I could to learn the ins and outs of the team. And, as the cherry on top, I didn't just rent a place in Chicago. No, renting insinuated that I was temporary, that I was only staying for a little while.

Instead, I bought a condo.

Buying instead of renting spoke volumes. It was a symbol of my commitment. It was a good omen to turn my dream into fruition.

It was a mark of my permanence — in this city and on the Chicago Bears team.

"*Braddah*, look at this view!" My sister, Oliana, ran to one of the floor-to-ceiling windows overlooking Lake Michigan, pressing her face right up against the glass. She was the youngest of our siblings, seventeen, about to enter into her senior year of high school. Her jet-black hair hung to her waist, the front twisted into a braid that wrapped around the crown of her head. "The water is so *blue*."

"It is nothing compared to home," my mom said, dabbing the corners of her eyes with a tissue I knew was too damp to do anything anymore. Oliana looked a lot like our mother, both with the same wide, chocolate-brown eyes and dimples. Both thick with curves that all my sisters had. My eyes favored my father's, a sort of golden maple syrup, but I had the same goofy smile as my mom, one that took over my entire face and usually garnered me a comment or two every time I met someone new.

Your smile is so unique!

You have such a big smile!

That's the best smile I've ever seen!

Of course, I learned early on that to the girls, that smile told them one thing and one thing only.

Put this guy in the friend zone.

But we'll get to that.

"Ah, my beautiful Mah," I said, pulling my mom into my arms and kissing her temple. "No more tears."

"I just cannot believe you'll be so far from home now." She sniffed. "California, not bad. But this... this *city*... in the Midwest?" She shook her head, like the mere thought of it made her want to faint.

"Did you forget that you have a spare key *and* a card that you can book as many flights as you want to on?" I smiled. "Consider it a second home for all of us."

"You say that now. But when I start showing up every other weekend, you are going to take my key away."

"Never," I said, giving her another kiss before I joined Oliana at the window.

"I'm moving here with you," she said just above a whisper, her wide eyes sweeping over the lake, the pier, the sky-rises in the distance. "I'm so tired of the island. The same food, the same people, the same ocean and mountains and trees. I mean, just *look* out there." She shook her head. "It's like a whole new world."

"Good luck telling that to Mah, *Tita*," I said, elbowing her ribs. I usually reserved the Pidgin nickname for when she was acting particularly sassy, but I knew more than anyone that she loved the nod of acknowledgement that she was a spitfire.

She smirked. "Yeah, I'd be getting *lickens* if I so much as muttered it."

"Yes, you would," Mah said from behind us, where she was surveying the rest of my new condo skeptically. If it wasn't home, it wasn't good enough in her eyes. "So do not even think about it."

Oliana and I shared knowing looks and smiles, and then I followed Mah around the apartment, making a mental list of things I'd need while she made an *actual* list that included far more than mine. It didn't bother me, though — that was just who my mom was. And being that I was her only son, and a not-so-discreet mama's boy, it didn't surprise me that she wanted to make sure I was taken care of before they got on the plane back to Hawai'i.

Remember how I mentioned that love was the other thing I'd always wanted? Well, I had my four sisters to thank for that — and maybe my mother and father, too.

The Kumaka family was a big ball of sleeve-worn emotions, and we always had been.

I grew up watching Disney movies and rom-coms and talking about my feelings far sooner than any other boy or man I'd ever met. I remembered my first crush, in the second grade, when most boys could only focus on video games. I, on the other hand, stayed up all night before Valentine's Day making a homemade card for the blue-eyed girl in my class who always smelled like citrus and vanilla. I gave it to her along with a box of chocolates and a teddy bear that I used my hard-earned chore money to buy.

She'd called me sweet, thanked me, and told me I was one of her best friends.

Friend.

It was the first time that word scarred me, but it wouldn't be the last.

Maybe it was because I had the best mother in the world, and a father who treated her like gold. Or maybe it was because I had four sisters — two younger than me, two older than me — and a fierce determination to protect and respect every single one of them. Maybe it was because I grew up hearing everything a girl wanted from a guy, and I thought I knew exactly what I was doing.

Turned out, I didn't know anything.

I could blame it on my big, goofy smile. I could blame it on the fact that I made it a point to get to know a girl before I asked her on a date. I could blame it on the cheesy lines I'd learned from the movies, the ones that always made my sisters swoon but seemed to make girls in real life grimace uncomfortably. I could blame it on my incessant need to ask permission before I even attempted a kiss, but regardless, one thing remained true.

I was always the friend, never the *boy*friend.

No, it seemed *that* title was reserved for the assholes who made all my girl "friends" cry and question their worth. The guys who didn't text back quickly or call the day after a date, the ones who flirted with other girls right in front of the one they were dating, the ones who said they wanted something "casual" and made it seem like the girl was cool if she was down for just having sex without expecting anything more.

Somewhere along the way, I got my wires crossed on what girls were *actually* looking for.

Of course, when I signed with the NFL, my trouble with love shifted. I went from being perpetually friend-zoned, to never knowing if a girl I was on a date with wanted *me* or *my money*.

Luckily, it never did take long for the truth to come out. A gold digger showed her true colors early enough on that I never really risked being hurt. My first run in with this type of woman was with Kelly, a hot little volleyball player who I nearly did a backflip for when she agreed to go out with me. But she showed me her real intentions regarding our "relationship" at a dinner with a few of my teammates and their wives in San Francisco, when she commented about how big one of the wives' wedding ring was and said to me, in front of everyone, *mine better be bigger*.

Zariyah was next, and she made it perfectly clear when she hinted that plastic surgery would be *a lovely Valentine's Day gift*.

And my favorite, the beautiful, sweet, seductive Lucia, who truly had me fooled for about two months — until the first time we had sex, and she asked me *so how does this whole sugar daddy thing work?*

So no, as much as it hurt, it wasn't hard to figure out if a girl only wanted me for the things the NFL had brought into my life — whether that be money, fame, or connections. And honestly? I was glad for it. Those women showed me everything I didn't want. They taught me the hard lessons that put me on guard, that gave me pause and reserve with every woman I'd met since then. I was spared a lot of disastrous relationships by seeing those signs early on, and I was tougher for it.

Still, I longed for a true connection, one that was more than friendship and one not born out of a desire to use me for the dollar signs or possible fame attached to my name. I wasn't well-known enough in the NFL to cause a scene yet, but I planned to be one day, and I wanted someone who would support that without exploiting it.

What I *really* wanted, more than anything, was a girl who didn't know me at all, one who I could tell my *own* story to, one who loved me for me.

What a sap, right?

The main point here is that while football was second nature to me, love was a fleeting fantasy.

But being in a new city, with a new team? Everything felt possible.

Maybe my dream girl was hidden somewhere in the Windy City.

Maybe, with a little luck, I'd find her.

And maybe, with a *lot* of luck, she wouldn't have any clue who I was.

"Where are you going to sleep tonight?" Oliana asked, scrunching her nose as she looked around at the empty space.

"I'll get an air mattress."

Mah's eyes lit up with horror. "No, no, no! You cannot sleep on an air mattress, that is terrible for your back."

"We used to sleep on air mattresses all the time when we had sleepovers!" I reminded her.

"You were ten. And about half the size you are now."

"It's just for a little while, Mah," I assured her with a smile, framing her arms in my hands. "I'm meeting with an interior designer later this week, and she's one of the best in the city. Next time you visit, it'll be a whole new place."

"*I* could be your interior designer."

I chuckled. "I know you could be. But hey, this is a new city with a new style. It's different from anything we've ever seen. Don't you think it'll be fun to let one of the Chicago professionals who knows the city best bring that new style to life?"

"I think no matter how *professional* they are, there is nothing Chicago has that is better than Hawai'i."

Oliana laughed, wrapping her arms around our mother to replace mine. "Alright, I think it's time we leave Makoa and let him settle in. We should get some sleep, anyway."

"But our flight is not until ten in the morning!"

"*Makuahine*," Oliana said, giving her a look. "Kiss your one and only precious son goodbye and let him breathe for once in your life."

Mom pouted, but I had her smiling at the end of a bear hug. And with a whispered *Mahalo* in my little sister's ear when I hugged her, we said *a hui hou* — until we meet again — and then I was blessedly alone.

The sun was slowly setting over the city and the lake, casting everything in a warm, orange glow that leaked into my empty condo like rays from heaven itself. Slowly, lights twinkled to life, and I smiled, feeling the newness that only a big move like this one could ever bring.

Moving to California had felt big, but not in the same way. After all, I was still close enough to catch a short flight home to feel the culture and warmth of Hawai'i, and my family was never too far away. But now, I was in Chicago — the Midwest, a city as unfamiliar as the team I was about to play with.

And I had something to prove.

I wasn't a rookie anymore, but I was new to the team, and that meant I'd have to fight for my spot. While the veterans could rest easy knowing they had a position regardless of what happened in the pre-season, I would have to work my ass off at training camp just to earn the chance to play and show coach what I could do if he kept me on the team.

And I wanted more than just *a* position.

I wanted a *starting* position.

Or, at the very least, enough playing time to surprise anyone who picked me up for their fantasy football team.

I blew out a breath as the last of the sun dipped away, the city somehow coming more alive in the twilight. There was no ocean, but instead, a grand lake that seemed to hold completely different possibilities. The palm trees had been traded in for European buckthorns, the albatross for starlings, the city on the bay for the city by the lake.

There at the window in my empty condo, despite the mounting pressure I felt and the uncertainty of a new home, I smiled.

Because everything was different.

And I was ready for a change.

CHAPTER 2

Belle

I smiled at the family photo in my hand, one from a couple with their newborn child in their lap. The little threesome was situated right in the middle of the grand family room I'd designed and decorated for them in the spring when Mrs. Albers was pregnant. That family room was only a small piece of the re-design, as I'd done everything from the nursery to the master bath. But that room had been the one that stole my heart.

There was always one.

It was a bright room, with all white walls and white trim, save for the cherry wood beams that sprawled across the ceiling. We'd chosen a gorgeous French empire chandelier for the centerpiece of the room, and it hung over the luxurious cream push pin couch that the family sat together on, the new parents smiling down at their baby. The Albers already had an impressive art collection, it was just moving those pieces into the right place that made everything come together, like the Kara Walker silhouette pieces hung in symphony over the couch.

What I loved most about that room was the fireplace.

Ever since I first studied interior design, I'd been fascinated by the concept of Hygge. It's a Danish word that essentially means cozy, warm, safe and comfortable — at least, that was always my interpretation of it. You could make a room Hygge by using low, warm lighting — like candles and fireplaces and chandeliers, as opposed to bright fluorescent or white lights. Add in some cozy blankets, plush furniture, hot tea, and some board games, and you've got the Hygge effect.

Looking at the picture of the Albers made my heart squeeze and float on butterflies like no man had ever accomplished in my life. I didn't fall in love with men. I fell in love with homes, with rooms, with spaces that would play host to memories for years to come. The Albers would put up a Christmas tree in that room. Their baby might take her first steps there. Mr. Albers might doze off on the couch one cold Sunday afternoon, with his sock-covered feet being warmed by the fireplace.

With the right eye, the right furniture, the right art and curtains and rugs and plants and tables and vases and candles, I could take a room from *just a room* to an entire experience.

That was the magic of interior design.

I was still smiling at the photograph when my office phone rang, Gemma's extension lighting up the little green bulb next to her name.

"I've got your eleven when you're ready," she said when I answered.

"You can send them in. Still on for lunch at Suko's?"

"*Yes,*" she answered desperately. "I'm famished."

"I'll make this quick," I promised.

Tucking the Albers's photograph away, I stood, smoothing down my pencil skirt and checking my lipstick in the large mirror across from my desk. It played off the windows across from it, making my little corner suite feel even bigger than it was, and filling the room with soft, natural light.

I stood in front of my desk, hands folded in front of me and a smile plastered on and waiting. My eleven was a new client, and I didn't know much about them other than they were new to the city and had bought one of the penthouse condos in the newest skyrise in Grant Park. My mouth was already foaming thinking about the views of Lake Michigan and the pier and the downtown skyline.

I hoped they'd give me full reign to do whatever I wanted.

I heard Gemma's soft laughter on the other side of my office door before she pushed it open, holding it for our new client.

And when he stepped through the arch, he sucked up all the air in the room with one giant, dazzling smile punctuated by two deep dimples.

Aside from that smile, the man was an absolute beast.

He was the kind of tall that towered, his broad shoulders held high and straight, his chest barrel-shaped and straining against the fabric of his suit. That suit was the only thing light about him, covering him in a soft, harbor gray. Everything else was dark — his pitch-black hair cut into a short fade, his warm brown skin almost golden in the natural light filling the office. At first glance, while he smiled down at Gemma, even his eyes appeared dark.

But when they lifted, when they met my own, I saw the sparkling golden honey they truly were.

"Well, Ms. Monroe will take over now," Gemma said. "You're in good hands, Mr. Kumaka."

"Thank you, Gemma. It was a pleasure meeting you."

God, even his voice was somehow dark and delicious, the kind that made your fingers slip under your panties on a late-night phone call. His face was boyishly handsome and strikingly severe at once, like a walking art piece that would make you stop and tap your finger to your chin, pondering what the artist's intent was.

Gemma quirked a brow, still staring at Mr. Tall, Dark, and Sinfully Handsome. "I swear, you look so familiar..." She chewed her lip. "I can't quite place where I know you from."

Mr. Kumaka shifted a bit. "Maybe we knew each other in a past life. I've always felt like I was a hawk." He smiled, and I didn't know why I realized in that very moment how different that smile was from Jordan's. It was endearing, a little crooked and wide and flashy, but it suited him in a way I couldn't put into words. "Maybe we flew together."

Gemma returned the smile. "Maybe we did."

She gave me a wink on her way out of the office, one that to anyone else would have looked like a fun exchange between boss and assistant. *Have fun, good luck, see you for lunch!* But since we'd been best friends for decades, we had a whole conversation with that wink.

Um, do you see how hot this guy is?

Look at his freaking muscles!

That smile, I've never seen anything like it.

He's so tall and big. I bet he could throw me around like a rag doll.

And I bet you're going to do whatever it takes to find out if that's true.

I smirked, and then the door shut, and I slipped into business mode.

"Mr. Kumaka," I said, extending a hand for his. "I'm Belle. Welcome to Monroe Designs."

"Lovely to meet you, Belle," he said, taking my hand in a handshake that was equal parts firm and gentle. It made me tingle, thinking what else that hand could do. "And please, call me Mak."

"Mak, huh? Not exactly the first name I expected to be paired with your last."

I gestured to the handcrafted leather and teak chair in front of my desk, and let my eyes linger on his fingertips as they unfastened the button of his jacket before he sat.

"It's short for Makoa."

"Ah, that makes more sense." I took a seat behind my desk, folding my hands on the sleek marble top and squeezing my arms together just enough to put my subtle cleavage in prime viewing. "So," I said, picking up his file. "You're new to Chicago. What brought you to the Windy City?"

"Work," he answered casually, and the way he watched me was as if he expected me to already know the answer to the question I'd asked.

"And if I remember right from what Gemma told me about your email, you moved here from Hawai'i, right?"

His smile sparked to life again, and I found I liked it more and more each time I saw it. "San Francisco, actually. But yes, I was born and raised on Maui." He frowned a little. "You really don't know who I am, do you?"

"Should I?"

He wet his lips, pink tongue swiping out just long enough to catch my eye. "I just never know. I'm..." He paused, like he was hesitant to tell me the truth. "I'm in real estate, and with you being in the field..."

I chuckled. "I assure you, I don't keep up with the high-profile real estate agents in Chicago, much less the ones across the country. Now, if you were a *Broadway* star?" I grabbed a pen to make notes in his file, pointing it at him briefly. "*Then* you might have a stalker alert."

"Theatre girl," he said with an appreciative smile. "What's your favorite show you've ever seen?"

I scoffed. "You can't pick a favorite show. That's like being asked to pick a favorite child."

"*Hamilton* is mine. Hands down."

I jotted down a note in his file, sitting back with the pen still in hand and what I'm sure was a shocked expression. "Is that right? You see it with the original cast?"

"The only way to see it."

"Agreed," I echoed, and a new appreciation for him grew in my belly along with a desire to see what was under his suit. "Gun to my head, I'd say *The Color Purple*."

Makoa nodded, lips pressing together as respect twinkled in his eyes. "LaChanze is incredible."

Surprise found me again. "Indeed, she is."

I chewed my lip, basking in the golden wheat field rays of Makoa's stare as I tried to figure him out. "So," I said, tapping my pen on each fingertip. "A theatre-loving, possibly famous real estate agent from the west coast."

That earned me a chuckle, one that I longed to hear again.

"And now you're looking to build a home in the Midwest."

"And somehow make it *feel* like home, too."

I nodded. "I think we can make that happen." My eyes had a mind of their own, and they trailed Makoa greedily, my knees squeezing together where I had them crossed.

When I met his gaze again, it was just as hungry as mine.

"You're in the new condominium in Grant Park, right?"

"I am."

"I haven't seen it yet," I confessed. "Not the inside, anyway. I know it's not what we originally discussed, but... perhaps we could move this meeting there, just so I can get an idea of what we're working with past the photos you sent in."

"Are you sure?" Makoa frowned, and damn it if he didn't look even hotter with those brows bent together, with that little wrinkle between them. "I don't want to put you behind schedule."

"It's no problem at all," I decided, and I stood to finalize the choice. Gemma would understand, especially if I brought her back some ramen.

Double especially if I came back with a full description of what Mr. Kumaka here looked like under the suit.

"I'd love to see the space in person, and get a little more feel for who you are," I said.

Makoa's lips crooked up at that, and he stood with me, fastening his jacket once more. "Lead the way."

I smiled.

Oh, I will, Mr. Kumaka.

Hopefully all the way to your bed.

Except, there was no bed.

In fact, there was *nothing* in the massive condo, aside from twenty or so unpacked boxes, a single folding chair, and an air mattress right in the middle of the living room.

"Sorry, I should have warned you," Makoa said, grabbing the back of his neck sheepishly as he looked around the empty space. "It's kind of a mess."

"I think you have to have more than just a folding chair in order to make a mess," I commented, cocking a brow. "Are you waiting on the movers?"

"Nope. Afraid this is it."

"No furniture, no art..." I dragged a finger over a few of the boxes on my way to the windows, which had a view that put mine and Gemma's condos to shame. "But hey, I guess this isn't so bad."

"Not the *worst* view in the world," he echoed, sliding up beside me, and I smiled when I realized he was watching me, more so than the lake. His jacket brushed my bare arm, and I chewed my lip, wondering if he'd take me up against this window, or bent over his kitchen island, or hell, I'd even let him lay me down on the stupid air mattress — which,

28

judging by this place alone, he was *entirely* too rich to have slept on for even one night.

But before I could turn and make a move, Makoa put space between us, sliding his hands into his pockets. "So, want the full tour?"

Does the tour include the master shower where we both get naked?

"Lead the way," I said instead, using his own words.

To my dismay, Makoa was a complete gentleman as he showed me around his new home. It was a three bedroom, two-and-a-half bath, with a living room, dining area, sitting room, and one of the most beautiful modern kitchens I'd seen. It had an extra room that was more open and a bit smaller than the rest, one that could be used as an office or in-home gym, if he wanted.

As we walked, I made notes in my phone and in his file, took measurements, listened as he told me what he liked, what he didn't like. I was thrilled to hear him mention his love of wood and warm lighting, since most of the modern condos I designed were all about bright light and minimalistic design. Makoa, on the other hand, wanted to fill his new home with art and color and warmth.

"I want it to feel like home, not just for me, but for anyone who comes through the door." He wrinkled his nose as we rounded our way back to the kitchen. "The last thing I want is for it to feel like a model home, or like something not lived in. Does that make sense?"

I smiled. "It does. You don't want people afraid to sit down on your plush white couch or feel like they can't use the hand towels in the bathroom."

Understanding bloomed in his eyes. "Exactly."

"I'm surprised you don't have even one piece of furniture, or art, or décor," I mentioned, eyeing the boxes. "You were in San Francisco for a while, weren't you?"

He cleared his throat. "I was young," he said. "And a little more focused on... other things."

I smirked, because he and I both knew *other things* was code for girls, and with a face and body like that, I didn't blame him one bit.

I just hoped to be first in line to welcome him to Chicago.

I had to chuckle to myself at his comment at being young, like it was past tense. His file revealed his age — twenty-seven — and at thirty-two myself, I felt a little like a cougar imagining what his massive hands would feel like wrapped around my waist.

Then again, a body like his and money like the one it took to buy a condo like this told me Makoa's age didn't have anything to do with how grown he was.

"Have no fear, Mr. Kumaka." I looked around the space, design ideas dancing in my head like a ballet troupe. "When I'm done with this place, it'll be everything you wanted and more."

"I don't doubt that."

His voice was a low rumble, one that had my neck heating when I turned to meet his gaze again. Now that the tour was done, the measurements taken, and the design imagined, there was nothing more to discuss — not until I could draw up some samples, at least.

I had a feeling we'd have a lot more fun without words, anyway.

It wasn't my usual style, to sleep with a client. Then again, *most* of my clients were couples or families or corporate assholes who didn't stand a chance.

Mr. Kumaka was in a completely different category.

And I filed him right under *fair game.*

Perks of being your own boss.

Makoa's eyes slipped to my lips, and I sucked in a hot breath with an unwhispered *yes* reverberating through me. I couldn't wait for him to touch me. I couldn't wait for us to bust through the niceties on the pretense of being professional. I wanted his mouth on me, and I wanted to devour all of him.

"At the risk of being too forward," he started, stepping just an inch closer to me.

I held my hands at my sides with every ounce of willpower I had left, waiting for his move.

"Could I take you out to dinner sometime?"

My next breath was a cold one, and I blinked, wondering if I heard him correctly. "Dinner?"

He nodded, and then immediately looked like he regretted the question. "I mean, of course, if that's not appropriate... I'm sure you don't normally date your clients." His eyes widened. "Not that it would be a date. Well, I mean, it *would* be a date. At least, I'd like it to be a date. If you'd be interested." He swallowed, and I could almost see the little voice in his head telling him to shut up. "In that."

I couldn't help the smile that curled on my lips, or the giggly schoolgirl feeling that flowered in my stomach watching this grown, tall, incredibly cut man stumble over his words as he asked me out. In one instant, he'd gone from this enigmatic suit-clad mystery, to a blushing high school boy.

Part of me was pissed that I'd have to wait, noting that there was no time quite like the present.

The bigger part of me was flattered, and curious, and intrigued.

"You don't have to play this role forever."

Gemma's words drifted through my mind like smoke, but I blew them away with the next breath, reminding myself that as much as everything around me was changing, my view on dating never would.

But if Mr. Kumaka wanted to wine and dine me before I took his pants off?

Well... why not?

"Dinner sounds nice."

He blew out a breath. "Yeah?"

I giggled. "Yeah. Unless you just talked yourself out of it in the time it took me to answer."

"Contrary to my performance just now, I assure you, once I commit," he said, inching a little closer, just enough that his cologne washed over me in a subtle rush of spice and oak. "I commit."

That word made me want to sprint out of his condo and slam the door in his face, but I hoped that commitment he was referencing would be to my orgasms, and convinced myself that was the true underlying meaning.

"So, dinner."

"Dinner," he echoed.

"Tomorrow night?"

He couldn't hide his surprise, or the goofy grin that was quickly becoming my favorite thing about him. "Tomorrow."

I smiled, letting my eyes trace him one last time before I grabbed his file off the counter.

"One more thing," he said before I made it to the door. When I turned to face him, his eyes were wary. "Do you like football?"

"*God*, no," I answered quickly, practically spitting out the words like a bad bite of food. I watched him carefully, hoping like hell I wasn't about to miss out on what was sure to be a fun romp just because I didn't like to watch guys throw balls into hoops and score goals and shit. "That's not a problem, is it?"

His smile slipped back, easy and confident, and something sparked in his eyes. "Not at all. In fact, it's perfect."

I narrowed my eyes on a confused smile. "Okay, then."

"Until tomorrow, Ms. Monroe."

My name on his lips left me with a shiver when I walked out of his door.

And I was already counting down the minutes until I'd see him again.

CHAPTER 3

Makoa

"**B**ro, you're the only guy I know who wants to *hide* the fact that he's in the NFL," Colby said to me the next night, and even on the phone I could imagine him shaking his head, his thick curls bouncing with the notion. "It's like an instant free ticket to Kinky Sexville, and you just tore yours up."

I chuckled, putting him on speakerphone so I could finish mixing the ingredients for the coconut-crusted crab cakes I planned on making as an appetizer for dinner. "You forget that a ticket to *Kinky Sexville* isn't exactly what I'm looking for."

He scoffed. "Oh, that's right, you want the ticket to *Love Me Forever Island*."

"Don't laugh. You don't have a right to laugh at that anymore, not now that you're *on* that island."

"Yeah, well, sometimes I miss the trips to the other place."

"Bullshit," I said, calling him out. He'd married Cheyenne last year, and I knew as well as anyone that he was head over heels for the girl. I was waiting for the day he'd tell me he had a kid on the way, because as much as those two banged, it couldn't be long now.

"Okay, fine, you're right. But still, I don't see any reason why *you* shouldn't be wearing your damn jersey around the city right now. And carrying a football, too. Maybe a couple-hundred-thousand dollars in one hand. Oh! Let's make you a billboard that says *New to Town, Seeking Pussy, Have Enough Money to Fly You to Bahamas.*"

If he were here, I'd have punched him in the arm. Colby was my closest friend, and had been since we played offense together at UH. He was one of the fastest running backs I'd ever played with, and he'd be one of the best in the NFL now, too, if it hadn't been for a career-ending tackle our senior year.

It was one of the risks we took every time we stepped on the field, but we always hoped it'd never be us.

Colby had taken it in stride, though, and he'd effortlessly moved into a career in finance and bought a house in the suburbs of California with Cheyenne. When I was in San Francisco, we saw each other at least once a week.

I had no idea what I was going to do without him.

Especially in a new city, with a new team that I'd have to prove myself too.

"I'm telling you, Colby," I said, setting the bowl of crab cake mixture in the fridge to cool as I moved on to make the salad next. "This is my chance. This girl... she's the kind who knocks you on your ass from the first time you lay eyes on her. And she's smart, and funny, has her own business."

"And she has no idea who you are."

I smiled. "The gods are smiling down on me."

"Do you really think you can keep it a secret? I mean, once you go to training camp, your name is going to be all over that city."

"We don't know that," I pointed out.

"*I* do. Because you're going to kick ass and then it'll be all the Bears fans can talk about."

"*Da* Bears," I corrected, embodying the fandom.

"Whatever."

"Well, lucky for me, Belle doesn't seem remotely interested in football. I asked if she was a fan and she practically gagged."

Colby chuckled. "Well, that should work out great, if you do end up dating her. I'm sure she'll love the lifestyle that comes with being a pro player's girl."

I paused where I was cutting tomatoes. "Damn. I didn't think of that."

"Hey, who knows if it'll even get that far, right?" he said before I could go down the rabbit hole. "Just have some fun tonight. Wine and dine, get laid, you know — the fun stuff."

"You and I both know I don't fuck until the third date, but I like the sound of the first two."

Colby sighed at that. "You're the strangest man I know."

"Tell me something I haven't heard all my life."

"Okay, how about this. You not telling her who you really are yet? I just want to go on record and say I think that is a terrible idea. But after the hell these girls have put you through over the past few years..." He paused, and I wondered if the horror reel of my ex-girlfriends was playing in his mind the way it was in mine. "I don't blame you. Just be careful, man. Any relationship that starts on a lie..."

"I know," I said, not wanting him to continue that thought. It was one I'd beaten into my skull enough times over the past twenty-four hours that I didn't need him to echo it. Besides, it wasn't like I was going to keep it from Belle forever... just until I could gauge more about who she was and what she wanted. "She should be here soon. I'll give you a call later this week."

"Good luck, my friend."

When we ended the call, I checked on the ribs cooking in the oven — far from my favorite way to cook them, but without a grill on my patio yet, I didn't have much choice. I'd gone out after my workout this morning to buy everything I'd need to make dinner, but had decided not to get more than *just* what I needed — mostly because I knew Belle had a plan for my place, and I didn't want to screw that up.

Thinking about her being here often, putting her hands on everything, leaving her mark... it gave me a thrill I couldn't explain.

I checked my appearance one more time in the mirror, turned on my favorite jazz playlist, and finally let my mind wander to the absolute enigma that was Belle Monroe.

When I walked into Monroe Designs, I expected to discuss furniture. I expected to answer questions about what kind of art I was into and the importance of chi. I expected to cut a check and set a date for the work to begin. I expected it to be a quick meeting before I had lunch and my first off-season, low-key workout with Gerald, the second-string quarterback for the Chicago Bears.

I never expected Belle Monroe.

The moment her office door swung open and I found her on the other side of it, I was swept up in everything that she was. Her long, copper-blonde hair had been curtained over her shoulders, which were tall and straight, her bow-shaped lips curved into the slightest smile as I stepped into her space. Her eyes were a delicate mixture of crystal blue and sea green, and they seemed to shift in the light, changing back and forth between the colors until I decided there was no possible way to say which one was more dominant. She was tall, and slim, and she held herself with an air that told me she took no shit.

The way I was instantly enamored by her was unlike anything I'd ever experienced.

It was like I'd been struck by Cupid's arrow.

I wanted her from that very first moment, and when she didn't recognize me, when she didn't question my lie about being in real estate, the hope in my heart bloomed like a lotus out of the mud.

Now, I realized I was getting ahead of myself. I just met the girl. She could be boring, or a psycho, or completely pleasant but just not my type. We could be looking for different things. She could change her mind and decide dating a client is completely off-limits. It was ludicrous that we hadn't even had our first date and already I was imagining her as my girlfriend.

But for the first time in years, I didn't feel like a piece of meat, and I didn't feel like just a friend, either.

It was like the Goldilocks *just right* girl had fallen into my lap, like the reason everything before now hadn't worked out had just walked into my life.

And I was determined to play my cards right so I could keep her long enough to find out if I was correct in that assumption.

I blew out a breath, adjusting the cuffs of my long-sleeve button-up so they rested just below my elbows, and praying like hell that I could pull tonight off. Volunteering to cook dinner for us had been a risky choice, but I wanted to impress her — and if I knew anything by my first meeting with Belle, it was that she'd seen it all.

If I wanted to impress her, I'd need to play my *best* cards first.

Unfortunately, as much as I loved to cook, I wasn't exactly *good* at it. My mom had joked all my life that I could burn water, and though I'd managed to perfect a few recipes over the years, I mostly tended to ruin the dishes I attempted to cook, no matter how I followed directions.

But tonight, I'd taken care with every ingredient, double and triple checking temperatures, marinade times, and notes for how to get every dish just right.

I crossed my fingers I wouldn't fuck this up.

My phone buzzed with a call from the front desk downstairs, and they let me know Belle was here. I told them to send her up, and then I tried not to pace a hole into my new floor as I waited for the knock to come.

When it did, I double-checked the setting one last time — candles lit, jazz playing, city lights acting as the perfect backdrop. The Kalbi ribs made my entire place smell like home, like we were having a luau on the island, and with a satisfied smile, I smoothed my palms on my jeans and opened the door.

Belle stood on the other side, holding a bottle of wine in one hand and a small clutch in the other. She was dressed to kill in a short, form-fitting black dress, the neckline plunging, straps barely two centimeters thick where they wrapped over her shoulders. Her hair was swept back in an elegant up-do, the side of it braided, and with all that hair pulled back it was impossible not to notice the length of her neck, the dainty necklace resting around it, the small diamond centered right in the middle of her chest. Her eyes were smoky and sultry, the curl on her pink lips one that told me before she even said a word that she was trouble.

And *God*, did I want whatever trouble she was.

"You going to let me in, or should I open this out here?" she asked, her brow arching on a wide smile as she held up the bottle.

Be cool. Be cool. Be cool.

I stepped to the side with an easy grin, taking the wine from her, and before I could speak, Belle slipped easily into my arms, lifted onto her toes, and pressed a kiss to my cheek.

"It smells amazing in here," she said, pulling back just as easily, like it was nothing, like our bodies pressed together and her lips so close to mine hadn't affected her, whereas they'd left me dizzy and reeling.

"I'm making an island specialty, Kalbi ribs," I said, guiding her farther inside before I shut the door behind us. "Hope you're not vegetarian."

"Vegan, actually," she said, setting her clutch on the kitchen island before she turned to face me.

All the blood drained from my face.

Shit-shit-shit.

"Oh God, I'm so sorry," I rushed out. "I should have asked before I... *fuck.*"

I was already on my way over to the oven, like if I tore the ribs from the rack and tossed them off the balcony, I could somehow still save this date. Luckily, Belle laughed before I could get my hands in the oven mitts.

"I was kidding," she said, folding her hands easily on the granite island, her eyes dazzling and playful. "Ribs sound amazing. Although, I'm kind of wishing I would have waited to see what you were about to do to rectify the situation."

I chuckled, backing away from the oven and swiping my brand-new bottle opener off the counter next to it. "You were about ten seconds away from seeing a rack of ribs go flying off the balcony."

"Would have been a most unfortunate night for some unsuspecting Chicagoan down below."

"Indeed. No matter how delicious these things are, I don't think they'd feel great falling on your head from thirty-seven stories up." I nodded to the bottle before opening it. "Thank you for the wine, by the way. You didn't have to bring anything, but I appreciate it."

"It's the least I could do," she said, biting back a smile as she surveyed my condo. "Especially since you went to so much trouble to host."

"Are you making fun of my dinner table, Ms. Monroe?" I asked when I finally wriggled the cork free. I watched as she took in the setting, which was nothing more than two giant boxes covered by a tablecloth in the center of the living area.

Those boxes were the ones with all my football memorabilia in them, but that was a little secret I'd keep to myself.

I'd also picked up two plush cushions for us to sit on, placed on either side of the boxes, like we were having dinner in India or Japan. It was all I could do without any furniture, but when I'd set it all up, I'd actually kind of liked it. And I'd at least bought some flowers for the middle of the make-shift table, along with a candle on either side.

"Not at all," she said, taking the glass of wine I'd just poured for her. She kicked off her heels, looking back at me over one shoulder. "But I hope you have a blanket somewhere, otherwise you might get dinner and a show."

I frowned, confused, but when Belle gestured to her tiny dress, realization hit me like a defensive lineman.

Fucking idiot, how was she supposed to sit on the floor in a dress?

"Fuck, I'm sorry," I said, rushing over to the pile of boxes along the wall. "I do have some blankets." I murmured the next part more to myself. "I just have to *find* them."

Belle chuckled, and I felt her hand wrap around my biceps as I shuffled boxes around. She squeezed until I stopped and turned, and then those blue-green eyes danced in the candlelight as she looked up at me.

She took a long, deep breath.

I mirrored it, letting her calmness soak into me.

"It's okay," she said, her eyes still captivating mine. "You go back in the kitchen and do whatever needs to be done in there. I'll look for a blanket. Deal?"

How the hell did she do that?

How did she calm me with just one look, one breath?

God, she was gorgeous. That was all I could think as I stood there, staring down at her, the candlelight playing with the shadows in her eyes.

After a moment, I nodded, stealing her glass long enough to take a sip of wine before handing it back to her. "Deal."

Her eyes heated in approval, and she took her first sip of wine from the same place I had, licking her lips as if she'd tasted mine on the glass.

The sight of her tongue sweeping across her lips sent a bolt of electricity right to my cock.

I cleared my throat, stepping past her and back into the kitchen where it was at least twenty degrees cooler. "So, Belle Monroe, interior designer," I said, picking up where I'd left off working on our salads before she'd arrived. "How did you end up owning your own firm?"

"I think I learned relatively quickly when I was interning that I didn't like working for anyone else," she answered, opening the first box against the wall and sifting through it. She balanced her wine in one hand while she looked with the other. "It just felt stifling, to be told what I could and couldn't do, which jobs I could take on, to have all these limitations. And not just as an intern," she added. "Even the associates had to work within parameters."

"Something tells me you're not the kind of girl who colors inside the lines."

Her eyes sparkled when she flashed me a smile. "Far from it." She took a sip of wine, setting her glass down long enough to move that box to the side and open the next. "So, as soon as I graduated, I took out a business loan to start my own firm. I already had clients lined up at the door, so it wasn't long before I was able to pay off that loan and start netting a profit."

"That's really impressive," I commented, genuinely, my hand hovering over where I'd been mixing all the salad ingredients in a mixing bowl.

"Thank you," she said, and then she whipped a blanket out of the box she was digging in, smiling at me victoriously.

At least, until she recognized the logo on the blanket.

She wrinkled her nose as my heart stopped and kicked back to life. "The San Francisco 49ers," she read, heaving a sigh. "God, you're a sports nut, aren't you?"

Relief found me in my next breath.

She really didn't have a clue.

I lifted a hand. "Guilty. Not to mirror your question yesterday but... is that a deal breaker?"

"No," she said on another sigh, but this time it was with a smile. "Just seems to be the kind of people I surround myself with. Although... is this a football team?"

I chuckled. "It is."

"Well, we're going to have to convert you to a Bears fan. I say this only because my best friend — you met her, my assistant, Gemma? — well, let's just say she might be the *biggest* Bears fan, and she'd have a fit if I was hooking up with a guy rooting for an enemy team."

Shit.

I poured the salad into two bowls, lightly mixing in the dressing. "Well, lucky for us, they're not in the same division," I said with a smile. "And we haven't hooked up yet."

There was something in her smile at the word *yet*.

Still, my attention was still on the fact that her best friend followed the Chicago Bears. That could potentially be an issue in my little plan. I tried not to sound too interested when I asked, "So, Gemma's a big fan, huh? Does she keep up with all the players?"

"Oh, I'm sure she does — not that I ever ask. But the girl has at least half a closet of jerseys with different names on the back," she said with a laugh, draping the blanket around her shoulders before she picked up her glass of wine again. "Although, she's been a little pre-occupied planning her wedding that's in a few months. Haven't heard her talk much about football this season."

"Ah. Tying the knot," I said, telling myself to be cool. The chances of her friend knowing a trade from a different division who barely had any playing time on the field was slim.

At least, until training camp.

Deciding I'd cross that bridge when I got to it, I set our salads down on the tablecloth-covered boxes, gesturing for Belle to sit with me. "Are you the Maid of Honor?"

"I am, indeed," she said, taking a seat and covering her lap with the blanket.

And damn if she didn't look good wrapped up in my old team's colors.

"Excited?"

She smirked, but something in her eyes told me that wasn't the word she'd use. "I guess. I mean, I'm happy for her, I really like her fiancé, and I know *she's* happy — which she deserves to be after all the shit she's been through. But... it's just hard. Everything is changing. I can't just show up at her place and demand she go out with me, or surprise her with a bottle of wine and some popcorn for a girls' night in." She shook her head, like she'd already said too much. "I'm sure that sounds selfish."

"No," I said quickly. "It sounds honest."

She smiled, shrugging as she picked up her fork and stacked her first bite of salad on it. "Honesty isn't as shiny as everyone makes it out to be."

I swallowed, but before I had the chance to feel guilty about my *own* dishonesty, Belle took her first bite of salad.

And then her face puckered like she'd bit into a lemon.

"Mmm," she said, smiling, but it didn't take a genius to see how it was forced.

I took my own bite, grimacing along with her. "Shit," I said. "I think I put too much vinegar in the dressing."

"No, it's good," Belle said, taking another bite.

I laughed when her face wrinkled so hard it made her shiver.

"Here, give me that," I said, reaching for her bowl. "I have crab cakes for an appetizer. Let's skip the salad."

"I really like it!"

She tried defending her bowl, but I stole it from her grasp, already up and halfway to the kitchen when I said, "It's okay. I guess I should have warned you... I'm not the *best* cook." I dumped our bowls into the sink to tend to later. "But these crab cakes? They're going to blow you away."

Spoiler alert: the crab cakes did *not* blow her away.

I'd added too much flour to the mixture, which made them tough and dry. Then, I'd nearly burnt the ribs, cooking them past the fall-off-the-bone point I'd been aiming for, and landing us somewhere in the zone of *just barely edible.*

I knew cooking dinner was a risk, and that risk had *not* paid off.

To her credit, Belle laughed through it all — including when I realized I hadn't bought any steak knives to help with the ribs situation. So, instead, we tore them off the bone with our teeth, getting sauce all over our faces, which somehow made Belle even more enticing than she already was.

Not only was she gorgeous, and funny, and driven, but she was also chill and down-to-earth. She rolled with the punches and made light of it all.

I drank up every word she said like it was the most expensive bottle of wine I'd ever tasted. She told me about her travels all over the world, how that was how she found inspiration — seeing new places, talking to strangers, visiting restaurants and open houses in other states and countries. That shifted us to talking about my place, and we walked around with wine in hand, me completely enamored as she spilled out the vision she had for each room.

She was brilliant.

And I was a smitten fool already.

What I loved most was when the conversation shifted to me, football didn't come up once. We talked about Broadway, about movies, about music, about what it was like growing up in Hawai'i. We even talked a little about how I liked to dabble in woodworking — which gave Belle inspiration for how I could help with the condo design — and for the first time in my entire life, the conversation didn't center around when I first fell in love with football, how long I'd been playing, what my career goals were, or what my plan was if I got hurt.

And it wasn't that I didn't *want* to talk about all of that with Belle. I did, someday.

But for now, I just wanted to be *me*.

The night slipped by easily as we talked, and the candles burned down, working with the glow from the city lights to showcase every edge and curve of Belle's face.

"What do these mean?" she asked when we'd made our way back into the kitchen. Her fingers traced the black ink on my right arm, the light scratch of her nails sending chills down my spine.

I rolled my sleeve up a little farther to reveal more of my tattoos. "That's a very long story with a very complicated answer."

Her fingers traced up and over each marking. "Give me the abbreviated version."

"Ever heard of Kākau?"

Her arched brow was my answer.

I chuckled. "It's the traditional art of tattooing in Hawai'i. Polynesian tattoos are sacred. It's all done by hand, not with a gun, and every symbol has meaning." I shrugged. "It's an honor where I'm from, to tell your story on your flesh, to bear the pain that comes with telling that story."

Belle smiled in awe, tracing over the lines that made up the ocean, the tail of the lizard that wrapped up my biceps. When her eyes met mine, they were heated, her finger sliding under the sleeve of my button-up. "Can I see the rest?"

My next swallow was like trying to gulp down a mouthful of peanut butter, and Belle didn't wait for me to respond before her fingers were working at the buttons of my shirt. She popped the first one, stepping into me, the scent of her invading every sense. When she unfastened the second button, her fingers brushed my chest, and my heart tripled its pace, my cock responding to the touch like a well-trained dog.

Her mouth was on a track for mine, and *God,* I'd never been so close to throwing every rule out the window as I was in that moment. All it would take was one slight pressure increase where I held her for her to know I was all in. One squeeze, one breath, one little move and I could have my lips on hers, her ass in my hands, her legs wrapped around my waist. My dick throbbed at the possibility.

But somehow, I managed to keep the game plan in place. I wrapped my hands around her arms to stop her advance, putting some much-needed space between us.

"I have cheesecake for dessert," I said.

But Belle was persistent, and she closed the space between us again, her lips pressing against the hollow part of my neck.

"I think dessert is right here," she whispered, nipping at my earlobe.

Dear God.

I inhaled a searing breath, grabbing her arms more firmly and putting two feet between us.

Belle's pouty lip and wrinkled brow nearly had me throwing in the towel, but I cleared my throat, mentally reminding myself that it would be worth the wait.

"Is something wrong?" she asked, chest heaving, tongue skating out to lick her lips as her eyes fell to mine.

Fuck me.

"No, not at all... It's just... I'm kind of old-fashioned," I said with a grimace, rubbing my thumbs along her arms before I released her. My hand grabbed for the back of my neck next, and I kept it there, watching the confusion wash over Belle's face.

"I don't understand."

God, she's really going to make me say it.

"I don't want to have sex tonight."

She blinked — once, twice, then a flurry of blinks like she was sure she misheard me.

"I know it's kind of dated," I admitted. "I just... I want to get to know you, Belle." I was already regretting my next words before I said them. "I like you. And I don't want to fuck that up by going too fast."

I waited for her to laugh, or to press, or to grab her purse and leave me in her dust. But after a long pause, she inhaled a breath and let it out slowly. Her smile was the only relief I found. "Okay, then."

"Okay, then?"

She chuckled. "I'll behave. Promise."

I smiled, ignoring how my heart flip-flopped in my chest like a freaking teenager.

"Alright," she said on an exaggerated sigh, motioning to the fridge. "Get the cheesecake before I change my mind."

I hated how fast dessert went by, and hated it even more when Belle was standing at my door, high heels back on, clutch in one hand while the other held mine.

"I had a really nice time tonight," she said.

I snorted a laugh. "Hopefully the conversation was better than the dinner."

"It was delicious," she lied, but then her hand squeezed mine. "Maybe next time, though, we go to a restaurant."

I laughed. "Deal."

We stood there for a long moment, her eyes searching mine, my thumb brushing circles on her wrist.

She hadn't even left, and already, I couldn't wait to see her again.

"I'm going to call in some orders this weekend, just some essentials, so we can get started on Monday." She arched a brow. "We're starting with the bedroom. It's a crime that a man your size is sleeping on an air mattress."

I chuckled. "No arguments here."

"I'll send over a couple of options in the morning, and we'll go from there."

"Sounds good."

Belle bit her lip. "So, goodnight, then."

"Goodnight."

But she didn't move. Instead, she huffed, hanging the hand holding her clutch on her hip. "Do I at least get a kiss?"

I chuckled, leaning in and pressing my lips to her cheek. I held them there longer than necessary, inhaling everything that she was before I pulled back and released her hand, too.

Her little mouth popped open. "Oh, you are *cruel*."

"Waiting is half the fun."

"Says *you*."

I smiled, reaching for her hand again and pulling it to my lips. "*A hui hou*," I said. "Until we meet again."

She sighed, brushing my cheek with her thumb before she pulled away, and with one last wave of her fingers, she disappeared down the hall and into the elevator.

CHAPTER 4

Belle

I burst through Gemma's door at seven on the dot the next morning.

"We have a problem."

Zach and Gemma were both in the kitchen, their hair a mess, sleep still in their eyes, Gemma mid-yawn while Zach hadn't even poured the coffee grounds into the filter yet. He cocked a brow at Gemma, who managed a smile before leaning her hip against the kitchen counter and addressing me. "Well, good morning, Belle. Happy Saturday to you, too."

"I know we agreed I couldn't come over before ten on the weekends, but this is an emergency," I said, nudging Zach out of the way and taking over where he was in the coffee-making process. I'd barely slept, and if I didn't get some caffeine in the next ten minutes, I'd become a monster. "Shoo."

Zach chuckled, throwing his hands up and backing out of the kitchen.

"What's the emergency?" Gemma asked, wrapping her arms around Zach's waist when he joined her.

"He didn't want to have sex with me."

Their silence was my only answer, and I huffed, slamming the top of the coffee pot closed as I thrust the carafe under the faucet and turned it on.

"I'm confused," Gemma finally said.

"HE DIDN'T WANT TO HAVE SEX WITH ME," I repeated.

"Like, he's not interested?"

"No, like, he had a thick, raging hard-on threatening to break loose from his jeans, but didn't do anything about it." I turned the faucet off with more aggression than necessary, slamming the carafe into place and flicking on the power switch. I crossed my arms and faced them when it started brewing. "He kissed me on the freaking *cheek,* guys."

Gemma chuckled, and Zach looked at her before he turned his confused expression on me. "That's not an emergency. That's not even a problem at all. That's him being a gentleman."

Gemma and I exchanged looks this time. "Please tell me you're not on his side here."

"I mean..." Gemma bit her lip, looking at her fiancé with a shrug. "That *is* kind of weird nowadays, anyway."

Zach's mouth popped open.

Gemma threw her hands up. "I mean, even we hooked up on our first date. Remember?"

Zach didn't respond to that.

"Thank you," I said, gesturing to Gemma before I let my hand fall to slap my thigh. "I mean, there we are, post-dinner and all talked out, and I'm running my hands all over his freaking tattoos. I start unbuttoning his shirt and he stops me." I pause for dramatic effect. "The man *stopped me from stripping him.*"

"Maybe he's really shy," Gemma suggested.

"I don't think that's it. I mean, you saw him in the office. The man is confidence embodied."

"True," she agreed. "Oh, what if he's into really freaky stuff? You know. Whips and chains, nipple clamps, all that. And he wants to ease you into it."

I considered it, and I wasn't *mad* at that possibility. "A Christian Grey, perhaps?"

"Could be! Did he have a room locked off that he wouldn't let you go in?"

My shoulders sagged at that. "No, I saw his whole place. And the man brought everything he owns from California in *maybe* two-dozen boxes. I think he hired me because he lived like a college bachelor before now." I shook my head. "I don't think it's because he's so kinky he thinks he'll scare me."

"Maybe he just wants to get to know you before he has sex with you," Zach said, deadpan, as if he couldn't believe he even had to say that out loud.

I scoffed, crossing my arms again. "We talked all night. He knew me plenty well enough to bend me over his kitchen counter." Then, all the blood drained from my face. "Oh my God, what if he has a micropenis?"

Gemma's eyes shot open, and she covered her mouth. "No! You don't honestly think?"

I shook my head, slumping against the counter once more. "Nah. I saw his bulge. No way was that a sock."

We stood in silence for a bit, thinking.

"Maybe he has a weird-shaped dick. Or a mole or something," Gemma said.

"He wouldn't let me take off his shirt. Maybe it's a third nipple," I guessed.

Gemma lit up like I'd told her her hair looked pretty. "Oh, that wouldn't be so bad!"

"Maybe it's the three-date rule."

I blinked a few times before I turned to look at Zach, confused. "Three-date rule?"

"Yeah. You know... he doesn't want to have sex until the third date. It's like the classic dating handbook rule number one."

I looked at Gemma, who tilted her head to the side as she considered it. "That does make sense."

"So, you're saying I'm not going to get any until he takes me out on *two more dates*?" I groaned, pulling three coffee cups from the cabinet and topping them all off. I handed one to each of them before wrapping my hands around mine. "Who on *Earth* still does that?"

"Nice guys. *Good* guys. Guys who are interested in more than just getting in your pants." Zach shook his head. "Belle, come on. This is a good thing."

"Tell that to my throbbing clitoris, Zach."

Gemma nearly spit out her coffee, and Zach chuckled, throwing up his free hand in surrender. "And on that note, I'm going to watch SportsCenter." He kissed Gemma's cheek before turning to me. "Good luck with your emergency."

I wiggled my fingers in a goodbye to him, and Gemma and I shared a knowing smile once he was gone.

"So, what was the rest of the night like?" Gemma asked. "I mean, aside from the lack of coitus at the end."

"It was..." I sighed, eyes falling to where the steam was rising out of my coffee cup. "Perfect. Like, straight out of a romance movie perfect. He cooked dinner — which was absolutely terrible, by the way," I added on a laugh. "But that almost made it better. He was so adorable, running around the kitchen, stumbling over himself to try to make everything. The salad was so bad, Gemma." I chuckled. "Tasted like straight vinegar and citrus, and not in a good way."

"Oh no," she said on a laugh of her own.

"But he was trying so hard. He made these crab cakes, but he put too much flour in so they were a little tough. And then the ribs, he cooked them too long, and we didn't have any steak knives, so we were like ripping the meat off with our teeth."

Gemma snorted.

"It sounds like a disaster," I admitted, but I couldn't stop my stupid smile. "But... I don't know. There's something about him. And *God*, he was so sexy, wearing these dark jeans and this crisp white button-up. He didn't have shoes on, either."

"Oh, fuck," Gemma breathed. "I love a barefoot man in jeans."

"I wanted to lick his toes, Gemma, and I swear I've never been into that."

She chuckled.

"What am I going to do?" I asked on a sigh. "If I have a three-date max rule, and he has a three date before we even *fuck* rule... where does that leave us?"

"Well... what if you ditch your rule and give him a legitimate chance?"

I flattened my lips, giving her a pointed look. "Come on, now. Did we not just see in live and living color what happens when I break my rules? Case in point: Jordan."

"That doesn't count."

I arched a brow.

"I'm serious," she said earnestly. "Belle, he's really nice. And *really* hot. What if he's different?" She paused, and I felt the words coming before she even said them. "I know you think every guy is going to be like Nathan, but..."

"Please," I said, holding up my free hand. "Don't."

"Nathan was young, Belle. He didn't know what he wanted. And I know that hurt you, but it was years ago, and don't you think—"

"Don't I think it's time to get over it and trust a guy again when he says I'm his one and only and we're going to get married, only to be completely crushed and heartbroken when he leaves me behind because I'm not the kind of girl you take home to Mom?" I shook my head. "No, thank you, I think I'll stick with the Good Time Girl title. It's a lot less complicated and reaps a *lot* more benefits."

Gemma sighed, taking her first sip of coffee. Silence fell between us as those words sank in, and my heart ached, as if it was just as pissed at me as I was that I'd brought up all those stinging reminders.

"Well, then, I guess you enjoy a couple more dates, and then you guys will have one night together," she finally said, her eyes sad when they locked on mine. "Better make the most of that date number three."

CHAPTER 5

Makoa

"Hike!"

I took off like a rocket, exploding from my crouched position and jetting off toward the agility cones laid out in front of me. As soon as I hit the first one, I side-stepped it, veering off to the right. Then, when my feet found the second one, I shifted again, sprinting left.

Back and forth, left and right, full sprint to dead stop and turn around until I cleared the cones. Then, I took off in a sprint down the field and looked over my shoulder just in time to catch the spiral throw from Gerald down the field.

"Nice!" I heard him call as I slowed my sprint to a jog and finally to a walk.

I wiped the sweat from my forehead with the hem of my muscle tank, taking a breath before I jogged back until I was close enough to toss the ball to Gerald.

"Way to explode off the line," he said with a grin, gripping the laces. "I can't wait to really see you in action at training camp."

"By the time you report, I'll be spending most of my days in ice baths trying not to die from soreness."

"Perks of being a veteran," he said with a shrug. "Ready for another round?"

I nodded, sidling up on the line next to him, and as soon as he called out *hike*, I was off again.

Over and over, drill after drill, we passed Sunday afternoon with sweat dripping into our eyes and our muscles aching for us to call it a day. But that was a mistake I'd seen too many young players make in the off season. They'd take a full vacation, eat whatever they wanted and barely work out, and then they'd report to training camp overweight, out of shape, and soft from too much time off.

That only did one thing: call coach's attention.

And not in the good way.

For me, the summer offseason was a break of sorts, but it wasn't full time off. I spent at least six hours a day working out, training, watching tape, and memorizing routes. And today, I'd convinced Gerald McNab, backup quarterback for the Bears, to come train with me.

I liked Gerald. I'd met him my first day in Chicago when I'd toured the Bear's facility with coach and the owner of the team. Gerald was one of the few guys there working out, and he had a smile almost as big as mine. He was a few inches shorter than me, stalky and muscular with long black hair that was dreaded and almost always pulled back in a low hair tie at the nape of his neck.

What I liked most about Gerald when I first met him was the firm handshake he greeted me with. It told me I should respect him. Not only that, but I'd seen him in action on the field. While he wasn't the star that Jonah Warren, our starting quarterback, was, Gerald was reliable, and consistent. And as a quarterback? There were no two qualities more important than those. When Warren needed to sit out, the Bears never had to get nervous with their backup QB going in.

I had a feeling it wouldn't be long before Gerald would inch his way up to that starting position. After all, Warren was getting old — for a professional ball player, anyway. Gerald was twenty-six, just getting into his prime, and after just one month of running drills together, I knew it'd be an honor to be on the field with him.

It was late afternoon by the time we called it, and we plopped down on one of the benches on the sideline of the high school field we'd secured to practice on. We couldn't use our own facilities until training camp, but that didn't mean we weren't resourceful enough to find a way to make it on the field.

After a long swig of water, I relaxed on the bench, taking in the Chicago summer heat and the familiar scent of cleated-dirt and fresh turf. I inhaled deep, letting out a sigh on a smile.

"That smell never gets old," I commented.

Gerald smirked, nodding as he took a swig from his bottle. "Can you imagine *not* being a football player? This — the smell, the ball in my hands, the feeling of being on the field — it's been a part of me since I was four years old. I can't fathom not having something like this in my life."

"I hear you. I've always wondered at what point we separate from the others, you know? There are the guys who see football as just a sport, or just a pastime when they're younger. And then..."

"There's us. The ones who can't separate it from the rest of our life."

"The ones who know that football *is* our life."

Gerald had his elbows on his knees, and he looked at me over his shoulder. "You're good, man. Really good. And you came to us at the right time. We need better receiving. I mean, we've got Howard and Thompson running for us, but our long game is weak."

I shook my head, chest tight with a familiar pressure that I somehow found comforting. "I'm going to give it my all at camp. And the preseason games..."

"They might as well be our Super Bowl."

I chuckled, but with his words, my mind was racing thinking about the upcoming season. I had one chance to prove I was worth the money they paid to get me here, one chance to secure my contract past the stage it was in now. And more than anything, I had one chance to prove that I deserved a spot on that field more than a spot on the sideline.

Gerald kicked back on the bench with me, and we were silent for a while before he nudged my arm. "So, you settling in alright?"

"Getting there. Starting to unpack what little I brought with me." I mopped the sweat off my forehead again. "Still not used to this humidity, though."

"Balmy as fuck, isn't it?" Gerald chuckled, wiping his own forehead. "You met anyone outside the team yet?"

The left side of my mouth curled up, and I knew the sheepish look I gave Gerald answered more than any words could have.

"Ah... who is she?"

I shrugged, trying to play it cool, though the truth was I hadn't stopped thinking about Belle Monroe since she left my condo Friday night. "The interior designer I hired to make my condo look like an adult lives there instead of the college bachelor pad situation I had in San Fran."

He chuckled. "I'm sure she'll be doing much more than designing your living room."

"Oh, for sure." I looked at him with a smirk. "She's gotta do the whole place."

"And do *you* in the whole place, too, right?"

I laughed softly under my breath. "We'll see if it gets that far."

At that, Gerald cocked a brow high. "You mean it hasn't already?" He whistled. "Honestly, that's a shock. In my experience, it's usually less than sixty seconds between the time they found out I'm a ball player and my pants are on the floor."

"Ha, well... she doesn't know I'm a ball player."

He frowned. "How the hell?"

"It's not like I'm famous."

"Maybe not, but to anyone who follows the Bears... you're exciting news. I take it she's not a sports girl, huh?"

"Not even close," I said, smiling at the memory of how she'd practically gagged at the mention of football.

"And you didn't tell her? That would have been the first thing out of my mouth. It's like an instant access pass."

I grabbed the back of my neck. "Let's just say I've been burned in the past by some girls who were *only* interested in the fact that I play football and what that can do for *them*. So, I'm playing my cards safe."

Gerald was quiet for a long moment, and when I turned to look at him again, he was shaking his head with a shit-eating grin on his face. "You really are a softie, aren't ya, Kumaka?"

I shoved him, and he laughed, using the momentum to propel him off the bench. "Alright. I'm going to get in some stretching before I head out."

"Give me a sec and I'll join," I said, fishing my phone from my gym bag. I thumbed through until I found Belle's number, biting my lip as I pressed the call button.

"Hello?"

"Hey, beautiful," I greeted. "Happy Sunday."

There was the distinct sound of music on the other end, but it was buffed out quickly, and then a breathy reply. "Happy Sunday to you." She paused. "You called me."

"I did. Is that not okay?"

"I guess I just expected a text more so than a call."

"You sound winded."

"I'm in the middle of a yoga flow."

I hummed my approval, which earned me a snort of a laugh.

"Perv."

"Texting is too informal," I said, ignoring the fact that I was *definitely* picturing her bent over and twisted up like a pretzel. "Besides, I wanted to hear the delight in your voice when I asked you to go out with me later this week."

She chuckled. "And you were so sure you'd get that reaction, huh?"

"After how smooth I was at dinner? The perfectly cooked food, the elegant ambience..." I scoffed. "How could you *not* be chomping at the bit to see me again."

Belle laughed, and I savored the sound, soaking it up like a ray of sunshine. When I glanced at Gerald, he was watching me with a knowing grin, and I flicked him off when he made a lewd gesture with big doe eyes, his lashes batting over and over.

"So, you want to see me again?"

"I do," I said confidently.

"Why don't you come by the office tomorrow and I can show you where I want to start with the condo?"

"I can do that," I said confidently. "But I want to see you *outside* of work, too."

There was a pause on the other end, and I closed my eyes, imagining that sexy, confident smile Belle wore so easily.

Okay, and maybe her ass in yoga pants, too.

"What did you have in mind?"

I smiled. "Would you say you're a competitive person, Ms. Monroe?"

Belle scoffed. "I think you already know the answer to that."

"Good. I'll come into the office tomorrow and get your address while I'm there. Save Wednesday night for me. I'll pick you up at seven."

"I like when you're bossy."

I rolled my lips together, shaking my head because I could see the devilish look in her eyes even when she was out of sight. "See you tomorrow."

"Tomorrow," she echoed.

Then, I hung up the phone and finished out the rest of our training session with a doofus smile firmly in place.

CHAPTER 6

Belle

"Just a minute!" I called when I heard the knock at my door. I already knew it was Makoa, since I'd buzzed him up from the downstairs lobby, but my stomach still did a little flip when the knock came.

And I instantly kicked myself for having that reaction.

I was too damn excited to see this guy. I mean, *usually,* I'd be so lackadaisical about the whole situation that I'd have Makoa driven mad by this point. But as it was, *he* was the one driving *me* insane.

Him making me wait was not something I was used to.

And for some reason, it really, *really* turned me on.

I checked my makeup one last time, dabbing at the corner of my mouth where a little gloss had gone rogue. Makoa had told me to dress casual, but I didn't really *do* casual. My wardrobe mostly consisted of tailored pant and skirt suits, chic business fashion, and designer high heels. When I wasn't in the office, I lived in athleisure or bohemian-style dresses. I wasn't even sure I owned a pair of jeans or a t-shirt — I always went to Gemma when I needed to borrow that style.

Tonight, I'd landed on a soft, baby blue romper with a deep V cut. It was loose and flowy, which was *casual* to me, and paired with my favorite wedges, the outfit accented my long legs and narrow waist. I'd just dyed my hair an even darker red over the weekend, landing me in the auburn family, and I wore it in large barrel waves that spiraled over my shoulders. It was so big and teased that it was practically *begging* to have a hand tangled in it.

I hoped by the end of the night, it would.

Ever since I left his place Friday night, I'd been thinking about Makoa. Sure, I'd worked, and worked out, and hung out with Gemma, and gone out with the girls for happy hour. And sure, he'd stopped by the office Monday long enough to hear my initial plans for his condo and get my address. But that interaction had been short and professional, and if anything, it'd only left me wanting more.

The majority of my thoughts since then had centered around the way it felt when Makoa almost kissed me, and the way his smile made my stomach dip, and the way I couldn't wait to have his condo furnished and decorated so I could fuck him in every corner of it.

Another knock came, and I scurried over to the door, putting my confident smile in place before I swung it open.

And there he was, the Polynesian dream boat.

It was a Herculean feat to keep my tongue in my mouth as I took in every inch of him. Makoa wore a cream linen shirt that cut off just under his elbow and had an open neckline — just enough for me to see a little more of those tattoos he loved hiding so much. His tan skin was ablaze against the linen, and the dark distressed jeans he wore hugged him in all the best ways. He had a gold chain around his neck, one that gave off major power vibes, and just with one inhale I knew I'd never forget that man's scent.

Earthy and warm, with a little spice and a whole lot of sex appeal.

His eyes hungrily devoured me in measure, and he let out a slow whistle when our gaze finally met. "I'm going to have to fight off every man in Chicago tonight."

I flushed, more out of practice than actual embarrassment. "Let me grab my purse."

I locked up behind us, and as soon as I was in the hallway with him, Makoa slipped his hand around my waist and pulled me into him from the side. His hand was the size of my ribcage, and when he tucked me into him like that, I felt like a baby kitten.

Maybe that's why I practically purred when he pulled me in even closer, pressing his warm lips to my cheek.

How I wished for those lips to be everywhere else...

He released his grip after the kiss, much to my despair, and we made our way to the elevator. Once we were downstairs, I followed his lead, holding my purse and wondering why the teenage love-sick puppy dog thought of wanting him to hold my hand had crossed my mind.

"So, where are we going?" I asked. We walked past a trio of women who practically slobbered on themselves as Makoa walked by, and I chuckled thinking about his comment before we left my place.

Maybe it would be *me* having to fight someone off tonight.

"Well, you see, I'm in a bit of a predicament. And I need your help."

"Do tell."

"Obviously, I'm new to town."

"Clearly."

"And, in San Francisco, well... I had a bit of a reputation."

I cocked a brow. "Did you now?"

Makoa nodded, completely oblivious to another group that ogled him as we passed. This one had a few dudes, too, and they seemed just as enamored with him.

Maybe Makoa Kumaka was the kind of handsome that could make even the straightest man stare.

"I was trivia champion at the local dive bar. And now that I'm in Chicago, I need to defend my title."

I laughed. "And what if someone else has that title?"

"I'm sure they do. That's why I asked if you were competitive."

"So, we're about to make some nerds cry when we kick their asses in trivia?"

"Precisely."

I grinned. "Did you have a place in mind?"

"I Googled trivia nights in Chicago. Looks like The Oaf Bar is the place to go."

I stopped mid-stride, tugging Makoa to the curb before I threw my hand up and hailed us a cab. "I know someplace better."

Doc's bar was absolutely packed. As it always was.

It didn't matter if it was Wednesday or Saturday or Monday at four in the afternoon, Doc's was the place to be in Southside Chicago, especially after a sporting event. Not that *I* ever cared about that, but I'd first been dragged to this hole in the wall by Gemma after a Bears win. Of course, back then, we didn't know that the insanely hot bartender would eventually become her fiancé.

And the owner of the bar.

The original owner, who the bar was named after, was somewhere in the Caribbean now living his best life. And since Zach took over, he'd only turned what was already a popular spot into one of the favorites for locals. There were new specials and entertainment every night, with a focus on sports, of course.

But on Wednesdays? It was dirty trivia night.

And on this particular dirty trivia night, Makoa and I were in dead last place.

"I thought you were the king of trivia?" I teased as he marked down our score from the last round — which was a measly two points.

"Well, I'm used to answering questions about pop culture," he volleyed, arching a brow at me. "Not questions like *what's the slang term most often used for a woman's labia* or *what sexual fantasy is the most popular in the United States?*"

I chuckled, lifting my Cosmo. "Well, you know what the end of another round means. Bottoms up."

"You trying to get me drunk so you can take advantage of me?"

I shrugged. "Maybe."

Makoa's smirk was sexy as hell, and he shook his head at me before taking three big gulps of his beer. My sip of Cosmo went down smooth, warming my chest as the DJ announced the next question.

"What percentage of people like dirty talk during sex? Is it thirty-two percent, fifty-eight percent, or seventy-one percent?"

"Seventy-one," I whispered, tapping the paper for Makoa to write it down.

He screwed up his face. "What? No way. I think it's thirty-two."

"*Thirty-two?* Are you kidding? Who *doesn't* love to talk dirty during sex?"

Makoa chuckled. "How about we compromise and go with fifty-eight?"

I waved him off in a sign of concession, and once our answer was on the sheet, he popped up to hand it in to the DJ.

"So, have you been to a show yet since you moved to Chicago?" I asked when he was sitting again.

"I haven't. I saw *Moulin Rouge!* is playing at the James M. Nederlander Theatre right now, though, and I'd love to see that one."

"Oh! I'm *dying* to see that!"

"Maybe we could go together," Makoa offered, and my cheeks heated as I sipped on my Cosmo.

"Maybe. Depends on how the rest of tonight goes, though." I wrinkled my nose. "Can't be seen with a trivia loser."

Makoa acted like a dagger had been stuck in his chest, and I laughed him off just as the DJ announced the answer. We'd decided right by compromising, and seemed to be the only team who answered correctly. And just like that, we went from last place to fourth.

"Next question. What popular TV character must have sex every seven years?"

Makoa threw his hands up so suddenly that I balked in surprise, and then I couldn't keep my laughter in at the genuine excitement on his face.

"Finally, a question I know!" He jotted down *Spock* and didn't even ask if I thought the same before he handed it into the DJ.

"*God*, I love a confident man," I said on an exaggerated sigh, leaning toward him with my lashes a flutter.

"Hey, I've been waiting to impress you with my vast knowledge of useless information all night. Let me have this."

I bit my lip, both loving and hating that I was completely enamored with this man. I mean, he had the body of an Olympian and the game of a high school freshman. Why was I so turned on by a hot, muscular man tripping over himself to make me dinner and nerding out at trivia night?

"Did you grow up in Chicago?" he asked while we waited for the other teams to submit their answers.

I usually hated these kinds of questions — the *getting to know you* questions that dating was full of. In fact, I hated them so much that I skipped them altogether. Every *other* man would happily let me distract them with a kiss or a moan or a fistful of their shirt as I dragged them back to my bedroom.

But not Makoa.

For some reason — a reason I refused to spend too much time digesting — I didn't mind answering his questions. I wanted him to know more about me.

And I wanted to know *everything* about him.

"Kind of. I grew up a little of everywhere until I hit high school. That was the only time I convinced my hippie parents to settle down for four years so I could have some actual friends."

"Hippie parents?"

"*Total* hippies. I'm talking marijuana smoking, peace-sign throwing, Fleetwood Mac junkies."

Makoa smiled. "They sound awesome."

"They really are. They're big into traveling and missionary work, so when I was younger, we moved around a lot. I even lived in Africa for a year when I was ten, but I don't remember much of it, other than the animals and the music. *God,* they had the best music. We would just sit around a fire at night and listen to the locals play for hours. Everyone would dance and laugh..." I smiled at the memory. "It was amazing."

"That sounds incredible."

I closed my eyes, remembering the big fires, the drums, the smiles of the locals as they danced and sang. "That was the first place that inspired me. I remember coming back to America and begging my mom to let me redo my entire bedroom with African-inspired design."

"At ten?" Makoa asked with a chuckle.

"Eleven, by that time," I corrected. "But, yeah. It was my first big project."

"And your parents were down for it?"

"Oh, they *loved* it. This was me stepping into my creativity in their eyes. They bought me whatever I wanted, within a budget, of course. They even let me paint the walls. And from that moment on, they were my biggest cheerleaders. They'd let me go wherever I wanted each summer to find new inspiration. They sent me to summer camps, to study-abroad programs, to visit family members and family friends wherever we could find them."

"That's really awesome that they supported you that way," Makoa remarked. "I mean, I know my parents have always supported me like that, too. And it makes it easier to go for the dreams that feel impossible."

I chuckled. "Yeah. Lucky for you and me, we're in a business that almost always thrives, huh? Not like your parents could really be upset with you wanting to go into real estate."

He smiled, taking a big gulp of his beer before he asked, "Do you have any siblings?"

"Nope, just me. Hence why I'm such a brat," I added with a wink. "You?"

Makoa grimaced. "Four sisters."

"*Four?!?*"

The DJ interrupted us with the answer to the last question, along with the updated scores, and with another correct answer, we were up to third place with just three questions left.

We submitted our best guess for the next question, *what is lectamia?*, before Makoa ordered us another round.

Just as the waitress walked away, a short, nervous, fidgety guy in a Cubs jersey approached our table. He looked nervous as he smiled at me first, and then turned his attention to Makoa.

"Welcome to Chicago, man," he said, a huge smile enveloping his face. He reached out a hand to shake Makoa's. "I'd really love to buy you a beer."

Makoa looked at me before forcing a smile and taking the stranger's hand. "Thanks, man. I appreciate that, but we just ordered a round, so we're all good here."

"I just know you're going to do big things for the team. We've had—"

Makoa shot up out of his chair, throwing his arm around the guy. "Alright, alright, you can buy me a beer. Come on, let's hit the bar." He looked over his shoulder at me as they made their way across the room, mouthing *sorry* before they elbowed up at the bar.

I frowned. How the heck did that guy know who Makoa was? Maybe he was more famous in real estate than I realized. I made a mental note to Google him when I got home.

The team...

What did that mean? I glanced at the guy at the bar with Makoa, noting the Cubs jersey again. Maybe Makoa was working with them, finding a new stadium or training facility?

My wheels turned until Makoa was at the table again, and as soon as he sat down with his new beer and nodded to the stranger who'd bought it for him, our waitress dropped off our other order.

I cocked a brow at the two beers in front of him. "Looks like I'll need to catch up."

He shook his head. "Sorry about that. That's Randy, he works in the marketing department for the firm."

Ah, the real estate firm. Now that makes sense.

Makoa's eyes found mine then, bright and wide with his matching smile. "Alright, now, where were we?"

I rolled my lips together, debating questioning him more on Randy and the firm, but the way he watched me told me it was the last thing he wanted to discuss. And when he'd come into my office that first day, he'd seemed pleasantly surprised that I didn't know who he was.

Maybe there was more to that part of his story, and maybe there was a reason he loved that I didn't have a clue.

I decided to cross Googling him off my mental list. If he wanted me to know him only through what he showed me, I was more than down for that. I knew what it was to be judged, to be put in a box according to who people thought you were, and I kind of liked getting to know him the old fashioned way.

"You had just blown my mind with your *Brady Bunch* family bomb drop."

Makoa laughed.

"How the hell did you survive with four sisters?"

"I learned early on to avoid them during *that time of the month* and to never give my opinion on their haircuts."

I laughed. "Smart man."

"No, honestly, we're all really close. I have two older sisters and two younger sisters, and my parents are big on family. We spend every holiday we can together, and growing up, the house was always full of kids, always loud and chaotic." He smiled, thumb sliding over the condensation on his glass. "I never thought I'd miss it, but when I moved out on my own, I realized there's a lot of comfort in the noise. When it's quiet..."

"It gives you too much space to think," I finished for him.

Makoa's eyes met mine, and a level of understanding settled between us.

I knew what it was like to live alone, to spend almost every night in the quiet of your own mind, where every thought was free to roam and keep you awake.

"Alright, so the question was *what does it mean to practice lectamia?*" the DJ said, interrupting our conversation for the moment.

But Makoa's eyes stayed on me, like he was digesting my last comment, like he wanted to climb inside my mind.

"The answer is... Lectamia is the act of caressing in bed *without* intercourse."

There was a chorus of groans, as well as a few cheers from the other teams, and Makoa shook his head, glaring holes into the DJ booth.

"You're never allowed to pick the bar we play trivia at again," he said.

I chuckled. "Hey, at least we're expanding our vocabulary. *Lectamia* sounds like it could be kind of fun."

Makoa licked his bottom lip, sitting back in his chair as his eyes appraised me. He traced the rim of his glass before lifting it to his lips and draining the last of his beer. "Maybe we should test that theory."

Everything in my body lit up with a whispered *yes*.

And with a *check, please* and an abandoned trivia game in our dust, we piled into a cab that took us back across town to my place.

We'd barely pushed through my front door before my purse was thrown on the floor and my arms were wrapped around

Makoa's neck. I was in the process of climbing him like a tree when he laughed, holding my hips in place to keep me on the ground and putting some space between us.

"Please don't tell me you were joking about testing the theory," I said, practically panting as my eyes fell to his lips with a desperate wish.

He chuckled, sliding his hands up my arms slowly. Then, those giant, beastly hands slid back to frame my neck, his thumbs on my chin, fingers tangling in my hair just like I'd manifested when I'd curled it.

"Not joking," he answered, his voice low. "But if I get the pleasure of kissing you, I'm going to take my time and kiss you right."

I swallowed, and inner me scolded my heart for doing a little flip at his words. The old version of Belle Monroe — the young, naïve one who didn't know where she fit in the world — leaned into those lush, romantic words like they were a field of wildflowers. I wanted to inhale them, feel them on every inch of my skin, pick a few petals and keep them in a book to hold onto long after this moment.

But I knew better.

I knew those words were just a ploy, just a cute, clever way to make me swoon and spread my legs.

And then, just like every other guy, he'd be gone.

I shoved those thoughts out of my mind for the time being, focusing instead on the way Makoa's eyes studied my lips like they were the answers to every quiz he'd ever take. He brushed his thumb over the bottom one, and I chased it with my tongue, eliciting a sharp inhale from him before his eyes met mine.

Then, carefully, with purpose and conviction, he pulled me into him, his fingers still in my hair, his breath warm on my lips until the very moment he pressed his own to mine.

I hated our first kiss.

It was the kind of kiss you saw in the movies, slow and sensual, his lips too soft and warm and perfect where they met mine. He held my face in just the right way, with confidence and care in equal measure, and he inhaled at the contact like he was breathing in all of me. His hands trembled a bit when he deepened the kiss, and I leaned into it, emotion surging through me no matter how I tried to fight it, like I was just deep enough in the ocean to get pummeled by wave after wave without being able to catch my breath.

That kiss was magnetic. It was fireworks and shooting stars and a million fairytales lived out in a single moment.

It was the kind of kiss that could ruin a girl if she wasn't careful.

If she didn't know better.

Luckily, I did.

Desperate to kill the romance threatening to pull me into dangerous territory, I wrapped my arms around Makoa to deepen the kiss even more, my tongue jetting out to meet his. He groaned at the sensation, and I smiled in victory, leaping into his arms without warning. I knew it would give him no choice but to let me fall or catch me.

And catch me, he did.

My legs wrapped around his waist, and before I knew it, I was pinned against my front door, Makoa's hands digging so deep into my hip bones that I prayed for a bruise to be left in their wake.

I sighed, letting my head drop back against the door and allowing access to my neck, which Makoa took greedily. His lips sucked and kissed along the skin, and I rolled my hips, letting out a moan of my own when I felt his hard length straining against his jeans.

It didn't take more than that brief moment of friction for me to know he definitely did *not* have a micropenis.

Wrapping one arm full around his neck to secure myself where he held me, I dipped one hand down between us, kissing him hard as my fingers danced down his chest, his abdomen. I slipped them under the band of his jeans, dragging a line from hip to hip, but his belt made it impossible for me to get any deeper.

Makoa groaned, biting my lip before he forced my hands above my head. He pinned them there at the wrists with one massive hand before the other palmed my breast, hard, and I leaned into the aggressive touch with a silent plea for more.

God, he was all man. He was all hard muscle and dominance with me pinned between him and the door, and I wanted nothing more than for him to devour me until nothing was left for any other man who dared try after him.

I bucked my hips again, catching a line of friction that made us both moan before I ripped a hand free and shoved it between us. This time, I rubbed his cock over the denim, eyes fluttering at the feel of how thick and hard he was even restrained by those damn jeans.

"Oh, fuck," he whispered when I gripped him, flexing his hips into my palm.

I kissed his neck, biting at the skin and rubbing his cock while my own need pooled between my legs. I was going to be so wet for this man by the time he took my clothes off that he'd need a fucking snorkel to go down on me.

The longer he kissed me and trapped me between that door, the more my impatience grew. When I couldn't stand it any longer, I unwrapped my arms from around his neck, confident that he had me, and slid the strap of my romper off my left shoulder.

But before I could wiggle out of it and go for the other, Makoa stopped me, dropping me to the ground and holding his hand over mine where it was on track to free the other strap.

I paused under his touch, both of us panting, his cock so hard it could easily destroy a cement block, and me so desperate to have him inside me that I literally whimpered when he broke our contact.

Makoa blew out a long, heavy breath, pressing his forehead to mine. "You are the sexiest woman to ever exist."

I bit my lip against a smile, my lips on track for his again. He caught my kiss with a groan, meeting me with hard, desperate movements that matched mine.

But then he broke the kiss again.

And said the worst three words I'd ever heard.

"I should go."

"No," I argued, trying to kiss him again.

This time, he obliged me with a sweet peck and a smile before he guided my hands from where I was trying to unbuckle his jeans to wrap around his neck instead.

"Trust me," he said. "I want to stay."

"So, stay," I begged.

"If I stay, we both know where this is going."

I pressed up on my toes to kiss him again. "Exactly."

"I think we should slow down a little, Belle." His eyes met mine then, and he chuckled at my pouty lip before he thumbed it. "I really like you. I don't want to mess this up."

I swallowed, heart pounding for a completely different reason now that he was looking at me that way.

Like he really meant the words he said.

Like he wanted more from me than I could ever give him.

Like I could trust him.

"We can't let this go to waste," I tried, trailing my hand down his stomach, over his belt, and wrapping my hand around his length again. I gave it just the slightest pressure, which had him closing his eyes and biting his lip against a groan.

"Devil woman."

"In the flesh."

He shook his head on a laugh, looking up to the ceiling like God could save him now as he peeled my hands off him and took a big step back. He twirled me around in a sort of dance move, until it was him closest to the door, and then he pressed two soft kisses — one to each of my hands.

"Goodnight, Belle."

I wanted to groan. I wanted to throw a freaking tantrum. But something about that man had me smiling in appreciation, like I'd finally found a worthy opponent to play this little game with.

"You're really going to leave me here..." I whispered, trailing my fingertips over my chest. "All alone..." I dipped my fingertips under the fabric of my romper. "To take care of myself when you could be the one to do the honors?"

I rolled my fingertips over my hard nipple, puckering it so that I knew he could see the outline of it against the fabric when I removed my hand.

Makoa sighed in misery, staring at my nipple like he wanted nothing more than to suck it between his teeth.

But the motherfucker resisted.

"I'll call you," he promised.

I sighed when he opened the door, and what was worse... I hated that I actually respected that he was leaving. Zach's words danced in my mind, and if Makoa really *did* have a three-date rule, then that meant we were already more than halfway there.

And maybe waiting *was* half the fun.

Maybe this torture would make the payoff just that much sweeter.

"Goodnight, Mr. Kumaka," I said when he was in the hallway.

He smirked, framing my face with his hands and a longing sigh that told me he *really* didn't want to leave. He sealed his promise to call me with a long, intimate kiss that left me breathless, and then he was gone.

And I stripped down for my second date of the night.

The one with my vibrator.

CHAPTER 7

Makoa

The first time I held a football, I knew it would be more than a sport to me.

I was only a tyke, and still I remembered watching football games on television with wide eyes and a yearning desire to be one of those players. Was it kismet that I was wrapped in a University of Hawai'i onesie shortly after I was born, or was it the stars aligning early on, putting me right where I needed to be? Was it natural for a kid to have absolutely zero desire to play video games when he could be outside running drills, or was that a sign, too?

It seemed like everything had pointed me to the NFL from the moment I took my first breath. I felt football coursing through my veins like it was the blood and oxygen that kept me alive.

Which was part of the reason I felt a little sick shoving everything related to my football career into my guest room closet.

I'd scoured through every box I brought with me, glad that I left a lot of my high school and younger memorabilia at Mom and Dad's on Maui. Even with just my college and after keepsakes, trophies, plaques, awards, uniforms, and gear, I'd filled three boxes, and had a bunch of stuff that couldn't fit in a box just lined up against the wall or along the top shelves of the closet. And when I closed the doors, I jotted down a note to get a lock as soon as possible.

I'd met with Belle on Monday, two days before our second date, to go over her official design and plan of attack for the condo. She'd been ordering furniture and rugs and plants and God knows what else all week, and I knew any day now I'd start getting deliveries.

And then she'd be here with her crew, unpacking, organizing, designing the space with the elegance that only she could.

I was reaching the point where I wanted to tell her about who I really was — mostly because I loved talking to her, and I wanted her to know my *true* passion. Every time we turned the conversation to work, I would find a way to change the subject, because I had absolutely nothing to say about real estate.

I could talk all day long about football.

The more I spent time with Belle, the more I believed that she really didn't know who I was. Hell, if anything, she'd had the opportunity to call me out on my shit when that guy bought me a beer at Doc's bar Wednesday night. But she hadn't probed at all, just changed the subject easily back to my family.

But as much as I *wanted* to trust her, to think I already knew her, I also realized this was part of my issue when it came to the girls I chose to date in the past.

I got swept away easily. I got caught up. I convinced myself there were no red flags until they were all waving in front of my face and it was too late to get out without getting hurt. Yes, I wanted to tell Belle about football... but the truth was that I didn't know her well enough just yet.

The nervous part of me wondered if she'd done it on purpose, ignoring the guy at the bar, the people staring as we walked *to* the bar. I wondered if she was playing a game with me like so many had before. *Oh, wow, you play football? I had no idea! You know what I'd really love? To interview a football player on my podcast...*

I mean, why *didn't* she question what had happened? I sure as hell would have if it were her in the reverse.

Maybe she's playing her own game...

Even as the thought hit me, though, it didn't sit right. It was clear that Belle was successful as hell without me. She didn't need my money *or* my network.

Still, there was something she wasn't telling me, too. I could sense it. I could feel her holding me just an arm's length away, studying me, like she knew something I didn't.

It had kept me awake all night after I left her house on Wednesday — that and the fact that I had blue balls like a motherfucker. A long, hot shower session didn't bring me relief, nor did the hours I spent tossing and turning, overthinking as I did so well.

It was then that I made a plan.

I decided the best time to tell her would be right after training camp. At that point, I would know if I had a chance at keeping my contract, or if I'd be hitting the road and trying to find another team to take me in. It would also mean that Belle and I had been seeing each other for a couple months. If we make it that long, I'll have no choice but to tell her if I want to take things to the next level.

Until then, there was no rush. After all, we were still new. We'd only been on a couple of dates. What was the harm in taking it slow and having fun?

I could get to know Belle and she could get to know me. Me, *without* the NFL.

The decision cemented, I pushed off from where I'd been leaning up against the closet and made my way into the living room. I needed to spend some time watching film, and then I was meeting up with Gerald at the high school for an evening of drills.

But when I rounded the corner, I heard a soft *click*. I frowned, leaning back into the guest room, and saw that the closet door had creaked back open, like it was mocking me, like it was pointing out the very obvious truth.

I'm not a secret you can keep for long, it whispered.

As if I didn't already know.

Belle

On Friday night, Gemma was sprawled out on her stomach on my living room rug, fuzzy slippers swinging in the air, paper and fabric and flowers littered around her like a shrine. I was on the couch above her with my laptop between my sweatpants-clad legs, fiddling with my designs for Makoa's condo, along with a few other projects.

Although, if I was being honest, Makoa had most of my attention — an annoying fact about most of my time recently.

A half-empty bottle of Malbec sat on my coffee table, and I topped off Gemma's glass before my own, finishing the job. Gemma sat up long enough to take a sip before a long sigh left her chest, and she dragged all her gorgeous brunette hair up into a messy bun.

"Why is this all so hard?" she whined, staring at the computer screen where she'd left off. She was currently trying to decide what kind of wedding favors she wanted, and after hours of narrowing down, it was a toss-up between football-shaped frosted sugar cookies with their name and date on it, or can koozies with the same.

Everything about their wedding was football themed, and trust me, I *tried* to talk her out of it.

"Look, cookies get eaten and then they're history. Besides, you're going to have a cake. Who wants wedding cake *and* a sugar cookie in the same night?" I shook my head. "Get the koozies. People will use them for years to come."

Gemma nodded, chewing on her lip and my suggestion. "They *would* be cute to have at our tailgates this season..."

"See?" I said, gesturing to her laptop. "Problem solved. Now, what's next?"

Gemma pulled her planner into her lap, thumbing through the pages. "I need to finalize the menu," she looked at me then. "I still don't know what to do about the vegetarian option. And I need to decide between the garlic mashed potatoes or the wedge fries. I feel like the wedge fries are more tailgate-ish, but are they *too* informal?"

She didn't wait for me to answer before she turned her attention back to the planner in her lap.

"And I need to finalize the flowers... and finish the program design so I can get those printed." Gemma tapped her chin with her pen. "I think that's it for tonight, the rest can wait until next weekend." She looked up to the sky with another deep breath. "You would think this would be my heaven, given how I love to plan so much."

I chuckled. "It's a little different when it's your wedding. I mean, you want everything to be perfect."

Her big eyes locked on mine. "I really do."

"Can I tell you something?" I asked, and when she nodded, I wrinkled my nose. "It's not going to be."

Gemma's shoulders deflated.

"I just mean don't stress yourself out over trying to make it all exactly as you think it should be, okay? It's a wedding, and hurdles are bound to happen. Just be as prepared as you can be and let the day-of planner take care of the rest. After all," I reminded her, reaching down to squeeze her wrist. "It's about you and that fine ass man three floors down getting married, not about the flowers or the football jersey guest book."

"That *is* pretty awesome, though," Gemma volleyed.

I rolled my eyes. "For some people, maybe." But then, I smiled, squeezing her hand once more before I let it go. "Just order those favors so we can turn on a trashy TV show and crack open another bottle of wine. I'm tired of working."

"Deal," she said, flopping back down on her stomach in front of her laptop.

Not even a full minute went by before my phone pinged from the coffee table, and when I saw the name on the screen, I squeaked, all but throwing my laptop to the side and nearly spilling my wine in the process of reaching for it.

"What? Who is it?" Gemma asked, eyes wide with concern.

"It's Makoa."

Gemma squealed, abandoning her laptop to jump up on the couch next to me. She was practically on top of me as I read the text.

Makoa: Hey, gorgeous. How's your Friday night going?

I hated how red and hot my cheeks were, how wide my smile was as Gemma squeezed my arm and shook me and giggled like a girl in the audience of a BTS concert.

Me: Well, I'm in sweatpants and already one wine bottle down, so I'd say pretty great. How about you?

Makoa: First you've got me imagining you in yoga pants, now sweats? You really are the devil.

Gemma quirked a brow at me then, but I waved her off just as a new text came through.

Makoa: My night is going okay, but I think my Saturday could be better.

I bit my lip, typing out *Oh, and why's that?* as my response. Gemma and I were glued to my screen as the little bubbles bounced, letting us know he was typing, but then they went away. I frowned, looking to Gemma just as the phone buzzed in my hand.

With a picture of two tickets to *Moulin Rouge!* at the Nederlander.

"Oh my *God!*" Gemma grabbed the phone from my hands, zooming in on the picture. "Belle. These are third row tickets. In the freaking *Orchestra!* What even?!"

I tore my phone out of her hands, smiling at the screen. "Those had to cost a pretty penny."

"I'd say," she agreed. "He's really showing out for you."

I smiled again, gripping the phone a bit tighter as my heart raced. And the longer Gemma watched me, the harder that grip became.

"Belle."

I refused to look at her.

"You like him, don't you?"

"Hush," I said, typing out my response to Makoa — which was just a string of excited emojis. Then, I asked what time he'd pick me up.

As soon as the text was sent, Gemma took my phone again, this time propping her ass up long enough to shove it under her and then sit on top of it.

"Hey!" I argued.

"You'll get this back when you answer my question."

I huffed. "Of course, I like him. Isn't it obvious?"

"I mean, you *like him* like him."

I blinked.

"Isn't this going to be date three?"

I smiled at that, shimmying my hips. "It sure is."

"Which means..."

"Bang town!" I jumped up, bending over the arm of my couch and arching my back as I looked behind me at Gemma. I made my best *"O"* face and twerked my ass. "Oh yeah, Zaddy Mak. Just like that. Right there, don't stop!"

Gemma swatted my ass in a fit of laughter, and I plopped back down, reaching for my wine glass.

"Okay, yes, that's one part of it," she said when she finally stopped laughing. "But... are you really sure you want to let him go after this?"

All the laughter left the room with that question, and Gemma watched me with a sobering look of pity while my phone pinged under her ass. I looked at her crotch hopefully, but she swatted my hand when I tried to reach for the phone.

"You'll get that back when I say you do."

I chuckled. "Okay, *Mom*."

"Answer my question."

I sighed, hopping off the couch to pace with my wine. I was far too uncomfortable to sit if we were going to talk about this.

"I don't know, Gem. It's not as simple as what I want."

"Yes, it is."

"It's not, though." I held out my hand, exasperated. "Look, you don't get it, okay? You were married to Carlo right out of college, and now you have Zach. You're the kind of girl guys find adorable and sweet. They want to protect you and take you home to meet their family. They want to marry you." I swallowed, turning for another pace. "Me, on the other hand? I'm the one they fuck a few times, send some dick pics to when they're horny, and — my favorite — the one they hit up as soon as their relationship ends to *take them out and show them a good time.*"

Gemma's shoulders slumped when I turned back around, and I tore my eyes away from her. There weren't many things I hated more than someone looking at me like they felt sorry for me.

"Belle, it doesn't have to be like that."

"I was assigned my role a long time ago. I've accepted it."

"Fuck Nathan," she said, grabbing my wrist when I paced by her and pulling me down onto the couch. "He was an idiot for letting you go. But what he said about you?" She shook her head. "It's not true. *He* does not get to define you."

My chest tightened with the force of a car crusher, my heart wheezing under the pressure. "Look, I appreciate you saying that. Really, I do. But... it's just safer for me this way. I mean, look, I broke my three-date rule with Jordan, and look how that turned out." I waved my hand as if he were there with us.

"That's not fair," Gemma argued. "You guys didn't have a relationship — not a real one, anyway."

"That's because I can't *do* relationships."

"But you *could!*" She shook her head, desperate. "Can't you see that this guy is crazy about you? He's pulling out all the stops to date you like you deserve to be dated. This isn't a guy texting you at two in the morning to come over and 'watch movies'. Makoa *wants you.*"

I swept my hair behind my ears on a shrug. I wanted to lean into those words. I wanted to believe they were true.

But... I knew better.

"And he can have me," I said. "For one night." I looked at my best friend, hoping she saw how much I hated having this conversation so we could stop.

"And after that? You're just going to, what, ignore him? He's your client, too, in case you forgot. Are you just going to let *me* handle his condo design?"

"If I need to. But my bet is we could keep it professional. Makoa seems like a rational guy."

Gemma sighed, reaching over to grab my hand in hers. "I know you hate talking about this, so I won't beat a dead horse. But just listen to me for a second. Okay?"

I nodded.

"You once helped me pull my head out of my own ass when I was too blind to see that Zach was a good thing for me. And I know it's early with this guy, but he seems *really* great, Belle. And I don't want you to miss out on what could be with him because you're still listening to your douchebag of an ex."

"Along with every guy I've ever been with since him."

Gemma frowned, squeezing my hand. "You are the author of your story, Belle. You get to decide what happens next." She held up her hands in surrender, pulling out my phone from under her ass and handing it back to me. "And now I'm going to open another bottle of wine and leave it at that."

She was up off the couch before I could respond, and I stared at my phone a long time before unlocking it and laughing to myself at the string of emojis Makoa sent in response to mine.

Makoa: Let's do dinner beforehand. I'll pick you up at five.

Makoa: Can't wait to see you.

I clutched the stupid phone to my chest, willing my stupid heart to stop fluttering, reminding my stupid brain that if we followed that stupid heart, we'd end up shattered just like we did before.

I *had* to remember that.

It was the only way I'd survive.

CHAPTER 8

Makoa

Not going to lie, I felt dapper as hell when I arrived at Belle's place Saturday night.

There was a cool breeze rolling in between the buildings of downtown Chicago, a blessedly rare occasion on a summer evening, and I was thankful for it. I was dressed to the nines in my best tailored suit, an anthracite mohair frock coat and matching slacks that was of the Italian style. My tie was navy and silver, and, because it was *Moulin Rouge!*, I'd even brought a top hat.

I carried that hat under my arm, whistling a tune as I strolled up to the lobby of Belle's building. I checked in at the front desk — with a girl who blessedly didn't recognize me — and after a quick ring up to Belle's place, I was granted access, and the elevator took me up to the twentieth floor.

The nerves didn't hit me until I was at her door, my knuckles rapping on the wood. And when that door swung open and Belle appeared like a vision on the other side of it, it was all I could do to keep my jaw set and my heart steady.

Her hair was darker than the first time I met her, the strawberry blonde more of a deep auburn now, and she'd curled all that luscious hair of hers and pinned it into an elegant updo, one that featured an intricate braid around the crown of her head, and dainty curls that fell to frame her face. Her eyes were smoky and blazing, highlighted with just a hint of shimmery green shadow and framed by long, gorgeous lashes. Her lips — which had been a source of torture for me since I walked away from their touch Wednesday night — were painted a warm hue of red-brown that matched her hair.

Those lips curled into a soft smile as I let my eyes wander the length of her, taking in the curves and lines of her body accented so well in her floor-length emerald gown. It was elegant enough to attend the Met Gala, and somehow she made it look effortless and casual, like she just woke up and threw it on without any intentional thought behind it. There was intricate beading and lace that played with each other along every inch, and through the long slit, I spotted high, strappy gold heels peppered with sparkling gemstones.

Belle was the kind of woman who could make any straight man fall over his feet to watch her pass by on the street, even on her worst days.

But tonight?

She was radiant.

"Did I render you speechless, Mr. Kumaka?" she teased, and I realized I'd been standing there for at least a full minute without saying a single word.

I cleared my throat. "You... Jesus, Belle. I don't even know what to say." My eyes met hers, and once again I felt taken in by their mischievous allure. "You're breathtaking."

Her eyes flicked down to her feet as a smile washed over her face, cheeks flushed, and she looked almost bashful when she found my gaze again. I held out my arm, and she threaded hers through it, making my heart pound a little harder in my chest when she wrapped her fingers around my biceps.

I remembered all too well how those fingers wrapped around another part of me just a few nights ago.

"I was thinking we could walk, since it's just a few blocks," I said when we were in the elevator. "It's actually pretty nice outside. But..." I looked at her feet hesitantly. "We can get a cab. I know I wouldn't want to walk three blocks in those bad boys."

Belle scoffed. "Please. I've been walking in heels since I was twelve years old. A few blocks is a cake walk."

"You're sure?"

"Positive," she said, leaning into my side. Then, just as the elevator landed, she looked up at me with those intense, ever-changing eyes of hers. In the soft light of the elevator, or maybe because of the hue of her dress, they looked more green than blue tonight. "So, do I get a kiss, or do I have to wait until the end of the night for that?"

I smirked, trying to seem calm and unaffected when, in reality, my stomach did a somersault and a backflip and a double roundoff at this mesmerizing woman asking me to kiss her.

Gently, I tilted her chin with my knuckles, angling my mouth down until it met hers. We both inhaled at the contact, her warm lips pressing into mine with a soft urgency, and if it weren't for her hair being in such an elaborate updo, I would have run my fingers through it and tugged her head back to grant me more access.

As it was, the elevator dinged softly before the doors slid open, and I broke our kiss just in time for us to be face to face with the lobby desk clerk and another guest.

The clerk cleared her throat, forcing a smile. "Ms. Monroe."

"Good evening, Bethany," she greeted, still flushed from our kiss.

We stepped out of the elevator, and my heart picked up its pace for a completely different reason when I realized the way the guy with Bethany was staring at me. I'd seen that look a thousand times — the quizzical brow, the slightly parted lips, the distant stare as if they're racking their brain trying to remember how they know my face.

Before he could put two and two together, I tugged Belle forward, out of the elevator and out of the lobby until we were on the sidewalk.

"Wait!"

I stopped mid-stride, and when I turned to face Belle, she was smiling, holding out both of her hands.

"You're missing a key part of your outfit, good sir," she said.

Her eyes flicked to the top hat under my arm, and I chuckled, handing it to her and bowing a bit to let her place it on my head. When I stood again, I smoothed my hands over the lapels of my jacket, casting my gaze off to the right like a model. "How do I look?"

She chuckled. "Like a gentleman. A fine, upstanding gentleman."

"And you're my lady," I said, holding out my arm again.

I loved the sound of her laugh when she slid her arm in to hook with mine. I loved even more how comfortable it felt to walk with her, to joke with her, to wrap my hand over where hers held my arm.

Every warning sign that had been installed in my brain from the Girlfriends of Makoa Past blinked in bright neon, reminding me to not dive head first into those feelings like I did so often.

But with Belle? It felt... different.

I shook my head, knowing it was too early to get so caught up in my thoughts. For now, I had a beautiful woman on my arm and two orchestra tickets in my pocket, and that was all that mattered.

"So, where are we going to dinner?"

"I found this great local place not too far from the theatre. It's got a slew of five-star ratings, and a lot of the reviews say they have the best pierogies in town."

"Pierogies! Yum," she hummed.

The breeze had picked up even more, and when we turned the corner, it blasted us back, making Belle hide a little behind me as she squinted against it.

"I guess they don't call Chicago the Windy City for nothing," I joked, but inside, I was cursing my decision to walk. When I looked up and noticed the sky darkening, thick clouds rolling in from over the lake, panic zipped through me. "Maybe we should get a cab."

"No way, we're almost there," Belle said. "Also, fun fact, did you know Chicago wasn't actually named the Windy City because it's windy?"

I cocked a brow.

"Well, I mean, of course the fact that we're on the water and get a nice breeze is *part* of it," she continued. "But another part of it is that when we were really establishing ourselves, we were very competitive and proud. We competed with Cincinnati in trade and baseball, competed with D.C. and New York for the World Fair, and were just generally very loud about our city. It was a nickname that *other* cities gave us, because we loved to brag so much. Hence, *the Windy City.*"

I smirked, nudging her. "Look at you, little fountain of knowledge."

"Hey, you may be the Trivia King, but *I'm* the Chicago Trivia Queen." She chuckled, completely oblivious to how much I ate up the fact that she'd just referenced us as a duo, a King and Queen. "I kind of have to be, with my job. I make it my mission with every design I do to incorporate the city, even if it's in small ways."

"I love that," I commented, genuine, and she blushed a little as she peeked up at me through her lashes.

Just as she did, I felt a rain drop on my hand.

I looked down at the affronting drop, my wide eyes connecting with Belle's next, but it was too late. In the next second, it seemed, there was the distant sound of raindrops hitting concrete.

"Shit," I whispered, and Belle and I took off as quick as her heels allowed.

"Where is this place?!" she called as we tried to outrun the rain, but it was already sprinkling, and I watched Belle try to cover her hair with her small clutch.

"Just around that corner, across the street!"

I unfastened the buttons of my jacket and ripped it off as quickly as I could given the speed we were moving, but it was useless. Just as I freed it from my last wrist to shelter her with it, Mother Nature poured buckets.

I tried anyway, holding my jacket over Belle's head as we scurried to the edge of the sidewalk and waited for the light to change so we could cross the street. The rain came harder and louder, pounding the hot pavement and creating a wave of steam. My jacket was soaked in two seconds, which only made more water dump onto Belle's head, and I cursed, giving up and reaching for her hand, instead, to help her cross the street.

When we finally ducked inside the restaurant, we were both drenched, Belle's hair a wet blob on her head, and my top hat sunken in. Our clothes clung to us, every inch glistening with water, and the only way Belle's makeup was still in place had to be from waterproof magic.

We were out of breath, panting, and even though it was the middle of June, the combination of the cool rain and the air conditioning in the restaurant already had me shivering.

I lifted my eyes like a coward, grimacing when Belle met my gaze.

But she just covered her mouth with both hands, and then burst into the loudest, longest fit of laughter I'd ever witnessed.

She bent at the waist, one hand covering her stomach like it hurt how much she was laughing, and the other hand reaching out to squeeze my soaked jacket on my arm. That made her laugh even harder, and in the next breath, she was in my arms, pressed up onto her toes, her mouth on mine and her arms wrapped around my neck.

I inhaled the scent of her, her perfume mixed with the rain, and even though she was trembling in my arms, her body was warm against mine.

"I'm so sorry," I breathed between a kiss. "I'm a fucking idiot for not getting a car."

"Stop," she said, pulling back with her hands still wrapped around my neck. "That was fun. Besides, I hated my hairdo anyway."

She shook her head like a dog, hitting me with droplets as she laughed again, and I pulled her into me for a kiss like it was the only possible thing I could do in that moment. This time, I held her close, wrapping her in my arms like I could warm her up from the inside out. I kissed her slow and sure, and it wasn't until someone cleared their throat as they walked into the restaurant and slid past us that I broke the kiss, putting marginal space between us.

"I'm starving," Belle said, and the way her eyes heated with those words, I wondered if it was the food she wanted, or me.

"Well, let's get you fed."

I grabbed her hand, turning and expecting to find us face to face with an annoyed hostess. Instead, I found an almost-empty room, with simple gray tile floors and high industrial ceilings, the brick exposed on either wall, and a whopping five cafeteria-like tables with four fast-food type chairs at each.

I swallowed, looking up at the menu on the wall, and then at the counter where it seemed you ordered your food.

It wasn't a restaurant at all.

I grimaced, looking down at Belle and expecting to find her nose wrinkled in the same way. But instead, her eyes were bright and diamond-like, fixed on the menu as she read off each item. "Oh, the spinach and cheddar ones sound *amazing*," she said. Then, she turned to me. "Are you going to get yours with sour cream and chives?"

I shook my head, watching her in awe.

"What?" she asked. "Why are you looking at me like that?"

Because you're the most fascinating, beautiful, wonderful woman to ever exist.

"Nothing," I said instead, guiding her closer to the counter. "You order for us. Let's get a smorgasbord and try whatever you want."

"Whatever I want?" she repeated, leaning into me as she lowered her voice. "I hope that offer stands at the end of the night, too."

Then, she was ordering almost every pierogi on the menu.

And I was thinking of football and stray dogs and my mom and anything else I could conjure up to ward off the erection threatening to grow in my very wet, very stuck-to-every-inch-of-me pants.

Despite its rugged, somewhat rundown appearance, it was easy to see how the restaurant had such great reviews once we'd finished eating. The pierogies were out of this world, perfectly fried little pillows of potato heaven, with different fillings and garnishes that left us both maybe a little *past* comfortably full by the time we were done.

The rain had come and gone, but we were still damp as we walked down the street to where the theatre was. I tried offering a car a million times so Belle could go back and change, but she insisted she was fine, and we walked into the theatre with our heads held high — despite the fact that our clothes were wrinkled and damp, Belle's hair looked like a bird's nest, and my shoes squeaked every time I walked.

"These seats are *insane*," Belle said when we were settled in, her eyes lighting up as she took in the stage design from our center orchestra view. She cocked a brow when she looked at me again. "Look at you, big baller. Real estate must pay well, huh?"

She said it with an easy chuckle, her eyes back on the stage design without a second thought, but just that little sentence had my mind racing, wondering if there was something more under the words. *Was she hinting that she knew I did more than real estate? Was she already thinking of all the other nice places I could take her, the things I could buy for her?*

As soon as that last thought hit me, I mentally slapped myself. I knew better than to think Belle needed *my* money. She could joke about me springing for the tickets all she wanted, but I knew that if she wanted, she could spend her own money and easily afford these, too.

Okay, maybe not *as* easily as I could, but I knew she held her own.

Again, my mind was racing, and the only relief I found was that the lights flickered three times, signaling that it was time for everyone to take their seats. Belle looked at me with an excited little wiggle dance in her seat, and then we both sat back, and the show began.

Moulin Rouge! was a new show on Broadway, based on Baz Luhrmann's revolutionary film that released in 2001. I still remembered the first time I saw the movie — not in the theater, because that was a rare occurrence for a family as big as ours — but in a pile of siblings on my living room floor. I remembered my two older sisters, Pania and Tamar, braiding each other's hair as we watched, their eyes lit up like they couldn't wait to be in love that desperately. My younger sister, Leinani, was a little too young to care about any movie that wasn't a cartoon, so she mostly played with her dolls next to me on the floor. Mom and Dad on the couch, Oliana growing inside Mom's belly, and I was right there in the middle of it all, pretending like I was bored, when the truth was that I was right there with my two older sisters.

Enamored, completely swept away with thoughts of Paris and freedom and love.

I was only nine years old. I should have been in my room playing with my G.I. Joes or out learning how to surf with my best friend, Akamu.

Instead, I was leaned back against the foot of the couch, arms crossed, acting like I was annoyed and couldn't wait for that movie to be over. But I loved every minute of it. And I'd watched it at least a dozen times since then.

But I realized before the first act was even over that *none* of those times would compare to this.

The costumes were dazzling and bright and luxurious, the stage design elaborate and magical. We weren't just watching *Moulin Rouge!*, we were *in Moulin Rouge!* Every new song pulled me in, deeper and deeper, and all the while, Belle was there at my side, on the edge of her seat just as much as I was, both of us enraptured by the actors and actresses and dancers on stage.

But, as amazing as the show was, there was one little problem that kept us both from being fully immersed...

We were freezing.

The air was turned down to combat the summer heat, which — on a normal occasion — would be a blessed relief for a man in a suit and a woman in a ball gown. But as it was, we were still damp, and the longer we sat there, the more we shivered.

By the time intermission rolled around, my muscles were stiff from trembling so much, and Belle's teeth were chattering enough to chew through a tree trunk.

"I'm going to run to the restroom," she said. "And maybe hold my hands under the hot water for a solid two minutes."

I chuckled. "I'll grab us some wine."

"Oh, good idea! That'll help warm us up."

We broke like two soldiers on a mission, me going one way and her the other.

I bought us a bottle of wine, along with some popcorn and chocolates. I was on my way back to our seats when I spotted the merchandise booth, and my eyes lit up at a particular item. I reached for my wallet again without a second thought, and with my new acquirements in tow, I headed back inside.

"Ohhhh, merlot," Belle cooed when I rejoined her at the seats. "Man after my heart."

I chuckled to hide the fact that yes, I was very much *indeed* after said heart. "Just wait until I show you what else I got."

I unloaded each item one by one, Belle lighting up at the popcorn first, and then the chocolates. But I saved the best for last, pulling the two hoodies I'd draped over my shoulder up for her to see.

"Oh, my God," she said, reaching for the smaller of the two and clutching it to her chest like it was a lifeline. "Where did you find these?!"

"Merch booth. Figured they could be a souvenir."

"A very *useful* souvenir," she said on a laugh, and in the next breath she had the hoodie pulled over her head. She sighed as the warmth surrounded her, and I was glad I bought the larger ones, because she tucked her knees up to her chest and covered her entire body with it. "Oh, my *God*, this is so much better." She looked up at me. "Not all heroes wear capes."

"Nope. This hero wears a hoodie that matches the damsel in distress."

Belle laughed as I pulled on the other hoodie, and then I plopped down next to her, pouring us each a glass of wine and carefully nestling the bottle on the floor between us.

"So, I've started getting deliveries," I said, cheersing her glass with mine.

"Oh?" She feigned innocence, but her eyes told me she knew exactly what had been delivered.

"Mm-hmm. I'm excited to see it all come together."

"One room at a time, but we'll get there," she said, and then she bit her lip, cupping her hands around her wine glass. The hoodie was so oversized that it practically swallowed her, just her fingers poking out from the sleeves. "I have an idea for the sitting room."

"Yeah?" I asked. We'd gone over plans for the bedroom, the living room, the kitchen and even the guest room. We were still trying to decide what to do with the extra space that could be an office or a workout area — mostly because I was keeping that space for football. Of course, I couldn't exactly tell her that. At least, not yet.

"Well, I know you wanted to make it feel a little like home, right? And, well, with your love of wood... I was thinking..."

She bit her lip again, shaking her head as if for courage before she took out her phone and pulled up a vision board.

"What if we did a Polynesian theme with a Chicago flare? Here, let me show you what I mean."

She swiped through each photo, which showed large wooden tiki totems, brightly colored Polynesian art, and lush tropical plants.

"Now, before you go thinking I'm going to turn your sitting room into a tiki bar, let me explain. I was thinking, what if we sort of told a story with the room? I know that's a big part of Polynesian tattoos." She paused, looking at me then. "Yes, I Googled. Anyway, what if we used each wall to tell a story, using the totems, tattoo-inspired art, like these?"

She showed me a mandala lined with symbols that I knew stood for war and love, and then a beautiful, oversized canvas print of lava flowing into the ocean in what looked like Kilauea.

"I thought we could paint a story of your homeland, but fuse it with the boldness of Chicago. We'd put in bright, statement furniture pieces, like this yellow couch," she said, showing me the couch, which had an older style to it, like it came right out of the 20s or 30s. "And we'd keep architecture in mind the whole way. I'm thinking huge wooden bookcases, geometric tables and lamps, low lighting, really hygge."

"Hyooh-what?"

She chuckled. "Hygge. It's a Danish word that essentially means warm and cozy."

I smiled. "I like that."

"I know you're here during the summer, which is *gorgeous*," she said. "But trust me when I say that the winters can be brutal. And *long*. So, having this nice, cozy space is an absolute must. And we can fill it with books and board games, make it a place you love to entertain your family and friends in. No television," she said quickly, holding up one finger. "That's reserved for the living room."

I chuckled. "I think this sounds perfect."

"Yeah?"

I nodded, taking the phone from her hands and swiping through a few more pictures. "It'll be a nice effect, taking the cold metal and contrasting it with the warm wood, the stark geo metal of the lights and the tables and chairs and mixing them with the soft swoops of the Polynesian art and the bright colors of the photography."

"Right! And, it'll be like a joining of homes — your old one, and your new one." She nudged me, taking her phone back. "I'll even let you put that stupid San Francisco football blanket in there to represent your in-between home, too."

I smiled at the joke, but mostly just watched her in fascination. "You're pretty rad, you know that?"

Belle laughed, the sweetest sound. "Rad, huh? I don't think anyone has ever called me that."

"Glad to be the first."

We shared a smile just as the lights flickered, and then we settled in, both warmer now and with a glass of wine and chocolates.

Just as the show started, I reached over and grabbed her hand, holding it in mine.

And she squeezed it, smiling against a flush I knew she thought I couldn't see.

The second half of the show was just as powerful as the first, and even more riveting, gripping me by the heart and holding me captive. And yet, as much as I watched the stage, I couldn't keep my eyes from drifting over to Belle.

I loved the way she watched so intently, the way her eyes watered when tragedy struck, the way her hand squeezed mine a little tighter when the drama surged. I'd never taken a woman to a show before — mostly because any woman I had asked had never been even remotely interested.

To see someone who loved it as much as I did, who felt it the way I did — deep down to the core — it was magical.

The end of the show brought us to our feet, along with the rest of the crowd, and we stood and applauded and cheered as the dancers, actors and actresses, and orchestra took their bows. We were both still bouncing and talking a hundred miles an hour as we spilled out into the streets of Chicago with the rest of the audience.

"And her *voice*," Belle said, mouth wide open. "I mean, I couldn't hold my shit together that second half. I was crying every other song."

"Their chemistry was so believable."

"And the *dancers*."

"Incredible. The design, the colors, the songs. Although, as much as I loved the mashups with all the familiar songs, I think an original score could have really set this show on another level."

"Yeah," Belle agreed with a click of her tongue. "I agree. I think it was lacking a bit there. But, otherwise?" She did a chef's kiss, smiling up at me. "Perfection."

I smirked, taking in the sight of her, the pavement wet from the evening rainstorm, lights playing off of it and sparkling in her eyes, too. Her hair was still matted to her head, and the hoodie fell down past her knees, a hilarious contradiction to the bottom grandeur of her gown and high heels.

Belle followed my gaze, covering her face with the sleeves of the hoodie — her hands completely hidden inside now — and shaking her head. "Ugh. I look like such a mess right now."

I shook my head, too, pulling her into me and tilting her chin up so I could see her eyes. "You look perfect."

Her eyes flicked back and forth between mine, and when they fell to my lips, I knew what she wanted without her asking. And I was eager to answer.

I tilted her chin a bit more, pressing my forehead to hers before I bent to capture her lips. They were warm and tasted like wine, and I leaned into them, soaking up every last drop.

Belle's hands wrapped around my waist, pulling me closer, and by the time we broke the kiss, we were both breathless, panting, tugging at each other's hoodies like they were the only things tying us to the Earth.

"You know, that big, fancy California King bed you ordered for my bedroom got delivered yesterday."

Belle snaked her tongue out over her bottom lip. "*Did it now?*"

I nodded. "Mm-hmm. Sure did. Complete with that plush, memory foam mattress, and the buttery-smooth, one-thousand-thread-count sheets."

She hummed. "That so?"

"Comforter, pillows, the whole shebang."

"Well, I *did* put in a rush order on all that," she confessed, pulling me closer, her lips dancing over mine. "Couldn't have you sleeping on an air mattress any longer than absolutely necessary."

"So thoughtful," I mused, thumbing her bottom lip.

She bit it as soon as it was free from the touch, and I inhaled a breath that stabbed my chest like a thousand tiny needles.

"So..." I said, caressing her cheek with my knuckles. "Wanna come see all your hard work?"

A devilish smile spread on those perfect lips of hers, and then with a brief, hot kiss and a wave of her hand in the air, we were in a cab on our way across town.

CHAPTER 9

Belle

We crashed through Makoa's condo door like we were bursting into a burning building to save a dozen kittens.

My back hit the wall with a loud thud, stealing my breath just before Makoa's lips were there taking whatever was left of it. He shut the door behind him with his foot, dropping his still-damp suit jacket on the floor, along with his top hat.

His hands were in my hair next, gripping and tilting, his mouth claiming me with every kiss.

I was perfectly warm, thanks to the massive *Moulin Rouge!* hoodie Makoa bought for me, but still, I trembled in his arms. Every new kiss elicited a new wave of chills, racing from every point of contact until they covered me head to toe. Makoa was a completely different man with his hands on me. It was like touching me brought out every carnal urge that lived inside him.

It'd only been a little over a week since I met this man, and somehow, it felt like I'd waited a lifetime for this moment.

As if he read my mind, Makoa's hands snaked under my hoodie, and he groaned when his hands palmed my breasts. "God, do you know how badly I've wanted to touch you all night?" He nipped at my bottom lip, trailing a line of kisses down my jaw line, my neck, until his next words were whispers right in the shell of my ear. "These tits, those legs, your perfect fucking mouth — they're all I've thought about for days."

I moaned when he hiked one of my legs up over his hip, my dress coming with it, pressing his erection into the heat of me. I remembered all too well how firm and thick it felt in my hands, and all I wanted was to free it from the fabric that I'd damned for separating us.

Makoa kissed me again, hard, and I shoved my hands into his chest until he bounded backward. Then, I lifted my hands with a smile. "Take this off."

Without hesitation, Makoa grabbed the hem of the hoodie and slipped it up over my head. He did the same with the one he wore, and I had about two seconds of appreciation for his Italian suit before I launched myself at him again.

We were a cluster of hands deftly making work of fabric, our lips fused together in a heated, almost hateful kiss. I unbuttoned his vest, he unzipped my dress. I tore open his dress shirt and he pulled every bobby pin from my hair, casting it down in a damp, curly, mess of waves over my shoulders.

"I can't figure this thing out," I cursed, yanking at his belt.

"That makes two of us," he said, panting as he tried to figure out the straps covering the back of my gown.

We exchanged a look, and then for only as long as it took to finish getting undressed, we took our hands off each other.

He watched me with a grin as I pulled at the straps behind me, freeing one shoulder and then the next. My dress fell in a puddle at my feet just as Makoa kicked off his dress shoes and yanked his pants down to his ankles. He stood there in navy blue dress socks and boxer briefs that hugged his thick, tight ass, thighs, and erection in ways that would make a photographer drool and beg for an exclusive shoot.

I stepped out of my dress, but before I could move for my heels, Makoa had me backed into the wall again, my hands over my head, his lips claiming mine.

"Leave those on," he husked.

His hands trailed down, working my strapless bra off with one easy snap. Makoa backed up then, his eyes drinking me in, and his fingertips cast more chills in their wake as they made their way to my breasts.

"Fuck *me*," he said, shaking his head. He palmed them, massaging them as my head fell back against the wall and I leaned into the touch. When he pulled at the nipples, gentle yet firm enough to make them pucker, I let out a little yelp.

And that must have done it.

He lost all control then, something of a growl ripping from his throat before I was hoisted up and over his shoulder like a bag of fucking potatoes. I would have laughed, if it wasn't so goddamn sexy. I felt like a prisoner, like he was a caveman about to have his way with me.

I expected him to carry me to the bedroom, but we only made it to the kitchen, and the granite was cool when he sat my thong-clad ass on top of it. As soon as I was stable, he bent, sweeping his tongue over my nipple before I had the chance to prepare for it.

A bolt of electricity shot through me, and I gasped, gripping what I could of his short hair in my hands. He moved to the other nipple, sucking it just as hard, and my pussy throbbed in anticipation of what his mouth would do to it next.

"It took every fucking bit of restraint I possessed not to take you right here," he said, sucking my nipple again and releasing it with a pop. "Just like this." He lifted one of my legs as I leaned back on my palms, and he placed my high heel on his shoulder, trailing his fingertips down my leg until they skated over the lace of my panties. "The very first fucking time you were here."

"You should have," I whispered, or maybe I panted it. I couldn't be sure, and I couldn't believe it was me making the desperate, mewling sounds of need as his fingers pushed my panties to the side.

"No," he said, and his eyes connected with mine. "You were worth the wait."

His middle finger slipped inside me, slicking through my wet folds and filling me as I trembled at the sensation. I let my head fall back, my eyes closed, embracing everything about the way it felt to have that massive, beastly finger inside me.

Makoa kissed all over my breasts, sucking and biting and licking as his finger curled inside me, and I swore to God I could come right there. I could detonate without him even putting that glorious cock inside me.

Makoa didn't give me the chance, though. As if he knew I was close, he flipped me before I could make sense of it, and I was bent over the kitchen island, the granite biting into my hips as he pressed into me from behind.

His hands wrapped in my hair and tugged, until my back arched, my ass cheeks framing the length of him. He sucked the lobe of my ear between his teeth, making me shiver and shake, and then he peeled my panties down over my ass, my thighs, leaving them where they fell at my ankles.

"Bend over," he whispered.

"I am."

He pressed his hand onto my back, flattening me against the granite. "More."

I wrapped my hands around the edges of the counter, bracing for impact with my heart racing out of my chest.

I expected to feel his cock ram inside me, but instead, he dropped to his knees.

And then he gripped my hips, pulling them back, arching me as much as humanly possible before he dragged his tongue from my clit to my asshole in one, full sweep.

I shook so hard I nearly fell to the floor, the heels adding to how difficult it was to keep my fucking legs working. Makoa took the hint, took my weight in his hands, and then he dove in for more.

His tongue was a whip, lashing me, over and over. He'd run the hot, flatness of it over and in, sucking at my ass, flicking at my clit. Gone was the fumbling, nervous, mess of a man I'd encountered the past few dates. It seemed whenever the clothes came off, Makoa became something else entirely.

A warrior. A beast.

A pussy-worshiping, unrelenting punisher.

My moans turned into something that would put even the hottest porn star to shame as he ate me out, but again, just when I was close enough to come, he leapt to his feet, and I collapsed into his arms.

"Don't give up on me yet," he teased, kissing my neck before he put my hands on the countertop, instructing me to wait.

He was gone only a minute before he returned to the kitchen, ripping a gold packet open as he did. Then, he ripped his briefs down, stepping out of them like it was nothing. Like he didn't just free the motherland of all cocks. Like his erection wasn't the hardest, thickest, prettiest dick I'd ever seen in my life.

"Wait, wait, wait," I said, panting, my hands pressing to his chest when he advanced on me.

Makoa frowned. "Are you okay?" Then, his eyes went wide. "Oh, God. Did I move too fast? Do you want to stop?"

I almost snorted. "No, stupid." Then, I pressed gently until he was standing a few feet away from me. "I want to admire the savage brute you just released."

Makoa's brow arched, and then he followed my gaze down to his length, smirking as he shook his head. He went to move for me again, but I held up one finger.

"Ah, ah," I said, waving the finger as I tilted my head to one side. I took in every blessed inch of that man's body, from his ridiculously sculpted abdomen and thick, tattooed chest and arms, to his tree-trunk quads and deep-cut V that led to the promise land.

His cock hung between his legs, so heavy it couldn't stand straight up even at full mast. It hung a little to the left, the tip mushroomed and thick, the base lined in veins.

It really was the most perfect cock I'd ever seen.

I almost wanted to cry.

"Are you done yet?" he asked with a smirk. "Because I'd *really* like to fuck you bent over this counter now."

I licked my lips, turning to face the counter again and bracing my hands on the edges. I bent at the waist, flicking my hair over my back, and then I looked back at him through my lashes with a *come and get me* stare.

Makoa bit his lip, shaking his head as he tore open what was left of the condom wrapper and slipped the magnum over his length. I watched hungrily as he stroked himself, striding toward me like he was about to conquer a fucking kingdom.

One hand grabbed my waist, the other lined his cock up at my entrance. I knew before he even pressed forward an inch that this was going to fucking hurt, but there was no way I was backing out now.

I arched my back, pressing my ass up to meet him, and Makoa kissed my neck, once, twice, three times before he pressed the first inch of his head inside me.

I gasped at the sensation, a combination of pleasure and pain ripping through me.

"You okay?"

"Mm-hmm," I think I answered, and I backed up, pressing him more inside me.

He hissed a breath, both of his hands finding my hips and helping. In and out, little by little, we worked together until I had that full behemoth inside me.

And when I did, it was pure ecstasy.

"Oh, god*damn*, Belle," he cursed, sliding all the way out before he filled me again. "You feel so fucking good."

I moaned, a whispered *yes* on my lips as he picked up the pace, finding a rhythm between my legs. I was so full, so fucking worked up that I didn't even need to touch my clit to feel my orgasm building. It was everything else making me come. It was the Chicago skyline through the windows, and the granite against my stomach, and his massive hands encasing my hips, and his breath mingling with mine in the sweetest, most seductive dance.

I didn't want to admit it out loud, but Makoa was right.

It was *definitely* worth the wait.

"*Fuck*, baby, I'm going to come," he breathed.

I ignored the fact that he'd just called me baby — a term *far* too intimate for my taste — and even more so the fact that I really, *really* liked it. Instead, I turned my focus to the more *pressing* fact that he'd just said he was about to come.

And I was *not* ready for that.

I pushed him backward, immediately pressing my lips to his and yanking him down to the floor. We crashed down in a tangle of limbs, and then he was on his back, and before he could even put two and two together to figure out how we got here, I climbed up to straddle him.

"Not yet, baby."

Shit.

Did that word just come from my mouth?

Again, I chose ignorance, at least for the time being. Reaching down between us, I positioned him at my entrance again and balanced on my feet. Makoa took the cue, his massive hands holding the weight of my ass, and then I lowered down, inch by blissful inch.

And this time, I got to watch his face as he filled me.

"Don't go until I do," I warned, and then, I started moving.

I worked slow at first, lowering down completely until I felt his balls on my ass before I lifted and repeated the motion. His hands supported me the entire way, and when I picked up the speed, he took the weight of me, helping me bounce on that glorious cock of his.

"Jesus *Christ*." His eyes rolled back, and I knew he was doing everything he could not to come.

I lowered down gently to my knees, still riding him, and moved his hands to grab my tits.

"That's not helping," he groaned, but his eyes shot open, watching in wonder as my tits bounced in his hands.

"Not yet," I warned, and then I reached between my legs, my entire body trembling when my fingers brushed over my clit. I was so wet, so fucking close that just the first touch had the blood tingling in every vein.

I rubbed slow circles at first, gyrating my hips, feeling his hands as they rolled over my nipples. Then, I worked my clit harder, faster, leaning back to feel him as deep as I could.

And with another warning from Makoa that he was going to come, I let go.

Moans and cries of pleasure ripped from my throat as the blood coursed through me, hot and electric, numbness invading every centimeter of my being. It was animalistic, the way I rode him in those last moments, with me coming on his cock and him pulsing out his own release inside the condom. Those little pulses only fueled my orgasm to last even longer, and by the time we were both spent, I collapsed on top of him, our bodies slick where they met.

Fucking hell.

I just laid there, panting, eyes closed as Makoa ran his fingers through my hair. He was still inside me, slowly growing soft, and with what felt like every ounce of effort I had left, I lifted my head to look at him.

"We didn't even make it to the bed."

Makoa laughed, brushing the hair from my face before he leaned up to kiss me, long and soft, maybe even a little too sweet for my taste.

But with him?

It didn't feel so weird.

"Well, let's fix that."

Makoa was up off the floor before I could register to do the same, and he picked me up easily, cradling me in his arms and walking me back through his condo to his bedroom. He laid me down in the plush, cool sheets, and I let out a sigh as he carefully removed my heels, one by one, letting them fall to the floor.

"Wow," I said, stretching out and wiggling my freshly freed toes. I didn't have to look to know I had blisters from the rain and the straps. "These sheets are what happen when velvet and silk have a baby."

Makoa laughed.

"Seriously. Come here. This is heaven."

"No, being inside you was heaven," he argued, taking the spot next to me before he rolled over to perch his head on one arm. The other drew circles on my stomach, and I purred like a kitten at the touch.

For a long while, we lay just like that, the only sound that of the city still alive outside in the distance. It was dark, save for the city lights outside the windows and the few we'd managed to flick on in the main living area streaming through the hallway.

I watched Makoa's eyes as they roamed over me, like he was a painter studying me for his next project. His fingers followed where his eyes were, and I wondered if he was memorizing every inch.

Maybe it was the rain, the way he'd looked running in it, the way he'd tried to shield me from it, the way he'd watched me in wonder when I'd laughed once we safely made it inside that restaurant. Maybe it was how easy the conversation flowed through dinner, or how making his condo a home was the only thing I could focus on, or how every time I looked at him I had a new question to ask, and every time he looked at me, I felt like the only woman in the world. Maybe it was how he'd called me his lady, and as cheesy as it was, it'd done something to my stomach, to my heart, maybe even to my soul.

Maybe it was *Moulin Rouge!*, the music and lights and colors. Maybe it was Satine's words in my ear, whispering, taunting.

Why else live if not for love?

I could blame a million different things for the way my heart beat loud in my chest there in that bed, in Makoa's arms, but I knew one thing for certain.

I couldn't walk away from him.

Not now.

Maybe not ever.

And that was a very, very bad thing.

I swallowed down the lump in my throat, tracing his tattoos as he traced the curves of my body. I was just about to ask him what one of them meant when he sighed, sweeping my hair back from my face.

"You're so far from any woman I've ever known."

I smiled, leaning into the touch. "What do you mean?"

He shrugged. "I'm just... I'm blown away with how you handled tonight. The rain, the restaurant."

"Those pierogies were like little potato puffs of heaven."

He laughed. "They were, but... I expected this high-end restaurant. And for us to both be dry and warm."

"Gotta roll with the punches," I said on a shrug. Then, I tapped his shoulder. "And *you* need to do better Google searches."

Makoa laughed. "That, I do." He shook his head, still watching me in awe.

And then, he said the worst thing he could have possibly said.

"You're such a good time."

My heart stopped, stuck in the grimy mud of what that line insinuated as Makoa kissed my forehead and popped out of bed.

"I'm going to take a shower. Wanna join?"

I shook my head, but he was already in the bathroom, the water running. I cleared my throat and forced out a croaky, "No, I'm okay."

A good time.

You're such a good time.

His words played on repeat in my head, over and over, again and again. I played them in every pitch, heard them as I thought back over the night, over our last few dates.

I'd read it all wrong.

All this time, even when I'd *warned* myself not to, I'd leaned into the possibility that maybe... just maybe... I was wrong. Maybe Gemma and Zach were right. Maybe Makoa wanted more. Maybe he was different. Maybe he was about to prove that I wasn't broken, damaged, washed up and only good for one thing.

And then as soon as he'd had me, he'd said the same words Nathan had all those years ago.

You're so far from any woman I've ever known.

AKA, you're not like the girls I take home to meet my family.

You're such a good time.

AKA, I really like fucking you, we should do that again.

We should do *just* that again.

I was such a tight bundle of anxiety that I didn't think to get dressed and get the hell out of Makoa's place until he was out of the shower and climbing back into bed with me. He pulled me into his chest, curling around me like a cat, and all the while, I stared out the windows wondering how I could have ever been so stupid to believe he would be any different.

I was a fool, a hungry little fool who ate into every line he fed me.

And because I'd believed in him, in the *possibility* of him, I was already hurt.

This was why I held up my guard. *This* was why I never entertained the option of being more than just the good-time girl.

This was why I had a firm three-date rule.

I blew out a long breath, reminding myself that I was still in a somewhat safe territory. I may have taken a few pieces of shrapnel to the heart, but this technically *was* date three. I could still retreat behind enemy lines.

So, when Makoa's breathing evened out, heavy and sound, I slipped out from under his arm, got dressed in my damp, cold dress, and put on my heels.

And I left.

CHAPTER 10

Makoa

It took me a week to figure out that I'd been ghosted.

I woke up early Sunday morning after my date with Belle, and was not-so-pleasantly surprised to not find her next to me when I rolled over in the giant California King bed she'd picked out for me. After all, I'd fallen asleep hugging her like a body pillow, but before the sun was even all the way up past the horizon, she was gone.

I'd frowned, rubbing the sleep from my eyes and attempting a phone call. When she didn't answer, I shot a text telling her what a great time I'd had and that I couldn't wait to see her again.

No text came in return.

I was busy Sunday. I met up with Gerald for more drills at the high school and spent the evening on a video call with my family. That call lasted four hours — which it often did. We had two parents and four siblings, which meant catching up took a while.

Still, I watched my phone and jumped any time it vibrated.

It was never Belle.

On Monday, my condo was a zoo of people delivering couches, chairs, tables, lamps, art, kitchen appliances, and more. It was the first of three back-to-back days of having people in and out of my condo, including Gemma, who was there overseeing where everything was placed, how it was built and set up, and adjusting things that didn't fit the way she wanted them to once they were placed.

But Belle was nowhere to be found.

By Thursday, I was worried. Had I said something wrong? Did I snore? Did the sex suck? But every question I came up with, I couldn't find a reason for her to completely ignore me. Combing over our date, all I could see was her smiling, all I could hear was her laughter and her moans in my ear, all I could think of was what an amazing night it had been — and I knew she felt the same.

I also knew without a doubt that she did *not* think the sex sucked.

The way we'd fucked... the way she'd moaned and arched into me, the way she rode me on my kitchen floor, the way she'd pulsed around me when we both hit our climax at the same time... that entire experience was out of body, out of mind, completely wrapped up in a connection that only happens once in a lifetime.

Had she not felt it, too?

When I still hadn't heard from her by Friday night, my worry was turning slowly to something else. It was all I could do not to drive over to her place, bang on her door, and demand she talk to me. I was tired of my emails and calls to her office being fielded to Gemma. I couldn't bear to open her name in my phone and see the five unanswered text messages I'd sent her before I told myself I was being pathetic.

Here it was. Saturday. A full week since our date.

And I finally understood.

When I woke up this morning, I'd started wondering if I'd imagined her. Was she a vision I'd somehow willed into being with wanting so desperately to find someone? Did I make up the way she felt in my arms, the way my name sounded when it rolled off her perfect lips, the way her blue-green eyes lit up when she looked at me?

I'd survived my workout as if it was someone else doing it altogether, and then numbly sat alone watching film that I knew I wasn't retaining anything from. Because my attention should have been focused on the television screen, but instead, my eyes kept drifting over everything new in my condo.

There was the giant sectional couch that I sat on, one Belle had carefully selected, keeping in mind how big I was, how I said I wanted to entertain, how I noted that I wanted warm, inviting colors. There was the bed I kept losing sleep in, and the geometric bar stools at the kitchen island, and the totem statue, made of teak, that was so far from the cheesy, commercialized tiki totem I'd imagined when she'd first explained it. It was modern and architecturally satisfying, a beautiful statement piece.

Every time my eyes wandered, I was even more upset. I'd see an art piece curated in my honor, or a combination of shapes and textiles and fabric that somehow captured exactly who I was as a person. And then, anger started seeping in.

It was when I got pissed that I could fully accept it.

She had ghosted me.

It didn't take long for hurt to push anger out of the way, and that hurt settled in for the long haul, pitching a tent and building a fire. Here I had been opening myself up to this girl, and she'd been waiting to fuck so she could ditch me immediately after.

At least, that was my assumption.

In reality, I had no fucking idea what happened. I knew I could be a sucker when it came to pretty girls, but damn... I really had thought she was different. For the life of me, I couldn't figure out how we had both been together for what felt like the most perfect date, and then woke up in two completely different realms.

Me, confused when I woke up alone and excited to see her again.

Her, already erasing me from her life.

And now, on a Saturday night I would have rather been spending with her, I was sitting at Doc's bar, alone, trying to convince myself it wasn't a big deal that I hadn't heard from her while I polished off my third beer.

My phone was face up on the bar, as if that would somehow conjure Belle to call it. I stared at that phone like it was a cornerback who'd just stolen my pass and I was about to pummel it into the ground.

"Another?" the bartender asked, swiping my empty glass off the bar as soon as I'd downed it. His name was Dave, and he was a Chicago native, born and raised and in love with everything that the city was. He'd recognized me as soon as I sat down, and what I liked most about Dave was that he didn't make a big deal of it. He didn't call a bunch of attention to me, ask for a photo or an autograph, or ask me a million questions about the upcoming season.

Instead, he'd just greeted me with a nod and a napkin on the bar, tapping it before he said, "What'll it be, Kumaka?"

I liked him instantly.

Still, at the present moment, it was difficult to be anything but salty and sour. I managed a tight smile when I nodded for him to bring another, but then my jaw was set with my gaze on the phone again.

"It's none of my business," Dave said when he plopped another full glass of beer in front of me. "But whoever it is that you want to call, maybe you should just bite the bullet and call *them* first."

I huffed, taking a big gulp of the amber liquid. It sloshed out onto the bar again when I sat it down with more force than I meant to. "Trust me, I've tried."

"Getting the cold shoulder, huh?"

I harrumphed.

"A girl?" he asked.

I practically growled in confirmation.

Dave planted both his palms on the bar, leveling his gaze with mine. "Alright, then. Here's the deal. Pick up that phone and call her."

I went to argue that I already had when he held up his hand.

"I'll give you three chances. This is the sensitive part of me, okay? Three calls, and if she doesn't answer by that third time, then you're handing your phone to me and I'm blocking her and you're paying your tab and letting me put your ass in a cab to go home and sleep it off. You leave that girl here in this bar, and you start tomorrow without giving her another piece of your time or energy."

I didn't like the sound of that, even though I knew he was right.

I couldn't hold on to the girl forever.

Why did that fact make me want to vomit?

"She's my interior designer," I tried. "I can't just block her."

"I'm sure she has an office phone. No?"

I couldn't argue with that point.

Dave slid my phone a little closer. "Three chances. Let's get this over with."

I looked at the device, at him, then back at the phone. "What if she answers?"

Dave watched me for a second before he offered a shrug. "You talk to her."

I tapped my fingers on the bar, shaking my head and taking a giant gulp of my beer. I held up the half-empty glass toward Dave. "I think you're going to need to give me a few more of these first."

Belle

I had my ass in the air and my left foot extended overhead in a three-legged downward dog when my phone rang from across the room.

"Shit, sorry," I murmured to Gemma, who was trying to stay Zen as she exhaled, crunching her knee to her chest in a plank.

She inhaled, lifting her leg back to three-legged downward dog. "It's all good. Just leave it."

"I'll go turn the ringer off."

"Leave it," she said again, giving me a pointed look before she blew out another breath and shot her foot between her hands, windmilling up to warrior one.

I joined her, forcing another breath and trying to ignore my phone going off. During a normal practice, that would have been achievable. I was a Zen master, after all.

As it was, I not only had to ignore the phone, but also the possibility that it was Makoa on the other end of the call.

I sighed on my next exhale, wishing with everything that I was that this yoga session would bring me some peace. It'd been a hellish week, to say the least.

Thanks to the Coffee & Cubicles contract that we weren't supposed to start working on until October being sped up, we were bombarded with more work than we knew how to handle that week at Monroe Designs. Gemma had taken over Makoa's condo project after I'd begged her to, explaining what happened between us at the end of our date. She wasn't happy about it, but with my hands tied up in the three floors of office space that I hadn't even started designs for, there really was no other option.

In a weird way, I was saved by the last-minute dump of work.

I didn't even mind being in the office or at the construction site from sun up to sundown. I lost myself in working with the architects and the engineers, in walking through each floorplan with the construction crew, in designing and re-designing every inch of every floor, from the cubicle areas to the conference rooms to the offices and the break rooms and everything in-between. Coffee & Cubicles was a shared workplace company, where small businesses and freelancers could rent office space. What set them apart from the other workspace companies I'd worked with was that they were high-end, with an emphasis on design, office view, and quality of the workspace they offered. This wasn't just throwing together some desks and thin walls. This was designing a workspace that felt like a penthouse.

So, yes, it was easy to get caught up in the brain power it took to create something like that.

And when I threw myself into work, I could ignore how much my chest felt like a giant hole had been kicked into it.

I'd taken today off only after Gemma had forced me to, locking me out of the work system until tomorrow at the earliest, but Monday if she could help it. *It's Saturday*, she'd argued, as if that was a reason to stop distracting myself from reality.

She'd dragged me to brunch this morning, toted me around on her arm while she shopped for lingerie for her wedding night and a swimsuit to wear on her honeymoon, and then convinced me to get in a yoga flow with her before we ordered dinner for the night.

She was in full-force, best-friend mode, and as much as I wanted to burrito up in my sadness all alone, I was thankful she wouldn't let me.

My phone finally stopped ringing after what felt like forever, and I blew out an audible sigh, following Gemma's lead as she transitioned into triangle pose. We left one hand on the ground by our foot, extending the other one in the air to get a good spinal twist, and I felt that detox goodness that only yoga can provide slowly filling me up.

And then, my damn phone rang again.

I growled, standing upright, but before I could take a step, Gemma's hand shot out to smack my thigh.

"Leave it."

"I'm just going to turn the ringer off so it doesn't bother us."

"It's fine. Get your ass back on your mat and inhale, exhale, bitch."

I made a noise in my throat, rolling my eyes with an exaggerated temper tantrum before I got back in position. Once again, my phone stopped ringing, and we started to slip into peace, flowing with the soft, new-age music.

Less than a minute later, my phone rang again.

"That's it," I said, and I scrambled out of Gemma's reach when she tried to stop me this time. In the process, she tumbled out of her fallen triangle and landed on her ass, cursing me and crawling to try to grab my ankles, but I skittered away from her.

I was in such a rush to get to my phone before Gemma could stop me that I didn't even think twice once it was in my hand. I saw Makoa's name, and I hit the ignore button once, silencing the tone without ending the call completely.

"Who is it?"

"No one," I said, but my stomach shriveled up at the sight of the letters that made up his name.

Gemma popped up, stealing my phone before I could register that it was her intention.

"Gemma, stop!"

"It's Makoa," she said, holding the phone away from me while I swatted around her to try to get it. "Belle, you *still* haven't talked to him?"

"There's nothing to say," I said, still trying to knock the phone out of her hands.

"I beg to differ," she said.

And then, the traitorous bitch answered the phone.

"Makoa! Hey, it's Gemma. What's up?" Her smile disappeared quickly, and she cocked a brow at me. "No, this isn't the office phone. This is Belle's cell." He said something, and then she chuckled. "Well, she was in the bathroom, but... oh! Look! Here she is. One sec."

This entire time, I'd been shaking my head with wide eyes that threatened all the harm I would bring that brunette bombshell if she didn't hang up the phone. And now, she was holding the phone out to me with her hip popped and eyebrow in her hairline.

"He's on mute," she said.

"Just hang up."

"No! Belle, you're thirty-two years old. Grow a pair of lady balls and talk to him."

I groaned, flopping down on the bar stool at my kitchen island.

Gemma put the phone in front of me on the bar, put it on speakerphone, and then took it off mute.

I cringed at the surge of noise that came through the speaker. Wherever Makoa was, it wasn't his condo. It sounded like a club or bar, and though every ounce of my being wanted to strangle my best friend and chuck my phone off the balcony, I heaved a sigh, squeezing both eyes shut before I muttered, "Hello?"

"Belle Monroe," Makoa said, slow and melodically. "Is that really you?"

"It is."

"Wow, so she *is* alive," Makoa slurred.

I glared at Gemma, but she just mouthed *talk to him* and pointed at the phone, ditching me long enough to grab our water bottles and bring them over to the island.

"She is, indeed."

"You ghosted me."

I sighed. "Makoa... I'm sorry. I've just had a really hellish week." I shook my head, annoyed with him for being so damn persistent, and annoyed with myself that I didn't want to just cut him off like I had a dozen guys before him.

"So come over," he said, his words heated.

I gritted my teeth, remembering his words like a branding iron that seared my skin off.

You're such a good time.

"Um, no, thanks. Sounds like you're out having a good time, anyway."

"I'm miserable."

His words took me off guard, and I glanced at Gemma, who was giving me a look that said she was going to throttle me.

I gave her an equally dirty look that said something along the lines of *what am I supposed to do here?*

"Please, Belle. Come over," Makoa said again, and this time, I couldn't keep my frustration contained.

"No!" I threw my hands up, letting them hit the counter with a slap. "I know you're probably tipsy and horny and want someone to fuck, and we *both* know that's all I'm good for. You said so yourself Saturday night. But I'm not in the mood, okay? So just... just stop, Makoa. Go home and leave me alone."

Gemma's eyes were wide, and she shook her head like I was insane.

"What are you talking about? Belle..." He hiccupped. "I would never... I don't think that. At all."

I huffed. "Right. That's why you called me a *good-time girl* on Saturday, right? Made it pretty clear what I was to you when you slapped that label on it."

"What?" There was a pause, a muffle of the speaker and what sounded like him talking to someone else before he said, "I said you were a good time, yes, but I meant that as in I had a fucking blast getting soaked in the rain with you, and eating pierogies, and geeking out over Broadway. I meant it as in I loved cooking dinner for you, even if I botched it. I meant it as in you have completely blown away everything I thought a girl could be," he said earnestly, pausing for a breath before he continued. "And I want to know everything there is to know about you."

My esophagus thickened with every word until I couldn't breathe past the knot in my throat, let alone swallow it down.

I realized distantly what it was that had me strangled.

Hope.

How dangerous it was.

"It's probably for the best that we stop now," I said after a long pause, shaking my head. "It's been fun."

"Oh, sorry, my mom is calling on the other line, hold on one sec," Gemma said, faking my voice as best she could before she hit the mute button on my phone.

And as soon as she had, she promptly smacked my arm.

"Ow!" I said, rubbing the spot.

"Well, that's what you get. *Why* are you being so dumb right now?"

"She says adoringly," I mocked.

"I'm serious. Makoa obviously didn't mean what you thought he meant when he said that last weekend. Do you not hear the guy? He sounds like a lost puppy dog that's been wandering the streets for days." Gemma shook her head. "Babe, I know that verbiage he used was a big fat finger in your most tender bruise, but Makoa isn't like Nathan. Okay?" She smiled. "He *likes* you. And I know you like him, too."

I sighed, trying to ignore the way my stomach twisted in a knot at the truth of her accusation. "It doesn't matter. It's good that it happened the way it did. I was getting caught up in the fantasy and I forgot reality." I shook my head, cementing it. "Three-date rule, Gemma. Our time is up."

Gemma glared at me, and then she swiped my water bottle off the counter, popped open the lid, and held it over my head.

"What the—"

"You've got approximately ten seconds to stop being stupid before I pour this water all over your head."

"You wouldn't."

Before she could argue that she very much would, we heard commotion on the other end of the phone. *We* were muted, but we could still hear Makoa, and he was currently fighting hiccups as he talked to someone.

"I'm toast." Hiccup. "That's it. It's over. I fucked up and I don't even know what I did."

"She hasn't hung up yet. Keep talking. Tell her what you want to tell her," another voice said.

"Is that *Dave*?" Gemma asked, looking at me. "I swear, that sounded like Dave."

"Why did I say that? *You're a good time,*" Makoa said in a deep voice, mocking himself. There was the distinct sound of a hand slapping a forehead. "What an idiot."

I bit back a smile as Gemma cocked a brow at me. Then, she tilted the water bottle until a trickle hit my head.

"Hey!" I swatted her away, but she just smacked my hand and held the water bottle even higher out of my reach.

"I am not messing around right now, bitch. I will drown your ass."

I had to laugh at that, because I was having flashbacks to when Gemma was trying to ignore her feelings for Zach when the poor guy was so wrapped up in her he couldn't see his way out.

My stomach free-fell at the comparison.

"I'm scared," I admitted, quietly, almost too soft for her to hear.

Gemma's expression softened, and she lowered the water bottle to the island, wrapping her arms around me in a hug. "I know."

I leaned into her, heart racing in warning of what I was considering.

"Just give him a shot," Gemma said, pulling back to frame my arms. "Okay? For me. Just... talk to him, hear him out, and give him a chance." She shrugged. "I know you're getting tired of playing all these games, Belle. And I meant what I said. You don't have to play this role forever. Maybe... with Makoa... it could be different."

"Or I could end up an even bigger mess than when Nathan left me."

"That is a risk," she agreed, which did nothing to make me feel better. She shrugged. "But I'll be here to pick you up off the floor, if that's the case. And isn't he worth it, to take that chance and find out?"

I chewed my lip, hating the way the butterflies in my stomach took flight at the thought of seeing him again.

Could Gemma be right?

Was I an absolute idiot to think that maybe, with Makoa, I could be more than just the fun girl?

Before I could overthink it, I grabbed my phone, hitting the unmute button. "Where are you?"

"Oh shit, she didn't hang up!" I heard Makoa say, then there was a rustling of the phone before his voice came in clearer. "You didn't hang up."

I chuckled. "I didn't."

"That's good. I like when you don't hang up." Hiccup.

"Where are you?" I asked on a laugh.

"I'm at the dirty trivia bar. Except there's no trivia tonight. But good ol' Dave here is keeping me liberated." A pause. "Er, *libated*." Another pause. "That's a funny word. *Liiii-bay-ted*."

Gemma giggled. "Sounds like Dave, alright."

I was smiling, too, and I knew it was less from how adorable Makoa was when he was tipsy, and more from the fact that my entire body was afloat with the hope and possibility I'd been suffocating all week.

Now that they could finally breathe again, they were all I had.

"Don't move," I said to Makoa.

Then, I hung up and grabbed my keys before I could wise up and change my mind.

CHAPTER 11

Makoa

My head was swimming when Belle walked through the door of Doc's, but as soon as she did, everything cleared.

She stood in the doorway, her unreadable eyes scanning the crowd that had formed as it got later. Her auburn hair was swept up into a messy bun, tendrils falling to frame her face, and she was an absolute smoke show even in black leggings and a hoodie.

The *Moulin Rouge!* hoodie, to be exact.

My heart leapt at the sight of her, and I fished in my pocket for my wallet, slapping a couple hundred-dollar bills on the bar and nodding at Dave before I hopped up from my seat. It only took me a few strides to reach her, and Belle didn't see me until I was just a step away.

In the next one, I swept her up into my arms, and I held her tight.

I thought I'd be scared when I saw her. I thought I'd be nervous and timid and wouldn't know the right words to say. But the moment I saw her standing in that bar, I knew the only thing that mattered was that I get her in my arms — and fast.

She was stiff when I first embraced her, and for a split second, I worried I'd ridden my hope too far. But she melted into me just as easily, and with a sigh, her arms wrapped around my neck, and she held me in return.

"Thank you for coming," I whispered, squeezing her waist. She smelled like lemon and honey and rain, like summer in a new city. "I'm sorry. For everything."

Belle shook her head, pulling back from my embrace before her eyes swept over the bar again. She nodded toward the door, and we stepped outside, into the cool summer evening.

"Don't be," she said when we were alone, crossing her arms over her chest. I hated that she wasn't still wrapped up in *my* arms, but I gave her space. "It's me who should be sorry."

I shoved my hands in the pockets of my shorts to keep myself from reaching for her.

Belle sighed, biting her lip as her gaze found the traffic whizzing by. She watched it for a long moment before she looked at me again. "What you said, about me being a good time... it triggered me." She blew out a breath, shaking her head. "God, I can't believe I'm telling you this."

"You can tell me anything."

"The fact that I already know that is part of what freaks me out."

I frowned. "Why did it trigger you?"

Belle smiled as if she were looking into a past life, glancing down at her feet before her eyes found me again. "I dated a guy for a really long time, practically all of college. He was good friends with Gemma's ex-husband, and we sort of all hung out, this big happy foursome."

I nodded, swallowing past the knot in my throat at the thought of her being happy with someone else. I didn't care that it was years ago. The amount of possession I felt in that moment surprised me, and again, my hands twitched to hold her.

"Carlo proposed to Gemma at the end of our senior year, and I thought for sure Nathan was next. That's my ex," she clarified. "And so, I waited, and waited, and helped Gemma plan her wedding while I checked under Nathan's socks and underwear in his drawer for a ring. But... he never proposed." She laughed. "He never planned to."

Idiot. Massive fucking idiot.

Maybe I should write him a thank-you card.

"Instead, the football-obsessed bastard *broke up with me*," she continued. "He played for our college team, hence why I hate *anything* football-related now."

I swallowed, but ignored that fact, focusing instead on the more important subject at hand — which was that this asshole had hurt her.

Belle looked like she was living in the memory when she continued, her eyes distant and sad. "He said that I was fun, that I was a perfect college girlfriend, but that he needed to get serious." She laughed at that. "As if we hadn't been dating for years. But what I hadn't realized until that moment was that he'd met my family, and hung out with my friends, but... the same wasn't true for me."

I frowned. "He never introduced you to his family?"

"Nope," she said, letting the word pop. "And that was the kicker at the end of it all. Nathan looked me right in my eyes when he told me where I stood in this world." Her gaze met mine. "I'm a good time, but I'm not the kind of girl you take home to Mom."

My own words from last weekend slapped me in the face, and even as tipsy as I was, I understood now why she'd ran away.

"Jesus... Belle, I'm so fucking sorry."

She shrugged. "Don't be. He was right."

I blanched at that. "Um, no."

"Yes," she argued, crossing her arms over herself even tighter, as if she wanted to shrink away. "I'm the girl guys call at two in the morning when they want to order a pizza and get their dick wet. I'm the one they call when they just got out of a two-year relationship and need to get over someone else. I'm the one on speed dial when there's a party, and one of their single friends says *hey, man, call up some hot chicks.*"

"Belle," I said, shaking my head as I reached for her. I couldn't give her space anymore, not when she was breaking right in front of me. "That is not who you are."

She pulled away from me at first, her glossy eyes finding the road again. She still couldn't look at me when I finally pulled her closer, and she was stiff until I wrapped her up, pulling her head to my chest.

"That guy, he was a young, stupid kid who didn't know what he had when he had it. If he didn't take you home to his mom, it's because *he* had issues — not you. Because trust me when I say anyone and everyone — Mom, Dad, brother, sister, or random stranger on the street — falls in love with you after just an hour of your time. And they're lucky if they survive that long."

Belle shook her head, but I tilted her chin until she looked at me.

"Hey, stop acting like that's not possibly true. You're not what that asshole said you were. He does not get to define you. Okay?"

I didn't miss the way her eyes teared up at my words, and she inhaled a stiff breath to keep those tears at bay, shoving her head back into my chest. "Stupid football players. I hate them. All of them. Never, *ever* again."

My throat ached against my next attempted swallow. *How the hell am I going to break it to her now?*

"I'm so sorry I said something that triggered that asshole's words in your memory," I whispered, rubbing her back and pushing what would be future Makoa's problems out of my head for now. "I meant what I said. I *do* have a good time with you, but I promise you, it has nothing to do with the sex."

She peered up at me then.

"Okay," I conceded. "You *are* a goddess in bed. Or rather, in the kitchen," I added with a smirk. "But that's just an added bonus."

Belle chuckled, and finally, she relaxed into me, her hands wrapping around my waist as she laid her head on my chest.

"I have a good time with you, too," she said softly, and I felt her swallow against my sternum. "And if I'm being honest, it petrifies me."

"Why?"

She laughed a little, pulling back so she could look me in the eyes. "I accepted the role Nathan gave me a long time ago, Makoa. And ever since then, I've had a three-date rule."

I cocked a brow.

"Not the same was what I imagine *your* three-date rule is," she clarified. "With mine, I don't see a guy past the third date. That way, I never risk getting caught up again. I never have to worry about falling for someone and thinking he's the one, only to be told I was never even in the running for his heart."

I closed my eyes, shaking my head and vowing to find this Nathan motherfucker and break his teeth.

"So, was this you adhering to your rule?" I asked.

When I opened my eyes, she was staring right through me. "It was me trying to."

The fear in her eyes killed me, because I knew it like it was my own soul. And I also knew, right then and there, that I had a new plan.

Make her fall in love with me.

Make her fall in love with me *and then* tell her about football. Because if I told her now, I'd lose her before I ever had the chance to have her at all.

But if we stayed on this course, if I got her to open up to me, to let me in, to lean into the possibility of what we could be together the way I was right now?

That would be it.

She wouldn't give a *damn* that I was a football player, not after I proved her wrong. Not after I put this shit rocket *Nathan* to shame.

Worst-case scenario, if I *did* lose her in the end... at least I could say I tried. At least I could say I gave it everything I could. It would kill me to lose her, that much I knew after just a week without her.

But she was worth that risk.

I thumbed her chin, letting out a long breath before I said, "Hey, have I given you a reason not to trust me?"

She shook her head, and I ignored the pit in my stomach that reminded me I was lying to her. But that was a mountain I could climb another time. A mountain I *would* climb, when the time was right.

Right now, I needed her to see that she could trust me. And even if I wasn't being honest about football, there wasn't a lie near my lips when it came to what I was feeling for her.

"Let's make a deal. Okay?"

"I'm listening."

"You break your three-date rule for me. Give me a chance. Don't judge who I am based on who you've dated in the past."

"And what do I get out of this?"

I shrugged. "Maybe a few dates. Maybe a few months or years of happiness. Maybe a lifetime. No one ever knows," I said, wrapping my arms around her. "But there *is* one thing I know for sure."

"And what's that?"

"I want to find out. And whatever the risk is, you're worth it."

Belle smiled, blowing out a breath as she laced her arms around my neck. "You're so cheesy sometimes that I swear you walked right out of a rom-com."

"I watched enough as a kid that I might as well have."

She laughed. "Ah, that's right. Four sisters."

"Name any rom-com from the 90s or 2000s and I bet you a hundred dollars I can quote at least ten lines."

Belle smiled again, but the smile leveled out when she pressed up onto her toes. Her lips found mine, steady and sure, warm and relieved as she melted into the kiss.

"So, we're going to jump?" she asked, pressing her forehead to mine.

I nodded, brushing a fallen strand of hair behind her ears. "I think we're already in the free fall, Ms. Monroe."

Her eyes found mine.

"I really hope this parachute works."

And I kissed her again, with my own heart wishing the same.

CHAPTER 12

Belle

When I was a little girl, I was obsessed with my bedroom. While my friends all wanted to ride their bikes or play with dolls, I saved up every penny I made from doing chores to buy a new comforter for my bed, or a throw pillow for my floor, or a swing chair, or curtains, or a frame for a photograph I begged my mom to have printed for me.

We moved around so much until I hit high school that every new room was a new adventure, and I would run into our new house wherever we were moving and stand in the middle of the room before the movers brought in any of our belongings. I'd close my eyes, soak up the energy of the room, and without even trying, designs would start popping up behind my eyelids.

It always came naturally to me. I saw the architecture, the shape of the room, the texture of the wall and the carpet or tile or wood. I felt every bedroom I had as if it were a piece of me, as if it were part of my soul, an outward extension of who I was inside.

According to my parents, I would spend nearly every weekend in my room, rearranging furniture, taking pieces off the wall just to replace them with others, organizing my closet, changing up the color theme or playing with textile and fabric combinations. At any given time, I'd have a dozen interior design and home magazines spread out on my floor, and I'd lay there on my belly, eating my weight in Twizzlers while I plotted out the next theme for my room.

It made sense, looking back on it now. After all, that little thirteen-by-eleven bedroom was the only space I had. And with a little imagination, it could be anything. It could be a jungle or an Indian oasis or an ode to punk music or a minimalist-inspired London flat. It could be modern and edgy, or vintage and warm, or colorful and loud.

It was all up to me.

Over the years, as I studied interior design, interned, and started my own business, the way I felt about the job shifted. It became more serious, with more on the line than just my opinion. When I worked with clients, it became so important to build *their* vision that I sometimes lost mine in the process.

But working on Makoa's condo?

It was just like being twelve again, like endless possibilities and a creative outpouring with nothing to stop it.

"I can see smoke coming out of your ears," Makoa said, slipping up behind me where I stood in the middle of his sitting room.

It'd been a week since he held me outside Doc's bar, since we made a pact to give this thing a shot, and every minute since that one had been terrifyingly blissful.

Work was still crazy, and Gemma still had to lead on Makoa's project while I handled the Coffee & Cubicles contract. But almost every evening I ended up here, looking at what had been done and tinkering with shit until it felt right.

And in the midst of it all, there was Makoa.

I smiled as he wrapped his arms around me, leaning back against his chest with my eyes still on the wall. "I'm just thinking."

"About how badass this room looks, thanks to you?"

I chuckled, rubbing his massive hands where they rested over my hips. I both loved and feared how comfortable it felt, that small, intimate touch. "It is coming together, isn't it?"

"I think it's the best room in the house. The way you've managed to bring Maui and Chicago together..." He kissed the skin under my ear, eliciting a shiver. "It's unbelievable."

"If you're trying to butter me up for a better price," I said, leaning back to kiss his neck. "It's working."

Makoa smirked. "Oh, no haggling going on here. You're worth every penny."

He smacked my ass with that affirmation, and I swatted him away, turning my attention back to the far wall of the room. We'd upgraded the fireplace that was there to one that lined the whole wall, one you could turn on with the push of a button. Gray rocks lined the bottom of it, and with the warm lighting and polished teak accents of the room, it felt akin to what I imagined being on the island during a hot summer night would feel like.

Everything I'd envisioned was coming together. Along with the warmth of the island, there was the cool, edgy vibe of Chicago weaved into every corner, too. The metal art print of the volcano pouring into the ocean was framed in a cold geo frame, one that played with the legs of the coffee and end tables. The soft hazelnut leather of the chairs and sofa were offset by the bright, smooth, pearl and pewter marble tops of the tables, and the plush fur rug that brought them all together seemed to capture both the island and the city as one.

Every piece of art, and furniture, every vase and plant, every inch of that room was a vision come to life.

But there was something missing.

"I think it needs a personal touch..." I mused, tapping my bottom lip with my index finger. I spun to face Makoa as the idea struck me. "How do you feel about family photos?"

"You want to hang some in here?"

I shrugged. "Why not? We could frame some, put them on the bookshelves. Oh! And maybe some childhood knick-knacks. Did you have a favorite toy that you kept over the years, or a book or movie or something?"

A knowing grin found Makoa's devilishly handsome face, and he held up one finger. "Hold, please."

I turned my attention back to the wall, imagining all the ways we could tie in those pieces of home. When Makoa came back, it was with a large box, and he dropped it to the middle of the floor before the beast of a man made his way to sit cross-legged in front of it.

He patted the floor next to him, and that childhood feeling found me again as I took a seat.

"One thing about my family," he said, popping the cardboard flaps open on the box and reaching inside. "We're possibly the most sentimental people on the planet." He pulled out an old, ratty, stuffed bunny with one eyeball missing. "And we *might* hold onto enough stuff to get us on an episode of *Hoarders* one day."

I laughed, taking the bunny from his hand and turning it over in mine. "Who is this cutie?"

"That's Mr. Bunny, of course."

"What a unique and unsuspecting name choice," I teased, cocking a brow at Makoa.

He grinned, taking the bunny and watching it with a distant smile as he plucked bits of damaged fur off it. "My oldest sister got this for me when I was... five, I think?" He shook his head. "I loved this thing. Took it everywhere with me. I remember one time, we used the bathroom at a gas station, and I left Mr. Bunny on top of the hand dryer. We were half-way home when we realized it, and Mah said the only way to get me to stop screaming was to turn around."

I laughed. "No bunny left behind." I took the stuffed animal when he handed it to me again, and he started rummaging through the box. "Remind me of the order of your siblings again?"

"It's Pania, Tamar, me, Leinani, and Oliana."

"I love their names," I said in wonder. "And yours, too. Does it mean anything?"

"Oh, trust me, a lot of meaning goes into *every* name where I come from."

"And Makoa means?"

He looked a little hesitant, and I wondered if it was rude to ask, or if it was reserved for just him and his family to know. But then, the corners of his lips curled up. "*Bold Man*," he answered.

I smiled in return. "Well, I'd say it fits. Takes a really bold man to attempt dating me."

He scoffed. "Takes a really stupid one not to."

We shared a look, something between *eww, that was so cheesy* and *ugh, but I kind of liked it*.

"So, Pania got you this?" I asked after a moment, trying her name out. I hoped I didn't botch it.

Makoa grinned. "She did."

"What's the age difference between you five?"

Makoa heaved a giant, dictionary-sized photo album out, wiping dust off the emerald leather cover before he positioned the book half on his knee and half on mine. "Let me show you."

I leaned in closer as he flipped open the album, smiling instantly at the sight of baby Makoa staring back at me. He was in a car seat, his black hair sticking up every which way, goofy grin in place even before he had teeth to fill it.

"Look at you!" I ran my fingers over the picture. "You were adorable."

"Were?"

I rolled my eyes as he flipped the page, and smiled again when I saw his entire family. They were gathered in the living room, it looked like — his mom and dad on the couch with a little girl between them, and then Mak and three other girls on the floor below them. A tinsel-and-ornament-covered Christmas tree was in the corner, and wrapping paper littered the floor around them.

"Okay, so, this is my mom, Aleyna," he said, pointing to his mother on the couch. One look at her and I knew where Makoa got his smile. "And this giant teddy bear is my dad. Loe."

"You have his eyes," I commented, laying my head on Makoa's shoulder. "And her smile."

"I also have his soft heart," he said with a smile, which turned downward when he added, "I wish I could say the same for my mom's superb cooking skills, but as you've experienced…"

I chuckled. "Hey, the macaroni and cheese you made us last night wasn't bad."

"It was Kraft. Not too many ways you can mess that up."

I kissed his cheek, and he moved on, pointing to the small girl between his parents on the couch. It was hard not to note the similarities between all of his sisters — their long black hair, bronze skin, soft brown eyes, and long lashes.

"This one is Oliana. She's the youngest of us, seventeen now, about to start her senior year. She loves Jiu Jitsu and surfing."

"What a little badass."

"And she'll never let you forget it," Makoa said on a laugh. He pointed to the sister he had his arm around in the photograph. "This is Leinani. She's twenty-three, in grad school at UH studying geology. And this," he said, tapping the girl on the other side of him. "Is Tamar. She's twenty-nine, and just got engaged. She and her fiancé live on the island, about twelve minutes from Mom and Dad."

"I'm sure they love that."

He snorted. "Oh, trust me — I'm the only one who's ventured off the island, and I get shit for it every time we talk."

"They miss you."

"They'd miss me if I went to the grocery store," he teased. His finger moved to the last sister, who I knew without him telling me was the oldest. She looked like a young woman, even in the photograph that was at least fifteen years old. "This is my oldest sister. Pania. She's thirty-one, and her primary focus is saving the ocean. She got her doctorate degree in biology and works with a non-profit on the island."

"You didn't tell me you came from a family of super humans," I commented. "I mean geez, leave some talent for the rest of us."

He chuckled.

"How in the world did you end up in real estate?" I asked, shaking my head. "I'm surprised you're not like... a rock star, or an actor, or a famous politician or something."

Makoa swallowed, grabbing the back of his neck on a shrug. "I don't know. Just kind of ended up in this job, I think."

He pointed to the tree and started telling me about their Christmas traditions, but I didn't miss the way he changed the subject, or the way his neck was still a little red from my observation. I wondered if he felt outshined by his siblings, if he worried being in real estate wasn't as impressive. He didn't talk much about his job, and now that I realized how impressive all his siblings were, I wondered if that was why.

"You know, I think it's awesome what you do," I said, cutting him off in the middle of him telling me how they decided who got to put the star on the tree.

He frowned, confused. "What?"

"Real estate is a tough job — and it's even harder to make a name for yourself the way you have. I mean, to be working with houses and clients of the stature I know you have to have in order to afford a place like this," I said, sweeping my hand around the room. "That's not easy to do. You have to be really talented, and knowledgeable, and charming, and a salesman on top of all of that." I squeezed his arm. "What you do is important, Makoa."

The corner of his lips curled up, but there was something hidden in his eyes — something that looked a lot like shame.

He blew out a sigh, shaking his head before he pressed his lips to mine. The kiss was too brief for my liking, but Makoa was already flipping the next page before I could try to deepen it.

"Wait, what's that?" I asked when he flipped past what looked like a greenhouse.

Makoa frowned. "What, this?" He pointed to the photograph, and I nodded. "Oh, that's Mom's hanging garden."

"Her *what*?" I asked, stealing the book and pulling it into my lap to get a better look.

He chuckled. "I don't know, that's what we called it. Mom used to macramé all the time, and she'd make all these holders for plants. Big ones, small ones, ones that hung over and drooped down with these leaf-ridden vines. We had a little sunroom, and she filled the whole space. It felt like a jungle when I was a little kid."

I shook my head in disbelief, eyes soaking in all the wondrous corners of the room in the photograph. There were plants of all shapes and sizes, all shades of green, some with flowers budding and hanging down, too. There was Burro's Tail and String of Nickels, Boston fern and a spider plant, Ripple Peperomia and Golden Pothos. My jaw dropped when I spotted pops of color in the background. "Wait... is that... is that a wall of *roses*?"

Makoa chuckled. "It is. They're her prized possessions."

My jaw was still hanging open as I shook my head, taking in every centimeter of the photograph. My eyes found Makoa's. "We have to have one of these here."

His eyebrows shot up. "A rose garden?"

"A hanging garden. This is... Makoa, this is beautiful. And it would be a piece of your childhood. We have so much natural light from the windows." I chewed the edge of my fingernail, thinking. "Maybe we could put it in here, in the corner. Or in the living room?"

"What about the bedroom?"

I frowned, but then the image became clear in my mind, and I gasped. "Oh, my God. That would be *perfect*."

In the next breath, I launched myself at Makoa, and he just barely had time to catch me before we rolled onto the plush rug. I straddled him, kissing him full and hard and breathless.

"Wow," he said on a laugh. "Interior design really does turn you on, doesn't it?"

"I promise, it's even weirder than what you're imagining." I kissed his next laugh to silence, rolling my hips where they met his. I grinned against his mouth at the feel of his erection already straining against his sweatpants.

"You're killing me, woman," he husked, nipping at my bottom lip.

"So take your pants off and let me bring you back to life."

He groaned again when I licked the side of his neck, sucking the skin between my teeth to leave the tiniest mark. I was already working a trail down to the promise land when I was flipped over on my back, and Makoa had *me* pinned instead.

"I like this view even better," I said, biting my lip and pulling his mouth down to meet mine.

Makoa chuckled, his tongue swirling with mine and shooting electric bolts straight between my thighs.

When he leaned up and put space between us, I stuck my bottom lip out in a pout.

"Trust me, I want to strip you down and break in this rug properly," he said.

"So, let's do it."

I reached up for him, but he caught my hands, kissing my knuckles. "We will. But not right now."

"Why not?" I practically whined, dragging out the words.

Makoa laughed, rolling onto the floor with me until he was on his back. He pulled me into his chest, kissing my hair as I settled in. "I took everything you said to me very seriously, Belle. And I meant what I said about you being more than just sex to me."

"That doesn't mean we can't have sex *at all*," I argued.

"I know. But... for now, I just want it to be about us getting to know each other."

I sighed, deep and heavy, which earned me another chuckle before Makoa tilted my chin with his knuckles, making me look at him.

"Hey... we can still have some fun."

There was a heat in his eyes with those words, and I smiled, running my hand down the length of his chest. "Oh yeah? What do you have in mind?"

"Mmm..." he hummed, tracing my bottom lip with his thumb. "Wanna make out and dry hump like a couple of horny teenagers?"

"Sounds like *lectamia* to me."

"Well, that is half the fun of trivia," he said, rolling me until I was pinned under him again. "You always learn something new."

I laughed, but it was silenced when he pressed his thick erection into the center seam of my leggings, catching a line of friction that had me remembering all too well what it was like to ride his cock until I came.

"Can you get off from lectamia?" I whispered against his lips.

Makoa grinned, rolling his hips and biting my neck as another shockwave of pleasure coursed through me.

"Only one way to find out."

CHAPTER 13

Makoa

The Fourth of July came in a sweltering, clear-blue sky heat wave that brought Chicago alive like I'd never seen before.

The city that was usually all business, with suits and dresses marching back and forth on the streets, climbing in and out of cabs, swiping their subway pass and boarding the L trains, was now pulsing with a completely different kind of energy. It was the kind, Belle informed me, that came about every spring, that grew in strength every summer, and seemed to shine just as bright as a firework on the day we honored our country's independence.

The beaches were packed, the parks bustling, boats peppering the lake everywhere you looked. Red, white, and blue swimsuits seemed to be the only acceptable attire — aside from perhaps a Cubs or Bears hat — and American flags flew proudly from every boat, every tent, every inch of the city, it seemed. Smiles were an accessory that every party wore, music blasted, people danced and drank and rejoiced over the heat and the holiday in tandem.

When Belle told me how excited she was for the Fourth, I insisted she let me charter a boat for the two of us and her friends, Gemma and Zach. Now, it was just after nine in the morning, and I was waiting at the DuSable Harbor for the three of them to join me, viewing the lively city through my polarized Ray-Bans.

And also getting my ass chewed by my best friend.

"You've got to tell her, man," Colby said. "Every day closer to the season puts you more at risk for her finding out another way. And trust me when I say you *don't* want that."

"I know, I know," I agreed, gripping the phone a little too tight to my ear as my eyes scanned the marina for Belle, Gemma, and Zach. They would be here any minute, and the last thing I needed was to be anxious the first time I hung out with Belle's friends. "And I will. It's not like I plan on hiding it forever."

"No, but it *is* like your reasoning for keeping it a secret has literally zero foundation now. I mean, you've been seeing her for... what... three weeks?"

"Four, if you're counting from the first time we met."

"Four weeks. A month, man. A freaking month, and you know damn well by now that she has zero motivation to use you for your money or your connection to the NFL."

"I know," I groaned.

"Then why are you still keeping it from her?"

I blew out a frustrated breath. "It's complicated — more now than before, if I'm being honest."

"Elaborate."

My eyes traced the boardwalk for signs of Belle, and when I found none, I turned toward the boat and lowered my voice just in case. "First of all, I've been lying to her for a month, as you so kindly just pointed out. *And,* her asshat ex-boyfriend who fucked her up and gave her not only a warped sense of who she is, but also a tainted view on dating, was a football player. He's the whole reason she hates the game, man. And I'm trying to convince her all the ways I'm *not* like that motherfucker — not all the ways that I am." I paused.

"She literally said she would never, ever date a football player again."

Colby was silent but for a long, exaggerated sigh.

"I know I'm in deep shit," I said after a minute. "But, trust me. I have a plan."

"And that plan is?"

I shrugged, as if it were obvious. "Make her fall in love with me."

A snort was my only answer from Colby.

"I'm serious. Look, if I tell her now..." My throat was thick with the rest of that sentence, so much so that I couldn't get it out.

"You lose her."

"I lose her," I agreed, hating the way that possibility crept under my skin like icy cold water. "But if we keep going down this path we're on... well, it'll get to a point where she won't even care. Everything else between us will be so strong, and she'll understand."

Silence passed between us before Colby said, "The fact that you've never really had a serious relationship is showing right now, man."

I swallowed. "Can you be a best friend here, and help comfort me somehow?"

Colby blew out another breath. "Well, I guess the silver lining is that it is still early. You've only been dating a month. It's not like you're about to propose or anything. Just... stick with your original plan. Hold out until after training camp. That gives you time to really get to know each other, and she doesn't follow football, so as long as you're not out on the town a lot, your cover shouldn't be blown." He sighed, like he still didn't like it, even as he was saying it. "Then, sit her down and explain why you didn't tell her up front, and then how it got more complicated once she told you about her ex. It sounds like you've been open with her so far, so if you keep that going, maybe she'll hear you out in the end."

"Maybe," I repeated, turning back toward the city skyline. When I did, I saw three figures walking down the dock toward me, and my chest tightened. "Why do I not want to place my bet on *maybe*?"

"Just enjoy the day, man. Take her out on the boat, get tipsy, kiss under the fireworks and save this for another day. I'm sorry I brought it up."

"No, don't be. You're right," I affirmed. "I need to tell her. I *want* to tell her. I just... I don't want to lose her in the process."

"I hate to break it to you, man, but... you might lose her, anyway."

My stomach soured with the thought, but it was just a flash in the pan. Because I could see Belle clearly now, and the way she looked at me, the way she smiled at me, the way those eyes told me she was in this just as bad as I was...

There was no way I'd lose her.

I just couldn't.

"They're here, I gotta go. Have a good holiday, brother. Thanks for listening."

"Good luck."

We hung up just in time for me to catch Belle, who ran the rest of the way down the dock and launched herself into my arms. She was an absolute vision in her white bikini, the red, mesh cover-up she'd paired it with blowing behind her, and one hand holding her oversized hat on her head until the moment she was in my embrace. I caught her with a swing and a kiss, one I wanted to deepen, but kept brief and PG-13 since her friends were here.

"Happy Fourth!" she said, her smile the widest I'd seen it since I'd known her.

"Happy Fourth," I repeated on a chuckle. "Someone's excited."

"We're going out on a friggin' *boat*," she said, gesturing to the thirty-nine-foot luxury sailboat behind me. "And there will be fireworks."

"And hot dogs!" Gemma chimed in, holding up her hand until I slapped it. "'Sup, Makoa. Nice to see you."

"You, too. Although I don't think I've ever seen anyone get so excited about eating hot dogs before."

"Don't even get her started," Zach warned from her side, smiling down at her when she leaned up to kiss his cheek. He unwrapped his arm from around her then, extending his hand for mine. "I'm Zach, Gemma's fiancé."

"Mak," I said, giving his hand a firm shake.

"Aww! Zach and Mak," Gemma said, threading her arm through Belle's. "I smell a bromance brewing."

Zach and I exchanged looks, and he shook his head, releasing my hand. "I wish I had the right words to warn you what it's like being with these two outside of the office, but I don't think I could even if I tried."

"We're adorable and you love us," Belle sang, pinching Zach's cheek.

"That's one way to put it," Zach mumbled under his breath, which earned him a chuckle from me. His eyes scanned the boat next, and he let out a long whistle, sliding his hands into the pockets of his navy board shorts. "Thanks for doing this, man. I haven't been on a boat in years. This thing is massive."

"Just wait until you see the wet bar downstairs. Come on," I said, gesturing to the boat. "Let's get onboard and check it out."

Zach took Gemma's hand, helping her onboard before I did the same with Belle. We spent the first half hour getting the full tour from the captain and being introduced to the crew who would be onboard with us for the day. When the girls had mimosas in hand and Zach and I were fixed up with Bloody Marys, we took a seat in the cockpit and off we went.

It was fascinating, being in a place where summer was so highly coveted. Growing up on the island, we really only had two seasons — summer and winter — and the only difference between the two was that the daily high went down about seven degrees in the winter. Overall, though, we had pleasant weather year-round, and it was the same when I lived in California.

But in Chicago? Summer was everything.

I smiled as I watched Belle and Gemma drink and laugh, each of them taking turns telling us stories from their youth. Zach would chime in from time to time to tell his *own* story about what he'd learned about them in the past couple of years. All the while, we were waited on by the boat staff, never without a drink in our hand, and the closer we got to noon, the stronger the smell of barbecue came from the grill hooked onto the side of the boat.

Belle assured me that after one winter spent in Illinois, I'd understand why days like this were so cherished.

As it was, I was cherishing it even without knowing what it would be like to face the brutal temperatures and snowfall.

Mostly because she was here, and she was happy, and that was all that mattered to me.

After lunch, Zach and I got on the topic of football. I played it cool, mostly talking about the teams I loved and how I used to play in high school. That's when I discovered that he *also* used to play back in the day. He didn't elaborate on why he stopped playing, but somewhere along the way, our conversation about that Friday night lights feeling, and how we felt after our first concussions, turned into which romantic comedy was the best of all time.

I wish I was joking.

"Bro, there's no contesting this," Zach said adamantly, abandoning his beer on the table so he could lean forward to emphasize his point. "*Silver Linings Playbook* is *the best* romantic comedy of all time. Period. End of story."

"It's a fantastic film, I agree," I said. "And maybe Bradley Cooper's best role. *But,*" I added, holding up a finger. "I'm sorry, man. Nothing beats *10 Things I Hate About You.*"

Zach threw his hands up. "You're kidding, right? Please tell me you comparing that movie to *Silver Linings Playbook* is a joke."

"Heath Ledger. Julia Stiles. Joseph Gordon-Levitt," I said, listing them off on my fingers. "Some of the most iconic lines of all time. Plus, it was nineties *gold.* How can you say otherwise?"

"Nineties gold is *When Harry Met Sally.*"

I pointed at him then. "*That,* we can agree on. Except *technically,* it came out in 1989."

Gemma stood, clapping her hands together. "Okay. I think this bromance needs a little room to grow," she said, leaning down to kiss Zach's cheek. She reached for Belle's hand next. "Come on. Let's get some sun on the front deck."

"The bow," Zach corrected.

"Whatever. I'm getting another hot dog, too." Gemma winked at Zach before she and Belle skipped off to the front, and I watched Belle go the entire way, biting my lip when she looked over her shoulder at me and smacked her plump, barely-covered-in-a-bikini-thong ass for good measure.

Zach and I chuckled to ourselves when they were gone, sipping on our beers with our arms outstretched on the back of the seats. I was just about to launch into my top ten rom-coms of all time when Zach said the absolute last thing I expected.

"I know who you are."

I swallowed down my beer carefully, not answering but with one raised eyebrow.

"Makoa Kumaka. Former third string wide receiver for the 49ers. Signed as a free agent with the Bears this spring." Zach took a drink before balancing his beer on the ankle he had crossed over the opposite knee. "But for some reason, Belle and Gemma think you're some real estate mogul. Wanna tell me why that is?"

All the blood drained from my face, from my neck, practically from my entire body as a whole. I wasn't sure how long I sat there and stared at Zach, but it was long enough for him to shake his head and check to make sure the girls were still at the front of the boat before he continued.

"Bro. What the hell?"

"I'm going to tell her," I said hurriedly, setting my drink aside and leaning toward him. "I swear. I am."

"Okay. Well, can I ask *why* you haven't already told her?"

I blew out a breath. "Let's just say that *before* the NFL, I was perpetually friend-zoned by any girl I was interested in. And once I signed, I started getting girlfriends left and right. But there was one problem."

Zach put the pieces together. "They wanted you for your money."

"Or my connection, or what they thought I'd be one day." I nodded. "You get the gist of it."

"So, you lied to Belle."

I swallowed, looking to where she was sprawled out on the front deck with Gemma. "I didn't mean to. I just... she didn't know who I was when I walked into her office, and I knew the second I met her that I wanted her." I snapped my fingers. "I've never felt anything like it, man."

Zach nodded, his own eyes casting toward the bow. "I know the feeling."

"I didn't think it through. I just saw this opportunity to be myself with her. I could be Makoa, the average dude who wants to take her on a date. Not Makoa, the NFL player."

"Have you seen yourself?" Zach asked, arching a brow. "I don't think you can call six foot five and two-hundred-twenty pounds of muscle *average*."

I chuckled. "You know what I mean."

Zach sighed, nodding again. "I do. I mean, I can't imagine what you feel, but it was something my parents talked to me about a lot when I was considering pro ball. They were worried about me getting caught up with the wrong girl, given what a softie I am."

"We have a lot in common."

He smirked, but it fell quickly. "Listen, no judgment, I get why you did what you did. But..." His eyes glanced at the girls again. "You need to tell her, and soon. My fiancée is obsessed with the Bears, and the only reason she hasn't figured out who you are yet is because she's been so focused on our wedding that she hasn't had time to think about the team. She's a little... addicted to details, I guess is the best way to put it. She loves her lists and her planning, so right now, between the wedding and work, she's completely occupied." He shook his head. "But that wedding is only two months away, man, and to be honest? The closer the season gets, and the more that gets checked off her list for the wedding, the closer she is to figuring it out. And if she does before you fess up? You're screwed."

I blew out a breath, scrubbing a hand over my head. "I appreciate the heads up."

Zach nodded. "Look, I'll do my best to keep it under wraps for you. I like you, and I can see you're a good guy. If there's anything Belle needs in this world, it's a guy who will treat her right. But... I'm not cool with the lying, man. And I promise — Belle isn't after your money."

"I know she's not," I said earnestly. "I mean, I know that *now*. But... the *new* issue is that I've been lying to her, and, even more pressing, she's already fucked up from a guy who strung her along on lies in the past."

"And he was a football player," Zach finished for me.

I pointed at him. "Do you see the issue?"

Zach sipped his beer, nodding more to himself than to me as he digested it all. "I do, especially since she's apparently put football players on her *Never Ever Again* list." He gave me a look then. "Don't ask me how I know that, and trust me when I say I wish I didn't."

I chuckled.

"I *also* wish I could tell you I was certain she'd be okay with you being a ball player, as long as you came out and told her. But... I don't know. If Belle is anything, it's unpredictable."

I laughed. "Well, now I feel encouraged."

Zach opened his mouth to reply, but before he could, the girls were making their way back to us, and he cleared his throat. "Don't even get me started on *Roman Holiday*."

Belle laughed, reaching down for my hand. "Alright. Gemma and I decided that's enough of the rom-com talk. Time for a dip."

And with one last look of understanding from Zach, the conversation was muted, and the secret sealed — at least for now.

Belle

I'd never been more scared in my entire life.

I still remembered the first time I rode a rollercoaster. It was at Six Flags Over Georgia, I was eleven years old, and I'd literally pissed myself before demanding that my parents take me home. I also remembered when I almost wrecked my car in high school because a damn jumping spider had me swerving and braking and gassing until I finally was able to pull over and get the motherfucker out. I even vividly remembered when I'd had a near-death experience in college, thanks to not chewing my steak enough and getting it lodged in my throat before a patron of the restaurant gave me the Heimlich and shot that piece of meat out of my mouth like a rocket across the table.

All of these things were terrifying.

And yet, none of them matched up to what I felt in Makoa's arms as we watched the fireworks over Chicago's Navy Pier.

I was just standing there, minding my own business, a content smile on my face as those balls of fire exploded in the sky and shimmered in a downward stream toward the water.

And then it hit me.

All at once, like a flash flood through a canyon, I realized it. I felt comfortable in those beastly arms of his. I felt warm and safe with my back leaning against his chest. I had zero desire to fuck anyone else, zero desire to put distance between us, and absolutely zero desire to break things off with him in order to save myself.

For the first time since Nathan, I liked someone enough to stay. I liked someone enough to introduce them to my friends, to spend nights at their house and have them spend nights at mine.

And that realization shook me worse than a ghost ever could.

I was still up in my head about it all when Makoa and I said goodnight to Gemma and Zach in the elevator of my building. They hopped off on the seventeenth floor and Makoa held my hand until we reached the twentieth, leading the way down the hall to my condo before I used my key to let us both inside.

Makoa headed into the kitchen to pour us each a glass of wine, and he was going on and on about the day, about how much he loved Zach and Gemma, how awesome the fireworks show was, how he couldn't wait for us to all go out on a boat again. It wasn't until he turned to face me again, two glasses in hand, and saw me standing like a statue at my kitchen island that he stopped talking.

"Belle?" He frowned, setting the glasses down on the counter before he made his way toward me. "You alright?"

"No."

"What's wrong?" he asked, instantly taking me into his arms.

I shimmied out of them, crossing my arms over my chest, instead. I hated the look on Makoa's face when I did, but being back in his grasp had my chest tight and my heart racing the same way it had on the boat.

"Did I... did I do something wrong?"

"No," I said quickly. "And that's the problem."

He arched a brow.

"Can't you see it?" I asked, tossing my hands up before I let them slap down to my thighs. "I *like* you."

His other brow joined the first in his hairline.

"Like... we're like... *dating*."

He chuckled, his tense shoulders deflating a little as he opened his arms. "Come here."

I shook my head.

"Belle," he insisted. "Come here. Let me hold you."

My brows tugged together, but with him standing there like that, with those words on his lips, I had no other choice. I slipped into his arms, and when he wrapped them around me, I melted, letting out the longest sigh of my life.

"I like you, too," he whispered. "And, as weird as it may sound to you, I assure you — it's not something to be upset about."

"I beg to differ."

"Tell me why."

"You know why."

He kissed my hair — *God, he actually kissed my hair, like they do in the movies!* — and then he pulled back so he could look me in the eyes. "We're on this ride together. Okay? And I promise to abide by the campsite rule."

It was my turn to quirk a brow. "The what?"

"The campsite rule. You know, when you go camping, you leave your campsite in the same or better condition than when you found it. No trash, no fires left burning." He paused when he saw the vacant look in my eyes. "Have you never been camping?"

"I have, I just can't believe you're comparing *dating* to camping."

"Kind of the same. I mean, it's mostly fun, but a little scary, a little dirty, a little out of our comfort zone. You know, no air conditioning, no showers." He smiled, running the back of his knuckles along my cheek. "What I'm saying is that it's okay to be a little freaked out. We have no idea which way this is going to go."

My stomach somersaulted.

"Are you having fun?"

I nodded.

"So am I. And right now, I think that's what matters. Let's just enjoy each other, and have fun, and take it slow." He shrugged. "And then we'll see where it goes from there."

"And if it goes nowhere?"

"I won't hurt you," he promised, and the way his golden eyes searched mine with the words made me feel stripped down to my soul. "I can't promise much, but I can promise that."

My throat was thick with an emotion I thought I'd never feel again, and I swallowed it down, nodding over and over before I wrapped my arms around his neck and kissed those stupid, perfect lips of his.

Makoa held me, strong and steady, kissing me with all the reverence his words had in the moments before. His hands found my face, framing it, tugging my hair just enough to lift my chin for better access.

My hands pressed into his chest, feeling the hard muscles there and groaning as I dragged my fingertips down over every mountain and valley of his abdomen. His board shorts were still a little damp from our dip in the lake earlier, but one firm grasp revealed his erection under them, and I gasped into his mouth, panting with need.

And that's exactly what it was.

Need.

I needed him to kiss me. I needed to touch him and be touched by him. I needed to turn off the words, turn off my brain, to lose myself in everything that he was physically.

My fingers slipped between the band of his shorts and his skin, and I tugged, guiding him backward and down the hall toward my bedroom with our lips still fused together.

"Belle," he warned, but it was a husky warning, one laced with a desire powerful enough to undo his restraint.

I kicked my bedroom door open with one foot, sliding my hands up his abdomen and under his shirt until he had no choice but to lift his arms and let me take it off.

"Don't overthink this," I whispered, stripping my cover-up off. With one quick pull of the string behind my back, my swimsuit top fell in a puddle on the floor between us, and Makoa swallowed, stepping into me with his hands palming both breasts.

"God*damn*, Belle," he groaned, kneading each one.

I arched into the touch, biting my lip when his thumbs skated over my nipples, puckering them to a hard tip. His mouth crashed down on mine, and I numbly felt for the strings of his board shorts, tugging them until they were untied.

"Shit," he said, stepping back. My body shivered at the loss of heat. "Maybe we should slow down."

"The hell we should." I was on him in the next breath, leaping into his arms so he had no choice but to catch me or let me fall. He stumbled backward, the back of his knees hitting the bed, and when he sat down, I was positioned on his lap with that hard, perfect cock thick and needy between my thighs.

"*Yes*," I hissed, nipping at his neck, his jaw, all the while rolling my hips to keep that point of connection hot. Makoa's hands wrapped around my waist, and I didn't know if he was trying to hold me still or rock me even harder, but I answered the second request greedily.

"You're impossible to resist," he breathed into my next kiss.

"So stop trying."

He answered my request with a spank to my ass, and then in one swift moment I was on my back, my head hitting the pillows in a *whoosh*.

Makoa's hands splayed my stomach, my hips, dragging down until he ripped my swimsuit bottoms off in one firm pull. I didn't even have to lift my ass, he had all the power to do it himself. And when I was fully nude, I opened my legs, trailing my fingertips down to slip between my wet lips.

He sucked in a breath, his eyes on the prize. "You have no idea how fucking sexy you are."

"Oh, I think I do."

Makoa smirked at that, but all the laughter left me when he made quick work of his board shorts, that glorious cock springing forward like it was eager and ready to report for duty.

I flipped over onto my stomach, crawling toward where he stood at the side of the bed. Propping myself up on one elbow, I reached for him with my free hand. I grabbed him at the base, rolling my hand down his shaft and up over his tip until his entire body shuddered.

I looked up, taking my time to appreciate the view of all the muscles lining his abdomen, his chest, his arms, even his thick fucking neck. Those Polynesian tattoos sprawled over him, giving him an even more godly appearance than he had naturally. My hand tightened a little more on the next plunge over his cock, and Makoa's eyes rolled up to the ceiling, his hand finding the back of my head.

I smiled when his fingers curled in my hair. "What do you want, Makoa?" I asked, but I knew already, and when his fingers tightened even more, I slipped my tongue out long enough to swirl it over his tip.

His answer was a growl, his eyes hooded when they looked back down at me. "Take my cock in your mouth, baby."

Those words. That monster of a man. The *command*. It all combined to send a shock straight between my legs, and I felt the need pooling there as I did just what he asked.

That first taste of him had been sweet, but it was nothing compared to the delicious power I felt reverberating through me when I took his cock all the way inside.

Well, as much as I could, anyway.

Makoa groaned at the feel of my tongue running along his base, and I swirled it at the top, puckering my lips before I dove down again. He couldn't stop himself from flexing into my mouth, and the way he held his hand steady at the back of my head had me releasing all control, letting him fuck me just the way he wanted.

I wrapped one hand around his base, using the wetness my mouth provided to slide it in tandem. Makoa moaned his approval, and then the hand not in my hair slipped over my spine, down, down, down, until he reared back and smacked my ass.

I yelped, wriggling from the sting, and when I took him in my mouth again, I moved my other hand to grasp his balls.

"Oh, *fuck* yes," he hissed, flexing into me. The hand that had smacked my ass slipped between my cheeks then, drawing a line from my asshole to my pussy. His fingers slid in with ease, curling against the tender spot of pleasure inside me.

I arched my back, giving him better access as I took him inside my mouth again. When he leaned forward to thrust his fingers in deeper, his cock went deeper, too, and with one last groan, he ripped free from my grasp.

"I'm going to fucking come if you don't stop," he said, smacking my ass.

"Why are we stopping, then?" I asked, peering up at him.

He shook his head on a smirk, picking me up and tossing me onto my back again like I weighed absolutely nothing. His knees found the edge of the bed then, and he hiked my ankles up onto his shoulders, pulling my thighs until his cock slid between them.

Makoa lined himself up at my entrance, and then his palms found the bed, and his mouth crashed hot onto mine, and he plunged inside me in one, full-to-the-hilt thrust.

We both exhaled a heavy, lust-filled moan of ecstasy into each other's mouth at the feeling of being connected. I wrapped my hands around his biceps, holding on for dear life and thanking yoga for the flexibility it took to kiss him while he fucked me with my legs on his shoulders like that.

I also silently thanked Gemma for convincing me to go on birth control in college, since there was absolutely *zero chance* of us stopping to put a condom on.

"God, you feel so good," Makoa breathed, rocking his hips out, and in, out, and in. He held one ankle on his shoulder, letting the other fall until I was practically in a split. "So fucking tight."

I didn't have it in me to break up his adoration with the fact that *any* vagina would feel tight to his barbarian of a cock.

Every thought and possible sentence I could form was stolen with his next thrust, anyway, and I surrendered to the feeling, to the way one of his hands held my leg steady on his shoulder and the other dragged through my hair, tugging hard enough to expose my throat for his mouth and take my next breath.

His thrusts were relentless, his kisses punishing, his hands bruising — and I loved every second of it.

When his hands were on me like this, when his teeth broke my flesh, I didn't have space in my mind to think about how much I cared for him, how much I wanted him, how much it would hurt to lose him at this point. Every new kiss shoved those thoughts further from my mind, and when he reached a hand down between us to rub my clit the way I had when I rode him our first time, thought ceased to exist altogether.

All I could do was feel.

His breath in my ear, whispering for me to come. His teeth on my neck in the next second. His cock, deep inside me, stretching me wide as his fingers rubbed slow, meticulous circles on my clit.

If I knew only one thing about Makoa Kumaka, it was this: That tank of a man knew how to fuck me.

"Coming," I managed on a whisper, eyes squeezed tight and muscles spasming as I reached for my climax. I caught it like the fuse of a firework, the burn slow and sizzling at first before it erupted through me in hot sparks, blast after blast, making me shake and writhe with every new wave.

When I creaked open my eyes, Makoa's were on me, the satisfaction from making me come written all in the honey pools.

I'd barely stopped shaking, barely caught a single breath before Makoa ripped out of me, yanking me up to stand with him. He had his hand wrapped around his cock, and just one glance of his eyes to the floor told me what he wanted.

I dropped to my knees, opening my mouth, eyes cast upward.

And with a groan and a flex, Makoa came, spilling his hot release on my tongue, my neck, the swells of my breasts, the tops of my thighs. He coated me with his desire, and I rolled my fingers in every stream I felt, rubbing it over every inch of me, tongue skating out to taste the bit left on my lips.

"Jesus Christ," he cursed, falling back onto the bed just as his legs gave out. He still had one hand wrapped around his dick, and his chest heaved with every new breath as he watched me, shaking his head. "What the fuck do you bring out in me?"

I laughed, wiping his cum from the corner of my mouth and sucking it off my finger. "The very best parts, I think."

He smirked, eyes bouncing over every inch of me. "I made a mess."

"Indeed, you did. But I think I have a solution."

"Shower?"

I nodded, hopping up to my feet before I made my way over to him. "Join me?"

"Like that's even a question," he answered, claiming my lips. His fingers dragged a trail over the cum on my tits, my stomach, and he slid his fingers down more to rub my clit.

I shivered at the feel of his hot release on that sensitive bud, even more tender after climaxing. "You're going to make me want round two if you keep touching me like that."

Makoa just smiled against my kiss. "Isn't that the whole point of the shower?"

I laughed, biting his lower lip before I released it.

And then I dragged that beast by the hand into the shower for what I was sure would be the first, but not the last time that night.

CHAPTER 14

Makoa

It occurred to me over the next three weeks that I was really, *really* good at making excuses.

The conversations I'd had with Colby and Zach were not forgotten, but I'd say they were sort of like the ugly gift from a great aunt, the kind you smiled at and insisted would be used but then shoved to the farthest, darkest corner of your closet where neither you, nor anyone else, would ever see it.

I'd think about sitting Belle down and telling her everything, but then we'd have an amazing night on the town, or spend the day lounging at her place, or go exploring the city, and I couldn't find it in me to ruin such a perfect day by bringing up something that wasn't *that* big of a deal.

It can wait, I told myself.

Belle grew busier and busier as the weeks went on, too — thanks to a job she hadn't planned on working on until October that was sprung on her early. There were days she was tied up at the office or on the construction site all day and night, where I wouldn't see her at all. Other times, she'd work long hours and then rejoice when I surprised her at her place, even if it was just to lay on the couch together and say nothing.

I couldn't tell her on an already long, bad day.

It can wait.

Work was picking up for me, too. With training camp quickly coming up, I spent every day on the field with Gerald, or working out on my own, pulling two-a-days and watching film to prep for what awaited me in Lake Forest. In a way, I was thankful Belle was busy, because I needed to devote time to my training if I wanted any chance of proving to coach he should keep me for the season.

With both of us busy, and so much going on... did I really need to add to it?

It can wait.

My thought cycle lived inside this tornado of reasoning until the very night before I left for training camp. This had been my original plan, anyway, and now that I was on the cusp of it, it just made sense to wait.

I'd go to camp, show the fuck out, and then come home and tell Belle everything.

For now, I had twelve hours before I had to show face at the stadium and be bussed over to Halas Hall for camp, and I planned on spending every minute of those hours wrapped up in Belle.

"I swear, cuddling with you is like cuddling a space heater," she said, pushing me off her on my giant, oversized couch. She kicked the covers off her feet, too, making a face. "I'm practically sweating."

"I can't help it. I've always been like a furnace." I wrapped her up again, holding her tight when she tried to squirm free. "And since I won't see you for a while, you can just stop trying to get out of cuddles now."

Belle snorted. "I can't believe I'm even *letting* you cuddle me at all."

"Not a big fan usually?"

Her pointed glare answered for her. "Three-date rule, remember? Belle Monroe is a strictly no-cuddle zone."

"Until now," I said, nuzzling her neck as I wrapped her up tighter. "Until me."

"Don't push your luck," she threatened, but her arms were already wrapping around me, too, and she settled into my warmth like it didn't bother her as much as she put on.

"I don't want to leave you," I said after a while, running my fingers through her hair with my eyes on the city sprawled out in the windows behind her. My chest was tight with the admission, and when Belle lifted her head to look at me, that grip strengthened.

"Stupid work trip. Also, quite possibly the *longest* conference to ever exist." She wrinkled her nose. "You sure you can't skip it? Didn't you say you already have a list of clients and connections here, anyway?"

I swallowed down the lies I'd sprinkled throughout our conversations, wondering how much they'd cost me in the end. "It's more than just a conference. It's like... the Super Bowl of Real Estate." I inwardly cringed at the comparison. "Good for networking. Besides, there's always something new, something hot."

I have no fucking idea what I'm talking about.

Belle nodded, resting her head on my chest again.

"It'll just be a couple of weeks," I said. "Two and a half-ish."

"Two and a half-ish," she echoed in a song.

"And you'll wait for me?"

I hated the desperation in my voice, and it lingered between us for a long while before Belle leaned up again, smiling. "You think I'm going to bail now?"

"You wouldn't be crazy if you did."

"Are *you* ready to bail?"

I scoffed. "Hell no. I'm just getting started on the long list of things I want to do to you." I paused. "Er, *with* you, I mean."

Belle pinched my side. "Mmm you have a whole list, huh? What's on it?"

"Wouldn't you like to know."

She kissed me on a giggle, but then she pulled back again, her eyes a sky blue tonight as they searched mine. "Am I an idiot if I say I can't even think about anyone else now that I've met you?"

My heart surged with hope. "Am I a fool if I say I've felt this way since the moment I saw you in your office?"

"We're disgusting."

"I kinda like it."

She smiled at that. "I think I kind of like it, too."

Belle nuzzled back into my chest, and I sighed, closing my eyes, fingers drawing circles on her back.

"Three weeks apart," she whispered.

"Two and a half-ish," I corrected.

She smiled against my chest. "I think if we can survive that, we can survive anything."

I nodded, kissed her hair, and prayed she was right.

CHAPTER 15

Belle

"Okay, so, at this one, we've got Luke, Dave, Mariana, Sasha, cousin Eddie, and his wife," I said, pointing at the table I'd drawn on the huge poster. Pink and blue sticky notes surrounded it, each with a name, so we could move them around easily, if necessary.

Gemma was cross-legged on her floor next to me, and she tilted her head, feeding herself popcorn from the bag between her legs. "I think that works. Let's leave that for now and move on to the next."

"Okay," I said, dragging my finger to the next circle over. I read off the list of names, nodding in agreement when Gemma said to switch a few people over to a different table.

Zach was at work, running Doc's bar for the night and leaving Gemma and me to our own devices. I'd been a little needier than usual the past couple of weeks, thanks to Makoa being gone for work. I'd expected it to be a little weird, but had *definitely* not expected to barely hear from him, and for me to be so up in my *feels* about not hearing from him. We had been talking, sure, but it was short — mostly at night for a half hour or so before he'd say he was exhausted and needed to get some sleep for the next day.

Who knew a real estate conference was so demanding? I sure as hell didn't.

Fortunately, Gemma rejoiced in the chance to have me help her with wedding to-do's, and I didn't care what we were doing, as long as I was out of my house and not alone.

When I was alone, I was thinking.

And when I was thinking, I was an anxious mess of *what the hell am I doing falling for a guy when the last time nearly broke me?*

"I don't see your parents on here," I commented when we'd gone through a few more tables.

Gemma shifted uncomfortably. "They're not going to be able to make it."

My jaw fell open. "You're joking."

She swallowed, shrugged, ate a piece of popcorn like it was nothing. Her parents were like mine in the sense that they were travelers at heart. Where my parents were obsessed with missionary work, hers were obsessed with motivational speaking, and where mine took me with them until I convinced them to stay still for my high school years, Gemma's parents usually went without her. She'd spent most of her childhood and thereafter with her grandfather, who was more like a dad to her than her actual father, from what I'd gathered. When her grandfather passed away, I'd hoped she and her parents would knit their relationship.

Apparently, that hadn't happened.

"It's okay. They have an event, and I get it. They book years in advance, and it'd be hard for them to change such last minute."

I blinked. "It's your *wedding,* Gem."

"I know. But I've already *had* a wedding, remember?" she said on a sad smile, as if the fact that they'd been there when she'd married asshole Carlo counted for something. "They'll celebrate with us another time." I saw the sadness in her eyes, but she waved her hand, like the hurt was a cloud of smoke she could waft away. "Anyway, let's move on."

I gave her a look that said *I love you enough for ten families*, and she smiled in understanding before I dragged my finger to the next table.

"Okay. Here, it's Zach's parents, his brother, his brother's best friend, me, and..."

Gemma smirked. "*Aaaand.*"

I rolled my eyes, but I knew my cheeks were flushed. "And my plus one, if I'm lucky enough to have one."

"Pshhh. Like you even have to question that." She snapped her fingers, pointing at the blue sticky note next to my pink one. "Erase that plus one shit and add Makoa's name."

I swallowed. "I don't think I should, Gemma. Not yet."

"It's been two months now," she pointed out. "You don't think you'll still be seeing each other in another month and a half?"

I shrugged. "I don't know."

"You don't know?" She looked genuinely confused. "Do you *want* to still be seeing him?"

I bit my lip before covering my face with both hands. "Ugh. You're the worst."

"Because I ask you about your boyfriend?" she joked on a chuckle.

I wrinkled my nose at the term, which earned me a deep belly laugh.

"Belle. He's your boyfriend. You're his girlfriend. And from the way I've seen you two acting together, and all the time you've spent together, I hate to break it to you, but... he ain't going anywhere."

"You don't know that."

"Apparently, I know it more than you do." She shook her head, grabbing my arm until I freed my hands from my face and looked at her. "Why are you hiding from it? I've been your best friend for years, and I've never seen you so smitten with a guy before."

"Except for with Nathan," I pointed out. "Which is *exactly* why I'm adverse to it."

Gemma shook her head. "No, Nathan was different. We were young. Sure, you guys had fun together, but Nathan didn't look at you the way Makoa does. He didn't care for you the way Makoa does. And he definitely didn't take the time to get to know you, your friends, your hopes and dreams and likes and dislikes the way Makoa has. I mean, I can see that clear as day. Can't you?"

I groaned again, and I didn't have to answer for Gemma to know that I saw it, too.

"I know this will sound crazy to you," I said after a minute. "But that's part of the problem. I *do* see it. And where I usually boot a guy to the curb after three dates, *long* before any of these kinds of feelings can develop, I find myself doing the exact opposite with Mak. I'm like... I'm leaning *all the way in* to this guy. And that means if he takes even one step backward, I'm going down. Hard."

"What makes you think he will?"

I shrugged. "My record. Statistics."

"Your record?" Gemma laughed. "Belle, other than Nathan, you have dated approximately zero guys. Unless you count Potato Face."

I smirked at that.

"Which I don't," she clarified. "But, from what I can tell, Makoa seems fully invested."

"He does, but..." I sighed, picking at my nails. "Again, don't think I'm crazy but... I feel like he's hiding something."

Gemma frowned. "What do you mean?"

"I mean, sometimes when we're talking about him, he'll change the subject suddenly, like he doesn't want me to pry too deep. I know the signs because I've used the same techniques on other guys. It's like a deflection, so we stay on lighter topics."

"Like, his family and stuff?"

"More like his past relationships, and work, oddly." I shook my head. "And he's been at this work conference... what if he hooked up with someone in his field or something? And he's with her now, and that's why I haven't heard from him very much? And maybe that's why we haven't talked much about his job, or his exes. Like... really, what conference do you know that lasts almost three weeks *and* takes up nearly every second of every day?"

All my insecurities rushed to the surface as soon as I opened the nozzle, the little droplets of *buts* and *ifs* rushing through and shoving each other out of the way in their desperation to be heard. My stomach catapulted, and I wrapped my arms around it, regretting that I was talking about the very thing I'd been trying to avoid.

"Oddly, I do get it," Gemma said after a minute. "Don't you remember how messed up I was after Carlo? I didn't want to give Zach a chance, even when he proved he deserved one. Even when I was so into him I couldn't see anyone *but* him." She shrugged. "I think that's our natural instinct. It's self-preservation, to be skeptical and cautious after being burned."

I sighed.

"But," she continued. "Here's the thing. All of that you just said? It's projection. You don't know any of that for sure. What's happening is that you're scared, and so your brain is in overdrive, trying to think of the worst-case scenarios so you'll believe it and throw in the towel and go back to the safety of not being at Makoa's mercy. Better to be the one to break things off and cause the pain than be on the receiving end of it, right?"

I deflated at the realization. "Self-sabotage at its finest."

"Mm-hmm." Gemma tossed another handful of popcorn in her mouth before she abandoned the bag and crawled toward me. Her petite arms wrapped around mine, and she rested her head on my shoulder, making a shelf for me to lean my head, too. "I wish I could tell you that there is absolutely zero chance of it not working out. But that chance is always there. It was there with me and Carlo, even after we got married. It's there with me and Zach, even though we're head over heels for each other right now. Love is scary that way, because at any moment, one person could change their mind and end it all."

"This is a terrible pep talk."

She laughed. "What I'm saying is, that niggling in your belly that's freaking you out?" She leaned up, looking at me. "It's trust."

I swallowed.

"You trust him, Belle. And that's a really, really good sign."

"The last time I trusted someone—"

"I know," she said, cutting me off. "But this isn't last time. This is this time. And you've got to let go of the *what ifs*. Maybe Makoa *is* keeping some stuff from you right now. Maybe he's been hurt, just like you. Maybe it's going to take some time. But don't judge him based off what you *don't* know about him. Judge him by what you *do* know."

My heart squeezed, and Gemma pulled all the way back, sitting in front of me. She held up her hand, fingers splayed. "Tell me five things you know."

I chuckled. "This is silly."

"Indulge me," she said, wiggling her fingers.

"Well... he's kind," I started, and Gemma smiled, knocking down one finger. "He's goofy as hell. He makes me laugh. He makes me feel safe." I smiled, looking down at the floor as my words carried me away. "He cares about my job. He didn't judge me when I told him about my past. He loves his family. He's a Broadway nerd like me, and he's *terrible* at trivia, but I find it adorable that he thinks he's so great. He's an awful cook, too, but I love that he wants to cook for us. For me. He trusts me with his condo, with everything in the design. He gives me room to be creative. He makes an effort with my friends, and the funny thing is that he doesn't even have to because he's *him*." I bit my lip. "And he has, quite possibly, the most perfect cock to ever be sculpted by the dick gods."

Gemma snorted a laugh. "I don't think the dick gods are a thing."

"Sure, they are," I argued, frowning when I met her gaze. "There are pussy gods, too. I thank them every day for this tight little slip and slide." I tapped between my legs with a proud smile, and Gemma rolled on her back in a fit of laughter.

When she sat back up, she watched me for a long while with a knowing smile. "Belle. I ran out of fingers." She held up all ten to show. "So, if we're going by what you *do* know about him... I'd say you've got nothing to worry about."

Nothing to worry about, I echoed in my mind.

I wondered if I'd ever be able to believe it.

Makoa

Training camp was a strange kind of torture.

Any player would be lying if they said they hated it. Then again, any player would be lying if they said they *loved* it. Because the truth of the matter lay somewhere in between, and which end of the scale that truth landed on depended heavily on the day and the *time* of day.

Of course, we were all ecstatic to get out and play. For a lot of the guys, it'd been weeks since they'd touched a ball or ran a play. Even if they hadn't taken a real vacation and had been running drills and working out as strenuously as I had, they hadn't played with their team, in their colors, with that familiar adrenaline rushing through their veins and reminding them that each second ticked them closer and closer to the first kick-off of the season.

The slate was clean.

We all had a chance to make it.

And the team had a chance to make it to the big game.

It was exciting, to see guys you hadn't seen in a while or, in my case, to meet a whole new team of guys. There was a lot of laughing, a lot of pranking each other, a lot of that high that comes only with getting the perfect snap or perfect catch or perfect block. There was a reason most football players would say their team is like their family, and much of that was born at camp.

All that being said, camp was also fucking brutal.

It was long days that started before the sun came up, and didn't end until long after it went down. It was hours of meetings, two-a-day practices, scrimmages and drills. It was watching film until your eyes crossed, being twisted up and mashed on by an athletic trainer before being sent out for more work on the field, and lifting weights even when your muscles were so sore it hurt to lift a toothpick. It was fine-tuning techniques, pushing even when you were exhausted to try to stand out to the offensive and head coaches, and above all, treating every second like it was your last chance to prove you deserved a spot on the team.

It didn't matter that no decisions would be made about who would be cut and who would stay for a few weeks yet. To even get *that* far, you had to get time on the field during the pre-season games.

That's what I was after.

When the team had signed me as a free agent, it wasn't lost on me that they signed at least a dozen other guys, knowing full well that they'd cut them just as easily if they didn't fit where the team needed them to. Fortunately for me, the Bears needed a better receiving game, and I pushed through every sore muscle and ounce of exhaustion to prove I was the guy for the job.

On the last week of camp, the fans were invited to watch us scrimmage, and the entire team was alive with the buzz that came from them cheering us on. Gerald and I were standing next to each other, signing a few balls and jerseys — though most of the fans were crowding the other end of the field, where our starting quarterback, receivers, O-line, and defense were.

They didn't know me yet, the few fans who passed me their balls with shy smiles or *you did great out there* encouragements.

But my hope was that by the end of the season, they'd be proud of that signature I left.

"I don't know about you, man," Gerald said, clapping me on the shoulder when the last of the fans were making their way out of the training facility. "But I feel like I could sleep for a week."

I chuckled. "Think you're going to have to wait until the end of the season for that."

"Or the first Tuesday off. I'd take even a full day of sleep if I can't get a whole week," he rebutted. Then, he nodded his chin. "I know we haven't talked much, with everything going on here, but... I heard the coaches talking on the sideline the other day. Your name came up quite a few times."

I arched a brow. "Yeah?"

He nodded. "I hope you feel ready for the exhibition season, man, because they're going to call on you."

"I'll answer," I said, determination bending my brows. "Did it sound good, what they were saying?"

Gerald smirked at that. "I wouldn't be telling you otherwise."

Hope bloomed in my chest. It was no secret that an invite to training camp didn't mean shit. You could work your ass off and still be cut easily, with about as much as an impersonal phone call midway through the pre-season. But ever since my contract ran up with the 49ers, I'd manifested that wherever I went next, I'd make the team. I'd make it my home. That condo I owned that overlooked the lake was proof of that.

In my mind, I was already a Bear.

And now, I was inches away from cementing that as truth.

I nodded in gratitude, and Gerald squeezed my shoulder once more before jogging toward the locker room. We'd all get a quick shower and a quick dinner before it would be time to report for evening meetings.

The locker room was loud and boisterous, with players laughing and dancing and making jokes about the scrimmage game, but I was quiet as I made my way to my cubby. I pulled my phone from my duffle, a relieved sigh finding my chest at a missed text from Belle.

Gemma and I figured out the seating chart for the wedding. Sorry, but you have to sit next to me. I tried to get you and Zach your own table, but Gem fought me on it.

I chuckled, heart aching with the urge to call her, to hear her voice, her laugh... and more than anything, to tell her about the day I'd had. I wanted to tell her how good I felt in the drills, how well I played in the scrimmage, how Gerald had heard the coaches talking about me.

I wanted her to know this part of me more than anything.

I swallowed down my regrets, typing out a response to her before I chucked my phone back in my bag where it would stay until ten o'clock at night when we finally called it in for the day. I hated that I didn't have more time to call Belle, even if just to sit on a video chat and listen to her talk about her day. It physically hurt some nights to know I was just an hour from her, but I couldn't go to her.

Right now, my focus *had* to be football. I had one shot to make this team, and I couldn't throw it away.

But camp would be over in just a few days, and then I'd be back in Chicago and she'd be back in my arms.

And I'd tell her everything.

I'd had both dreams and nightmares about what would happen when I did. The best of them left her smiling and laughing and shoving me playfully remarking *why didn't you just tell me from the get-go, silly?* The worst of them had her crying and screaming and slamming a door in my face as she repeated the one label I never wanted from her over and over again.

Liar, liar, liar!

Just like training camp, I imagined reality would lay somewhere between the two, but I was ready to face the consequences. In my gut, in my heart, I knew she trusted me. I knew, once I explained everything, she'd understand.

And then, this would all be behind us.

I closed my eyes, imagining her wearing my jersey, sitting with the other girlfriends and wives and cheering me on at every home game. I imagined her catching a flight to the away games, or me coming home to her after a loss on the road, or — even better — celebrating a win in the best way we know how.

My eyes fluttered open as optimism surged through me, swirling in a tornado with the hope Gerald had left in my chest before.

Everything I wanted was right at the tip of my fingers.

All I had to do was reach.

CHAPTER 16

Belle

I ran my fingers through my hair Friday evening, eyes nearly crossing as I checked the last of my emails. Being so consumed with the Coffee & Cubicles contract, I hadn't had time for anything else all week, and so I'd spent the last of my Friday afternoon and evening catching up as best I could on emails and tasks before I let myself call it for the night.

Gemma was already long gone, home with Zach after I assured her I was fine and she should enjoy her weekend. She didn't like leaving me to my own devices in the office, mostly because she knew I could stay here all night. I promised her I'd pack it in before sunset, and as golden hour lit up my office, I sighed, shutting down my computer and logging off.

You better be leaving the office, Gemma's text said.

I shot back a video of me locking up the office door.

Everything about me was dragging as I slugged into the elevator. I didn't need a mirror to know my eyes were weary, my shoulders slumped, my hair a disaster. I'd be shocked if my makeup had made it through the hellish day, but didn't care enough to check my reflection. All I wanted right now was a glass of red wine, my leftover pad Thai, and my bed.

The yawn I'd been fighting for the past hour stretched my jaw when I pushed through the glass doors of the office building and out onto the street. I covered it with my hand, closing my eyes and shaking it off as best I could to prep for the walk home.

But when I opened my eyes, all the fatigue left me in a *whoosh* at the sight of Makoa.

He was leaned up against a sleek black car, dressed casual in a pair of joggers and a muscle T that hugged his biceps and made it easy to see the definition of his abs underneath. There was an obnoxiously giant bouquet of flowers in his hands, a beautiful fall arrangement that I absentmindedly thought would look perfect as the centerpiece of his new dining table. His wide, goofy grin was at a new high, stretched across his face with his eyes dazzling in the last of the sun's warm glow.

He was back.

He was *home*.

"You catch any flies with that yawn?" He chuckled, pushing off where he was leaned up against the car and crossing the few feet between us.

"You're here," I said, shaking my head as he handed me the flowers. I inhaled them deep, but didn't admire them nearly as long as I should have before I almost dropped them to the ground when I threw my arms around Makoa's neck.

"I'm here, *Ku'uipo*," he whispered, holding me tight and kissing my forehead.

Cue butterflies.

I pressed up on my toes, sealing my mouth to his in our first kiss in nearly three weeks. We both inhaled at the contact, his grip tightening, my head fuzzy with the current of electricity that soared at the touch. I couldn't get close enough to him, no matter how tightly I held or how much I pressed myself into his grasp. My mouth opened, letting his tongue sweep inside, and we moaned in sync.

"*God*, I've missed you," he groaned, nipping at my bottom lip.

"I think you should show me how much."

Makoa growled, smacking my ass before he put a little space between us. He grabbed my hand, pulling me over to the car and opening the back door.

My purse and the flowers were both abandoned in the seat as soon as Makoa climbed in on the other side, and I didn't care about the driver when I heaved myself over to straddle him. He laughed into my next kiss, hands on my hips to keep me from grinding the way I wanted to.

"Woman," he warned, a snap of his fingers to the driver the only indication he could give that we were ready to go before my lips were on his again.

The car accelerated, and Makoa allowed me one little roll of friction to feel his erection against me before he picked me up at the hips and moved me to the middle seat next to him. He kissed me to cut off my protest, buckling me in at the same time.

"Safety first, you little siren," he said.

I tried to pout but couldn't stop smiling.

He's here.

He's home.

One arm found its way around my shoulders, the other slid between my knees to hold onto my thigh possessively as Makoa took my breath away with another kiss. This one held promises of what would happen when we made it to his place, and I leaned into it, stomach tight with anticipation of what that hand on my thigh would do once we got there.

We tore out of that car like it was on fire when it pulled up to the condominium, and Makoa tugged me by the hand to the elevator. We made out like a couple of teenagers on the way up, Makoa pinning my hips against the back wall, hiking one leg up and slipping his hand under my blouse.

The doors opened too soon for my taste, but as soon as they did, I was yanked out by the hand. I giggled as we all but jogged down the hall to his door, and as he fumbled for his keys, I wrapped my arms around him again, kissing all over his neck and rubbing against him in every possible way I could to make the feat harder to achieve.

We were still like that, a tangle of lips and hands and laughs, when Makoa finally got the door unlocked and we tumbled inside. The flowers I'd managed to hold onto until that point slipped to the floor, and I was in the process of climbing that hunk of man like a jungle gym when we discovered very abruptly that we were not alone.

"Surprise!"

It was a chorus of voices, one that startled Makoa enough to shove me behind him and shelter me like it was an attack while I screamed in surprise. I latched onto his shoulders, peering around them at a group of equally shocked faces, panic zipping through me as my heart raced out of my chest.

There was a split second of silence, and then the youngest girl laughed, pointing at Makoa with a victorious smile.

"Busted, *bruddah!*"

His baby sister laughed again, and then realization hit me like a bucket of ice water to the head as all those Kumaka eyes landed on me.

Shit.

Makoa

Shit. Shit. Shit.

The absolute last thing I expected to walk into on my first night back in Chicago was a surprise visit from half my family.

My parents, oldest sister, and youngest sister stood in the foyer, watching me with their own special kind of amusement. I didn't have to look in the kitchen to know there was proof there that Mah was making laulau and poi, one of my favorite traditional Hawaiian dishes, as the rich and distinct smell of the leaves steaming had filled my entire condo.

My family was here.

And now I was trying to figure out how to hide my erection and the fact that I was about to bang Belle against this door.

In the back of my mind, I realized it shouldn't have been that much of a surprise to see them all here. This was the whole reason I gave my mom an airline credit card and told her she could book a flight to see me any time she wanted to. This was why I'd given both her and my youngest sister a key to my place.

I just wished I'd told them both that I required at least twenty-four-hour notice.

Oliana was still laughing at me as I tried to figure out what to say, and my oldest sister, Pania, was fighting her own curious smile as she tilted her head, assessing Belle. But my focus was on my parents — Dad, who gave me a look that told me he was both impressed and surprised I'd landed a woman as hot as Belle, and Mah, who had a twitch in her eye but a smile on her lips. I couldn't figure out if she was pissed she'd just seen me making out with a woman she doesn't know, or if she was happy I had a woman coming home with me at all.

"Sorry we caught you off guard," Pania said when I was silent for too long. "We just wanted to be here for your first g— OW!"

Pania swatted me away when I flew from where I'd been shielding Belle over to her, instead. I pinched her side, throwing my arm around her with a louder-than-necessary laugh. "Are you kidding? I'm so happy to see all of you!"

Just please don't say anything about football.

I gave them each swift hugs and kisses on the cheek before I turned to Belle, who was nervously clasping her hands together now that I'd left her at the door alone.

"*Makuakāne, Makuahine, Kaikaina, Kaiku'ana* — this is Belle Monroe," I said, forcing my best smile. "Belle, this is my family." I hoped she could see the apology in my eyes. "Minus two."

Belle didn't miss a beat, her smile easy and confident as she extended a hand for Mom, first. "It's so nice to meet you, Mrs. Kumaka," she said. "Mr. Kumaka, Pania, Oliana." She nodded to each of them as she took their hands, and I marveled at how she remembered my sisters' names, at how I didn't even have to introduce them properly for her to know. "I've heard so much about you."

My mom arched a brow in my direction that said *that makes one of us*, but luckily, Dad was already putting on his charm.

"It's nice to meet you, too, Belle. So sorry we came unannounced."

Belle shook her head. "No apology necessary."

"I didn't realize my son was dating a super model," he added, to which Belle chuckled, her cheeks tinging pink.

"From what Makoa has told me about this family, I'd be the least of the super stars even if I *were* a model."

Mah beamed at that. "I raised my kids to reach for the stars," she said, looking up at me then. "I still remember the first time Makoa came to me with his little arms wrapped around a football and said—"

I cleared my throat, grabbing my mom by both arms before she could finish that sentence. "Belle, will you excuse us for a second?"

I was already ushering my family toward the balcony, and Belle smiled in understanding. "I'm just going to take care of these," she said, gesturing to the flowers that she'd dropped to the floor. Most of them were fine, but there were petals and leaves scattered around, and I gave her a look of gratitude before I turned to focus on the issue at hand.

"This is not the way you welcome your own family into your home," Mom chastised as soon as the sliding glass door was shut behind us. "It is also very *rude* to leave your guest inside that way."

"Oh, he can't help it. He's shook we just found him about to get it on with his *girlfriend*," Oliana said, singing the last word.

Dad gave her a look of warning, which shut her up and made Pania smile.

I grabbed the back of my neck, looking inside to make sure Belle was busying herself and couldn't hear us before I turned to all of them. "I'm sorry. I really am happy to see you, but a heads up would have been nice."

"That would have ruined the surprise!" Mom argued.

I sighed. "I know, I know. Uh... I just..."

"Didn't expect to have to introduce us to Miss Monroe in there?" Dad finished for me, arching his thick, dark brow.

I cringed.

"You don't have to hide her from us," Pania said. "I promise not to tell her about how you peed the bed until you were ten."

Oliana snickered.

"It's not that," I said, looking inside again before my shameful gaze found them. "It's just... things are kind of complicated."

My dad nodded in a sad understanding. "She has you friend-zoned, doesn't she?"

"What? No," I said quickly, narrowing my eyes at my giggling sisters. "Very clearly not friend-zoned, if you didn't catch our little entrance there."

"So, why haven't we heard about her, then?" Mah asked.

I looked up to the sky, like there was a god who could help me now. When I looked back at my family, I knew the only way to get this over with was to rip it off like a Band-Aid.

"Okay, don't freak out, and please don't make a commotion... but... Belle doesn't know I'm in the NFL." I swallowed. "She doesn't know I play *at all*."

"What?"

"Why not?"

"What in the world?"

"Why wouldn't you tell her?"

"How couldn't she know?"

"*Keiki kāne*," Dad's voice boomed the loudest, and we all silenced, looking at him in unison. The man was a teddy bear, but when he stood tall like that with his brows furrowed and lips flat, he made me and my siblings quake. "What's going on?"

"I know it doesn't make sense. Trust me," I added, murmuring to myself more than them. "If anything, I wish I could go back and change everything about the decision I made not to tell her. But, when I came here, it felt like a new chapter, like I was starting over in a way. And when I met Belle, she had no idea who I was. She's not a sports girl, couldn't care less about football, and because of that, *I* got to tell her who I was. I got to decide what she knew about me, what made me who I was."

"But football is your first true love," Mom said, her eyes sad as they flicked inside before finding me again. "If she won't understand that, then she's not the right woman for you."

"That's not it at all," I said, shaking my head as I tried to figure out how to explain. "What Dad said earlier was a joke, but we all know it was true for the first half of my life. Every girl I wanted saw me only as a friend. Then, I go to college, give my everything to football, and suddenly, I'm a pro ball player and all these girls want me. But they didn't actually want *me*."

Pania sighed, her eyes softening with understanding. "They wanted your money."

I swallowed, grimly nodding. Pania had been there for me when everything went south with Zariah and Lucia. If anyone understood, it was her.

"Or my connections, or what they thought I'd be someday, the places they thought I could get them," I added. "In whatever way you spin it, they didn't care about who I was."

"And does she?" Dad asked.

I glanced inside, chuckling when I saw Belle fidgeting with her hair and swiping the mascara from under her eyes in the reflection of the microwave.

"More than I deserve."

"Where does she think you've been the past few weeks?" Oliana asked.

I cringed. "At a real estate conference. That's what she thinks I do for a living."

Mom clucked her tongue, and when I looked at her, she looked more disappointed in me than she ever had been. "You can't hide who you are forever."

"I'm not," I said hurriedly. "At first, I just wanted to make sure she wasn't playing some game. I thought maybe she *did* know who I was and was just trying to get in with me, with my money. But it didn't take long for me to see that wasn't true."

"But you still didn't tell her the truth," Oliana challenged.

"Again, it's complicated. She's got scars of her own." I shook my head, because everything that came out of my lips made me feel more and more like a coward. "I just didn't want to lose her before I had her to begin with... I wanted to earn her trust."

"By lying to her," Dad said.

I sighed, pinching the bridge of my nose. "I'd planned on telling her tonight, but then..." I waved my hand toward all of them. "Please, just don't say anything about football. I'm glad you're here, I really am. I've missed you."

They all smiled at that, exchanging looks.

"Let's go inside, have a nice dinner, catch up. I want you to get to know Belle." It was my turn to smile. "I think you'll fall in love with her just as I have."

"Love?" Pania's eyes dazzled in what was left of the setting sun, the crook of her lips even more curious now. "I've never heard that word from you before."

I swallowed, not letting that four-letter word linger too long in the open air before I snuffed it out. "Please. Just hold this between us for tonight. I'll tell her tomorrow, and everything will be fine. Okay?"

The look in their eyes told me they weren't as sure as I was, but with them begrudgingly agreeing, we made our way back inside to Belle.

And I said a silent prayer for her that she'd survive dinner with the Kumaka clan.

CHAPTER 17

Belle

"**Y**ou cheated!" Oliana said, pointing her finger at one of the words Makoa had spelled out with his Bananagrams tiles. "That's not a real word."

"*Yas*?" Makoa shook his head. "That is absolutely a real word. Ask the internet, or consult the texts you've sent me."

"It's *slang*."

Makoa shrugged. "Still works. You're just mad because you can't beat your big brother. Haven't been able to since you were born. Well, unless you count the award for most drool on a pillow, because that one *definitely* goes to you."

Oliana narrowed her eyes before she was up out of her chair and around the table, latching onto her big brother's shoulders and driving her knuckles into his head. He laughed and spun around, tickling her sides before he threw her up over his shoulder as she screamed for him to put her down.

I laughed at the show, sipping the coffee we'd made to go with dessert and praying it would bring me back to life. The exhaustion I'd felt earlier had morphed into a new kind, one that was born from the adrenaline I'd felt when Makoa surprised me, followed immediately by the crash when we came in to find his entire family in his condo.

My heart was doing funny things in my chest as I watched him play with his little sister. It was a phenomenon that kept happening, over and over. I felt it when he set the table for his mom, when he hugged Pania and told me stories about the two of them when they were younger, when he and his dad sang one of their favorite songs and moved their hips like hula dancers by the fireplace, breaking us all into a fit of laughter.

It was one thing, to be in Makoa's arms at night, to hold his hand at a Broadway show, to spend a day with him and my friends on a boat.

But to see him with his family?

It tugged at heartstrings I didn't even know I had.

"Alright, you two. That's enough," Mrs. Kumaka said, and then her eyes wandered the sitting room, a small smile on her lips. "I love what you've done with this room. It feels like home, but different..."

"It's a combination of Maui and Chicago," Makoa explained, pointing out the details in the art and furniture as Oliana writhed to get free. Then, he smiled at me. "You can thank this design genius. She dreamed it all up and brought it to life."

"I wish I could see it," Oliana said, beating her brother's back with her little fists. "If someone would put me *down*, maybe I could."

"Why don't you give us a tour?" Dad suggested when Makoa finally set Oliana back on her feet.

That made his mom light up, and she and Mr. Kumaka stood to join Makoa and Oliana, while Pania slyly grabbed my arm under the table to prevent me from doing the same. I looked at her curiously, but she just smiled up at her family. "You guys go ahead. Belle and I will clean up in the kitchen."

Mr. and Mrs. Kumaka smiled at both of us, and Makoa took the lead, guiding them down the hall and back to the bedrooms. Oliana looked over her shoulder at us, winking at her big sister, and suddenly, my stomach was a bundle of nerves.

Anyone who thought facing a big brother was hard didn't have to face the oldest sister of the one and only boy in the family.

We were both quiet for a long while, gathering dishes from the table and taking them into the kitchen. Pania started in on the dishes while I put all the leftover food in plastic containers.

"So, is this the part where you grill me and threaten my life with a shot gun if my intentions with your brother aren't pure?" I joked, handing Pania the crockpot the pork was cooked in.

She smiled, and I marveled at how much that smile looked like Makoa's, how those same dimples framed her lips. "No guns, I promise," she said, her eyes finding mine. "I'm more of a roundhouse-kick-to-the-head kind of gal."

My eyes must have bulged out of their sockets, because she laughed, pointing at me.

"You should have seen your face."

I yawned, trying to cover it with the back of my wrist. "I have a feeling I don't want to see my face at all right now — threatened by my boyfriend's big sister or not." My stomach still did a little flip at that word... *boyfriend.*

"Long day?"

"Long couple months is more like it. I had a contract move up from October, and it's a big one, a three-story claim on one of the new office buildings on the river."

"Wow. And they hired you for the job?"

I nodded. "It's fun, but challenging, and apparently this is a company that isn't used to working with other people's schedules, because they didn't seem to mind blowing mine all to hell."

Pania smiled, working on scrubbing the serving spoon. She was quiet for a while before she said, "So, back to my brother."

"Subtle," I said on a smile of my own.

"You two seem really happy together."

I nodded, swallowing down my nerves as best I could. "We are."

"I really am sorry we bombarded you tonight. I'm sure the last thing you wanted to do was spend a night with family after he's been gone so long for ca..." She cleared her throat. "The conference."

I raised my eyebrows at that, scooping the last of the poi into a container before I handed the dish to her. "Yeah, I definitely didn't realize how long and time-consuming a real estate conference could be. But, weirdly... I'm kind of glad you all were here."

"Yeah?" Pania snorted. "Takes a lot to put up with us. And this is mild, compared to when the other sisters are here."

I smiled, stepping beside her to help load the dishwasher. "I don't mind it. I'm an only child, and my parents have always traveled a lot, so I grew up in a pretty quiet house." I shrugged. "It's fun, all the noise and commotion, all the laughter."

"We'll see if you say that again after spending a holiday with us."

I chuckled, but my stomach took a nose dive at the thought. Part of me could see it — me and Makoa on a plane, sitting on the floor by the Christmas tree in his old house, helping his mom in the kitchen, opening gifts, playing games...

The other part of me laughed at the audacity of it all, at the fact that I was even in a situation where going home for the holidays with the guy I'm dating was an option.

It seemed my heart was always at war with my head, one vying for hope and trust, while the other pointed at every scar I had to remind me of the risk I was taking, at the likelihood that I'd end up just as burned as last time.

"I don't know what he's told you, about his past," Pania said after a moment, handing me a casserole dish to dry. "But Makoa isn't like a lot of other guys."

I smiled. "I think I caught onto that pretty early."

"Did he make you watch a rom-com?"

I snorted. "No, but he did take me to trivia, and then to see *Moulin Rouge!* on Broadway."

She seemed proud when she smiled again. "He's always been a Broadway fan. Makoa, my sister Tamar, and I used to put on plays for our parents all the time when we were younger. Makoa thought he was *such* a good singer."

I wrinkled my nose. "Well, he's lost that over the years, I think."

"Oh, no — I said he *thought* he was a good singer." She waved a soapy hand. "That boy has always sounded like a bad mix of Bob Dylan and Miley Cyrus."

We both bent over at that, the exhaustion making me laugh harder than I normally would have. I was wiping the tears from my eyes when she continued.

"Well, if you know anything about my brother, then you know he wears his heart on his sleeve. And I can see it after just tonight." She paused, sponge in hand as she turned to look at me. "He cares about you, Belle."

I swallowed, nodding as my eyes found the dish in my hand again. "I care about him, too."

"I don't think you understand what I'm saying." She stopped the pretense of washing dishes, tossing the sponge in the sink and turning to face me completely. "I've never seen him like this with anyone else."

My heart stuttered, kicking back to life at a quicker pace. "Really?"

"Before you, Belle..." She sighed. "Let's just say my brother has been through some shit. He's not afraid to love, even when he's been burned so many times. But it worries me. As his big sister, to see him giving himself so fully, because so far, no one has been worthy of that kind of care. He's been kicked around by far too many girls, and I just..." She rolled her lips together, glancing down the hall before her gaze met mine again. "Please... don't break his heart. I'm not sure he could survive it. Not this time. Not with you."

I looked down at the rag in my hand, wrapping it up in my fists. I didn't know what she meant about Makoa, because we hadn't talked about his past that way. I didn't know about his ex-girlfriends, or what they'd put him through.

And I hated that he hadn't felt comfortable enough to tell me himself.

"I'm more worried about him breaking me," I whispered.

Pania smiled, reaching out to squeeze my upper arm. Her eyes flicked behind me before she said, "If he does, I'll give him the biggest wedgie since the one I gave him when he was nine years old. And trust me, that's one he still hasn't forgotten."

I laughed just as two big, warm arms wrapped around me from behind, and Makoa kissed my cheek, pulling me back against his chest. "I don't know what the first part of this conversation was, but please don't take her up on this offer. I'm still picking my boxers out of my ass all these years later."

Pania rolled the towel in her hands, winding up and swatting him with it before she winked at me and left us alone in the kitchen. The Kumaka family was gathering around the television in the living room, and Makoa spun me in his arms until we were facing each other. I wrapped my arms around his neck, and he kissed my nose, eyes searching mine.

We didn't say a word.

We didn't have to.

My throat was sticky and dry, heart pounding in my chest as we stood there, holding each other, his sister's words on repeat in my mind.

He's not afraid to love...

Makoa framed my face with his hands, kissing me sweetly and slowly and surely before he grabbed my hand and led me into the other room with his family.

And I realized that when it came to him, maybe I shouldn't be so afraid, either.

Makoa

It was after midnight by the time my family finally let me take Belle home. My mom hugged her for what felt like half an hour when the time came, and only let go when Belle promised to come visit them all in Hawai'i soon.

I drove her to her condo across town, and we were quiet the entire way, my hand holding onto her thigh. Belle was so tired she had her head against the headrest, eyes closed, dozing in and out while I watched the streetlights float across her face.

When we made it up to her door, I walked her inside, chuckling as she fought back yawns and peeled off her high heels.

"I'm going to sleep like a baby tonight," she said with a croaky voice.

"Hopefully better than a baby. Those things scream all night," I countered, pulling her into my arms as soon as she was barefoot. I swept her hair behind her ears, searching her eyes for any sign of her never wanting to see me again after everything that had ensued tonight.

"Hi," I breathed after a moment.

She gave me a sleepy smile, wrapping her arms around my neck. "Hi."

"You okay?"

She nodded, but just as she did, she yawned so long and big. I thought she'd get lockjaw.

I chuckled, leaning in to press a kiss to those lips as soon as she'd shut them again. "I had a completely different idea in mind for tonight when I took you to my place."

"That makes two of us." Her smile widened. "But it was fun."

"Yeah?"

"You didn't think so?"

"I did, I just... I know that had to be a lot for you, meeting my family. And unexpectedly so."

Belle tickled the hair at the back of my neck. "It was definitely a surprise... I haven't ever met a man's family before."

I shook my head. "That's so crazy and hard to believe, because you just knocked it out of the park."

"They're easy to get along with."

I scoffed. "You didn't grow up with them."

"Don't lie. You loved it."

I wrapped her up even tighter. "I really did."

We stood there for a long while with her in my arms and my heart in my throat. That heart beat faster and faster with every passing second, and every pulse said the same thing.

Tell her.

Tell her.

Tell her.

But when I opened my mouth to, Belle yawned again, and this one watered her eyes. She shook it off with a smile, laying her head on my chest. "Okay. You gotta put me to bed before I pass out."

I chuckled, kissing her hair before I swept her up in my arms and carried her back to her bed. I helped her undress, and it was then that I realized just how tired she was, because she didn't even try to make a move toward having sex. She climbed under the sheets, pulled the covers up to her chin, and sighed, wiggling around with a giant smile on her face.

"I think this is what it feels like to do a hallucinogenic drug," she said.

I barked out a laugh, brushing her hair back from her face. "That good, huh?"

"I'm the kind of tired only a straight day of sleep can fix."

"Well, get some sleep, then," I said, leaning down to kiss her. She held that kiss for a long time before she let me go. "Can I see you tomorrow?"

Belle sighed. "I'd love to, but I'll be working all day."

I frowned. "I hate that you're working on a Saturday."

"Again, that makes two of us."

"How about tomorrow night?"

Belle squeezed my hand. "Your family is in town. You should spend time with them."

My frown deepened.

"Hey, I'm not going anywhere," she said on a chuckle. "They flew a long way to see you. Besides, I really do need to catch up on rest. I'd really like to be in bed by seven tomorrow, if I can help it."

I swallowed past the knot in my throat. It was killing me, to keep the truth from her any longer than I already had.

I debated the consequences of just telling her now, but she could barely keep her eyes open, and she had work in the morning. It would be selfish of me to do it knowing both those truths.

"How about you come over Sunday night?" she offered when I didn't say anything. "I have something with Gemma during the day, but I should be home around six or so."

I blew out a breath, hating that I'd have to wait until after my game, but I would take whatever I could. "I'll be a little later, have some work stuff to do but... I'll grab takeout for us for dinner?"

"Only if you pick up dessert, too."

I smiled. "I can do that."

Belle's sleepy smile spread as she watched me, leaning into where I held her face. "I've missed you."

Her sentiment was punctuated by a hard thump of my heart. "I've missed you, too."

"Will you hold me for a while?"

I shook my head like she was crazy to even think she had to ask, and she scooted over until I could fit under the covers with her. I wrapped her up in my arms, pulling her back to my chest, pressing kisses along the back of her neck as she practically purred like a kitten.

I hated that I had to wait to tell her. I'd been thinking about the exact right words all day long, almost all *month* long at camp. And then, my family's surprise had thrown everything out of whack. But she was exhausted, and as much as I wanted to tell her *before* my first game, I realized it could wait. She didn't watch football, anyway. It wouldn't make a difference if I told her now or Sunday night.

A deep and heavy sigh found my chest, and I shoved it all out of my head for the time being. Just a couple more days, and she'd know everything. Until then, I needed to focus on football.

This first pre-season game would make or break me.

"Makoa," Belle whispered after a long while, her fingers drawing lines on the arm I had wrapped around her.

"Mm?"

"I realized something while you were gone. And maybe a little tonight, too."

"What's that?" I asked, nuzzling her neck.

She swallowed, staying quiet for so long I thought she'd fallen asleep. But then another whisper came in the dark, and this one knocked the breath from my chest.

"I think I'm falling in love with you."

The next beat of my heart was delayed, and when it finally came, it hit me like a punch to the gut.

I wrapped her up tighter, kissing her neck, her shoulder, the spot just under her ear. I kissed her reverently, like I didn't deserve to, because the truth was that I didn't.

"I think I fell a long time ago," I whispered back.

Belle twisted in my arms, her eyes finding mine in the dim lighting of her bedroom, and she pressed her trembling lips to mine. I held that kiss strong and steady, so she knew I meant every word I said, so that it sealed my unspoken promise that I wouldn't hurt her.

Would I?

I shook the thought from my head once more, reminding myself that until Sunday, there was nothing more to do or say. I'd tell her the truth by the time the weekend ended, and then it'd all be behind us, and everything would be okay.

Everything will be okay.

And like a sucker, I actually believed it.

CHAPTER 18

Belle

My best friend at a Chicago Bears football game was like a nine-year-old kid in a store full of Disney toys.

It didn't matter that it was a pre-season game, which even *I* knew didn't count for much. Gemma was clad in her favorite Bears tank top, ripped denim shorts and — this is not a joke — Chicago Bears *sneakers*. They looked like Keds, except each shoe was covered in the team logo, instead. She had a rally towel hanging out of her back pocket that I knew from past experience she would wave around like a madwoman when the defense was on the field, and she'd painted two thin orange and navy stripes on each cheek.

More than anything, it was the look in her eyes that really got me.

Those intense green eyes of hers were wide and doe-like, black lashes almost never meeting her cheeks because she didn't seem to blink at all as she took in the scene around us. Where all *I* saw was an obnoxiously loud crowd spilling beer all over the place, she saw her people. Her tribe.

Football fans.

Bears fans.

And to her, there was no better feeling than this one right here.

"Thank you again *so much* for coming with me today," she said as we pushed through the crowd to make our way to her seats. "I know you hate this."

"I really do. And I thought I'd gotten out of this forever with Zach being in the picture."

Gemma chuckled. "Well, if it wasn't for a family event, he'd be here and you'd be free of the torture."

"He's lucky I love him. And you. And his family, too, for that matter."

Gemma had had season tickets for the Bears for years now. She'd bought them with the intention of coming with Carlo, her ex-husband, but that was before that asshole cheated on her and then had the audacity to die of cancer before she could properly castrate and divorce him.

Jerk.

The only good thing that came out of that situation was that after she dragged me to a couple pre-season games, I convinced her to get on the dating apps and find a guy to take, instead.

Enter: Zach.

He was more than happy to be her football buddy, which meant I didn't have to be around the sport I loathed as much as the man who used to play it. Nathan had ruined a lot of things for me, and this was definitely one of them.

Still, I loved it any time I got to spend time with Gemma, even if I did throw a fit about being at a Bears game. And when she told me earlier this week that Zach couldn't make the first pre-season game because it was his mom's birthday, she asked if I'd step in as her date.

How could I say no to the girl who'd picked me up off the floor more times than I could count?

When we finally made it to her seats, we kicked back to watch the players warm up, sipping on our beers. Gemma already had a hot dog, complete with ketchup and cheese like the weirdo she was, and I picked at the plate of nachos I'd grabbed for myself.

"God, I'm so excited to see the guys play," Gemma said around a mouthful of bun and meat. "I've been so caught up in the wedding, I have no idea what happened at training camp or what we're looking like. It's always fun to see the new players on the team."

"Think you guys have a shot at the playoffs this year?"

Ohhhh, yeah. That sounded like you know what you're talking about. Good job, Belle.

Gemma shook her head. "Way too early to tell. I know one thing, if we want any chance in hell, we need a better offensive line and receivers who can move the ball when our runners can't."

I blinked when Gemma looked at me. "I understand approximately none of that."

She laughed. "Don't worry, I'll walk you through it."

"Oh goodie, a football lesson. Just what I've always dreamed of."

Gemma stuck her tongue out at me, but then her eyes were on the field, and she ate the rest of her hot dog with ravenous unawareness as she watched the players warm up. I couldn't help but chuckle at the sight, and I pulled out my phone, taking a video of the field and panning over to where Gemma sat transfixed.

I sent it to Makoa, smiling as I typed out a text to go with it.

This is why I couldn't hang out today. My best friend is a football junkie, and she's the only one I'll break my No Football rule for. Hope you're having fun with the fam. Tell them all I say hello, and I'll see you tonight!

I added a few kissy-face emojis before shoving my phone in my pocket, and when I looked up again, Gemma was watching me with a shit-eating grin.

"You are such a smitten little kitten."

"Shut up." I picked up one of my nachos, devoid of cheese, and pegged her in the neck with it. She just laughed, catching it before it fell and dipping it in the cheese before she popped it in her mouth.

As soon as the first whistle blew, I lost her.

She was a completely different person when football was being played. She hooted and hollered and growled and scrubbed her hands back through her hair and yelled at the players and cursed out the refs and hopped out of her seat like a banshee. What I found more entertaining than anything was how everyone else around us watched her more than the game.

Me, on the other hand? I had no idea what was going on.

I mostly checked my phone to see if Makoa had texted back — which he hadn't — or occasionally pointed out a player or two who had nice butts to Gemma. She would laugh and wave me off, because *obviously* there were more important things going on, but I still loved to try to distract her.

"Come on, boys! Let's make a conversion!" Gemma hollered out when the Bears offense took the field. She bounced on her toes, nudging me with her elbow. "There are so many new guys out there. This is what I love. They've all got something to prove. Did you know that at the end of pre-season, they'll cut the roster from ninety players to only fifty-three?" Gemma shook her head. "Can you imagine that pressure?"

I chuckled, shaking my head at my best friend and her glee that I'd never understand. "You're a nut."

She stuck out her tongue, but then the ball was snapped, and her hand wrapped around my arm as she watched the play. The play didn't last long, and to me, it looked like nothing even happened at all. But Gemma released her death grip on me, clapped, nodded, and said, "Good start, boys! Now, let's go!"

I found myself zoning out again, even when Gemma jumped up and down after the next play and cheers rang out around me. She said something about what an awesome catch it was, and I smiled, checking my phone again.

Then, the absolute last thing I expected to hear over the loudspeaker made me almost drop it.

"Pass complete to Makoa Kumaka! And that makes another Chicago Bears..."

The crowd cheered *first down!* to complete the sentence, but I stood there with my jaw unhinged, blinking as I tried to decide if I really just heard what I thought I did.

When I turned to look at Gemma, she was watching me with the same confused look until both of us glanced up at the scoreboard.

On the screen was a replay of the catch.

And beside it, a professional headshot of my boyfriend in a Chicago Bears jersey, smiling, his name and position and stats in a neat line underneath.

"Oh, my God," Gemma whispered, covering her mouth with both hands. She shook her head, looking from the board to me and back again. "That can't be... is that..."

"It's him," I confirmed. There was no mistaking it. That name, that beastly build, that goofy one-of-a-kind smile.

"I don't understand... I thought he was in real estate?"

My eyes scanned the field for his number, and when I found it, he was already lining up for the next play. The ball was snapped, but the guy carrying the ball was tackled down quickly, and then they were lining up again.

I knew it was him, the way he walked and carried himself.

I knew it was him, that broad chest, that tight ass, those monster thighs.

I knew it was him, and yet I still couldn't believe it.

I unlocked my phone so fast I nearly dropped it again, typing out his name in the Google search bar. I'd only written the first four letters when the search auto-populated the rest, and when I hit enter, the screen filled with pictures and videos and articles.

Makoa Kumaka Signs as Free Agent with Chicago Bears.

Chicago Bears Training Camp Spotlight: Makoa Kumaka.

Makoa Kumaka Leaves 49ers as Free Agent, Team Says "He Will Be Missed."

Makoa Kumaka University of Hawai'i Wide Receiver Stats

WATCH: Makoa Kumaka Catches Flimsy Pass, Runs for Fifty-Two-Yard Touchdown

Video after video, picture after picture, article after article populated as I scrolled and scrolled. One page, two pages, three pages. I shook my head the more I clicked, trying to swallow but coming up empty.

"Belle..." Gemma said, her hand softly finding my arm.

"He lied to me."

It sounded like someone else's voice instead of my own, and I kept scrolling, shaking my head as more and more proof popped up.

"I'm sure he can explain."

Those words almost made me vomit, and to stop it from happening, I jerked up out of my seat. "I have to go."

I shrugged her off before she could argue, muttering *excuse me* to all the other fans I passed in front of to get out of the row. Some of them cursed me for not waiting until the next play stopped, but I didn't care.

He lied to me.

The words flickered at first, like a neon sign slowly blinking to life, but then they were there, hot and bright, front and center with nothing else to focus on.

He lied to me.

He LIED to me.

My phone buzzed in my hand, Gemma's face on the screen, but I ignored the call. Then, I promptly turned the phone off completely, shoving it in my back pocket.

Question after question bombarded me as I rushed out of Soldier Field. Why did he lie? Why would he keep this from me?

What *else* is he keeping from me?

Is this just a game to him? Did he mean anything he said at all?

Who even *is* he?

Tears stung my eyes the more I shoved through the crowd, and it was all I could do to keep it together when I finally made it outside. I hailed the first cab I saw, climbing in and rattling off my address before my head hit the headrest and I closed my eyes, forcing as deep a breath as I could muster.

I thought he was different. I thought I could trust him. I thought, for the first time, there was a guy who could prove me wrong. I thought he meant what he said. I thought we had something real, something special, something unlike anything I'd ever had before. I thought maybe, just *maybe*, Gemma and Zach were right about him, about me not having to play the same role, about there being a chance to find something real.

I thought I was falling in love with him.

My chest ached so violently I surged forward, wincing against the pain. When my eyes blinked open, I saw his condo in the distance, and I shook my head as more tears blurred my vision.

I won't hurt you.

It was a lie.

All of it.

And I was a fool to have ever believed otherwise.

CHAPTER 19

Makoa

We won.

Sure, it was just a pre-season game. It wouldn't mean shit for our record, and for most of the players on this team — especially the veterans — the win was nothing to celebrate.

But for me and for any of the other guys vying for a spot on the team, this was huge.

Gerald clapped me on the back after my shower, ruffling my hair with his massive hand. "Eleven receptions, one-hundred-and-eighty-nine yards, *and* a touchdown?" He shook his head, his wet curls bouncing with the effort. "I knew you came here to prove a point, Kumaka, but damn, save some for the rest of them out there, eh?"

I tried to fight the cheesy smile that spread over my face at his words, but I couldn't help it. "What can I say? Just had a good game."

"I'll say."

I knocked him on the arm. "Look who's talking, Mr. QB of the game. You played three quarters and didn't have a single interception. And what was your final CMP?"

He smirked. "Sixty-seven percent."

I shook my head, holding up my fist for a bump.

"Get some good rest tonight," Gerald said. "I have a feeling coach is going to have a lot for you to do in practice this week. Can't have a game like that and go unnoticed."

He winked, clapping my shoulder again before he moved on to congratulate Sean Whacker, who was trying to secure his position as a running back and had a monster game, too.

Pride made my chest swell, and I dressed as quickly as I could with Belle on my mind, but took a moment to just sit and watch the locker room when I was putting on my shoes. At every locker, there were legendary men, giving legendary interviews or recapping a legendary game. It didn't matter to me if they didn't play at all tonight. In my eyes, these guys were the elite few, the ones millions of eyes watched every week, the ones who made *me* pick up a ball and devote my entire life to it.

And I was here with them.

Sometimes it didn't feel real, but in moments like this, after games like this... I couldn't imagine my life any other way.

I was born for this.

I was *made* to be here.

My goofy-ass smile was still plastered on when I dug into my duffle bag for my phone, eager to text Belle and tell her I was on my way. I was even more eager to tell her everything about what my real job was tonight — mostly, because I couldn't wait to celebrate with her.

I couldn't wait to share *all of this* with her.

It was a strange kind of excitement, one unfamiliar to me since the women I'd dated early in my career had built a wall so high I didn't think anyone would ever be able to climb over it. But I knew Belle. I knew who she was, what she wanted, what she cared about. I knew without hesitation that what I did for a living didn't matter to her, and if she wanted something in life, she'd kill herself to go out and get it on her own before she'd ever try to take advantage of me or any other man, for that matter.

She was everything I'd ever wanted, everything I thought didn't exist.

And she was mine.

I finally found my phone, pulling it free from my duffle and swiping to unlock it. I called my mom first, talking to her and my dad and both of my sisters for a short while before I assured them I'd be home in the morning to have breakfast with them. They'd been more than understanding that I wanted a night alone with Belle — especially with everything I needed to tell her.

Speaking of the angel, there was a waiting text from her that I'd missed before the game, and I smiled as I opened it.

Then, that smile was gone in an instant, along with every piece of joy I'd been floating on.

The video she'd sent played over and over, showing her feet up on the back of a chair here at Soldier Field, all of us warming up on the field in front of her before she panned over to show Gemma eating a hot dog. I let it play what felt like a dozen times, shaking my head, trying to convince myself it couldn't be real before I closed it and saw the text that came with it.

This is why I couldn't hang out today. My best friend is a football junkie, and she's the only one I'll break my No Football rule for. Hope you're having fun with the fam. Tell them all I say hello, and I'll see you tonight!

Bile rose in my throat, and I shook my head more adamantly, staring at the text and video as if I could undo them if I only stared long enough.

"No," I muttered, blowing out a breath and swiping my bag off the bench. I threw it over my shoulder and rushed out of the locker room. "No, no, *no!*"

She was here.

She was at the game.

And now, she had to know everything I never told her.

As soon as I was clear from the noise of the locker room, I dialed her number, closing my eyes on a silent prayer that she'd answer as I put the receiver to my ear. But the call went straight to voicemail, and I cursed, hanging up and trying again, only to get the same result.

"Fuck!"

I sped across town as fast as I could, running red lights and trying to call Belle the entire way, even though I knew she had her phone off. I didn't even take the time to park my car in the garage at her building, parking illegally on the street right in front, instead. I didn't care if I got a ticket or even towed — I'd deal with that later.

I ran inside, screeching to a halt when I realized I wouldn't be able to get up to her place without her buzzing me up. I ran my hands through my hair on a curse, trying to think of a solution. I was just about to call Gemma when Zach's hand found my shoulder.

"Hey, man," he said, squeezing. His eyes were laced with pity, his mouth tugged to one side. "Great game today."

I shook my head. "Please tell me you were there with her."

"It's my mom's birthday, I've been with the family all day." He frowned. "I'm sorry, man. I didn't know you hadn't told her yet. When Gemma said they were going to the game together, I just assumed..."

I shook my head again. "No, don't apologize. This is no one's fault but mine." I glanced at the desk clerk behind him, lowering my voice. "Any chance you can get me on the elevator? I have to talk to her, man."

Zach blew out a breath, looking outside before his eyes found me again. "If she doesn't want to see you..."

"Please."

There was an understanding in his eyes then, and he nodded. "Alright. Come on."

It felt like the slowest elevator ride of my life, and when it hit Gemma and Zach's floor, he paused, holding the door open.

"Just be honest, explain why you kept the truth from her. Belle... she's not as hard up as she wants everyone to think. She's soft just like the rest of us, but she's been hurt badly enough to know to hide it."

"I never meant to hurt her."

He nodded. "I know. But you did."

I swallowed down the truth in those words like acid.

I promised I'd never hurt her, but I did.

"Thanks for your help."

Zach tapped the doors where he held them before stepping out completely. "Good luck."

My heart thumped in my ears like a drum when the elevator reached Belle's floor, and I stepped out into the hallway in a sort of haze, something between a nightmare and a drunken stupor. My feet felt sluggish and heavy, the adrenaline fading.

And then I was at her door.

I knocked without hesitation, shifting my weight from side to side as I waited, and then the door opened, slowly at first and then in a *whoosh*, and Belle stood there on the other side of it looking like absolute hell.

Her eyes were bloodshot, puffy and swollen, morphing her face into something barely recognizable. Auburn hair sat in a pile on top of her head, falling out of the hair tie that tried to wrangle it, and she looked so small in the oversized sweatpants and t-shirt she had on. Her little nose was pink, too, and she sniffed, shaking her head with those blue-green eyes glaring at me like I was evil embodied.

"You've got a lot of balls showing up here."

"Belle, I can explain."

"You can explain that you lied to me? For months? Literally from the first day I met you?" She shook her head, eyes trailing over me like a bug she was about to smash with her heel. "No, thanks. I figured that out all on my own."

She went to slam the door, but I stopped it with my palm, stepping my sneaker against it for good measure. "Please, Belle. Just hear me out."

"What could you possibly have to say right now?" She thrust her hands out, mouth open as if to hammer home the point that I was an idiot for thinking there was any explanation that would undo the pain I'd already caused. "You lied to me, Makoa. You've been hiding this... this *huge* part of who you are, telling me you're in fucking *real estate*?" She scoffed, shaking her head.

"I didn't mean for it to go this far."

"No? Just how far *did* you plan for it to go?"

I shook my head, desperation fizzing in my bloodstream like bubbles. "I was going to tell you. Many times before, but every time it just didn't feel right. But tonight, I was absolutely going to tell you — no matter what."

"Guess I beat you to it."

She tried to close the door again, but I pushed against it.

"Belle, just... let me inside. For five minutes. Please?"

She inhaled a hot breath, blowing it out with a wave of her hands as she abandoned me at the door and walked inside. I followed her, gesturing for her to sit on her couch but she denied me, standing with her arms crossed, instead.

Everything inside me longed to hold her. I knew if I could just get her in my arms, if she could feel the way my heart beat only for her, if she could see the sincerity in my eyes when I told her I never meant to hurt her — this would all go away.

But one look at her from across the room told me there wasn't a shot in hell that I was getting close to her right now.

Here goes nothing.

"I have a complicated record with women," I started, knowing there really was no perfect way to say everything I needed to. "When I was younger, every girl I tried to give my heart to stuck me firmly in the friend zone. I was too goofy looking, too sweet, too nice. They all wanted men who treated them like they didn't matter, and I didn't have it in me to do that."

I thought I saw Belle's eyes soften just marginally, but it happened so fast I couldn't be sure I'd actually seen it at all.

"By the time I got to college, I'd been burned so many times that I just said screw it. I focused everything on football. It was all I did. I ate, slept, and breathed it. It was absolute devotion, the same kind I wanted to give to a woman, but never had the chance to." I swallowed. "Until Kelly."

God, just saying her name made my jaw tense.

"Kelly was drop-dead gorgeous, a volleyball player at UH on a scholarship. She was far out of my league in every way possible, but for some reason, when I graduated from college, she started paying attention to me. We went on a few dates and I... well, I was a virgin up until that point, but with her, it finally felt right. We were together several months, and I thought everything was perfect." I smiled, though it was far from joy I was feeling. "Until I took her to dinner with my teammates on the 49ers and she said, in front of everyone, that the rock I get her better be bigger than the other ones at that table."

Belle frowned.

"It doesn't seem like much, but it was the first clue that tipped me off. From there, I paid closer attention, and saw every sign I didn't see before — like how she always wanted to go out — on my dime, and how she always asked me to buy her an outfit to go out, and she was always pushing me to spend my signing bonus to get a hot new car or take her on a vacation or whatever else. I mean, she was part of the reason I didn't invest in my apartment in San Francisco. We were always out and going, and there was no time to sit at home, so why bother making it nice?"

I shook my head, running my hand over my jaw.

"Anyway, she was the first of a string of girls just like that. There was Zariah, who had me fooled until she started hinting at the fact that she wanted plastic surgery and *a good boyfriend* would buy it for her. And the final straw was Lucia, who straight up looked me in the face and asked me how it worked."

"How what worked?" Belle asked.

"The whole sugar daddy thing."

Belle blew out a sigh. "Jesus."

"Yeah." I chewed my lip, looking out at the city, the last bits of sunlight casting its glow. "All I've ever wanted was to be someone's person. I wanted to give them all of me and get all of them in return. But first, I was too nice, always the friend and never the boyfriend. Then, I was nothing but a piece of meat with dollar signs attached to it. So, when I moved here, all I was looking for was a chance to start over. A new chapter, a place where no one knew me and I could be whoever I wanted to be." I laughed. "I mean, I *literally* prayed for a girl who wouldn't have a clue who I was."

"And then you walked into my office."

I swallowed. "And then I walked into your office. And I just... here was everything I'd asked for. You had no idea about me or my past or my possible future. You *hate* football. And I just thought, I'll keep it to myself for now, get to know her better, and once I know she's not playing some kind of game... then I'll tell her the truth. I just... I worried that maybe I was being stupid again, that I was walking into some kind of trap. The way you were so eager to come back to my place, and those first couple of dates..."

"I'm just a girl with a healthy sexual appetite."

I couldn't help but smile at that. "Well, I know that now."

Belle didn't join in my smile, but sighed instead, crossing her arms even tighter as her gaze turned to the windows. She shook her head, thinking for a long moment before her eyes found mine. "I'm really sorry all that happened to you. It breaks my heart to know the way you were used like that." She paused, rolling her lips together. "But it doesn't make it fair to lie to me. You should have given me more credit than that, *especially* after those first few dates. I mean, did I ever take advantage of you or give you any indication that I gave a fuck about your money or what you did for a living?"

"No," I answered quickly. "You didn't. And I was going to tell you. But then you ghosted me."

She held up one finger. "That's not fair. Don't blame this on me."

"I'm not, I'm just saying that I was going to tell you, but then you disappeared, and then that night at the bar when we set things straight, you told me everything about Nathan and..." I threw my hands up. "Here's this guy who lied to you, broke your trust, ruined your outlook on love forever. *And* he played football?" I shook my head. "Belle, I was trying to convince you that I was everything he wasn't, that I would never do that to you. So, how could I then *immediately* tell you—"

"I would have understood!" She threw her own hands out at me in return. "Makoa, if you would have told me *then*, it would have been mutual. And that's the difference between us. In that moment, I opened up to you. I was the most vulnerable I've ever been with a man. I showed you my scars and made the choice to take a risk and give you a chance. But you?" She shook her head, her eyes glossing over. "You chose to lie to me. You chose to take that vulnerability I gave you and convince yourself that you were an exception, that the pain you'd cause me wouldn't count because, what? *Your intentions were pure?*"

I opened my mouth to respond, but she held up a hand to silence me.

"You've been hurt. I get it. I mean, if *anyone* gets it, it's me. But I showed you that pain. You hid yours. I mean, *Jesus*, Makoa," she said, swiping a loose tear away angrily. "You lied to me so easily."

Her voice broke on that last sentence, along with my heart, and I tried to reach for her but she tore away.

"If you could lie about this, you could lie about anything. Don't you see? I think that's what hurts the most. That's the biggest issue here." Her eyes teared up so fast she couldn't do anything to control the streams that escaped on her next blink. "Before this, I never thought it possible for you to lie to me... but now... I don't trust you anymore."

My chest ached, and I suffered a hot breath before trying to plead my case again. "Belle, please, I—"

"And you clearly don't trust me either."

I frowned. "What? No," I argued, rushing to her. I held her arms in my hands, thankful she didn't pull away but wishing she'd uncross her arms and let me in. Instead, she looked out the window, like she could never truly look at me again. "I *do* trust you. With everything that I am."

"Clearly, you don't. Or you would have trusted me not to hurt you the way those other girls did."

Another zing of desperation flew through me. "I'm sorry. I wish I could take it all back and do it differently."

"But you can't," she finished for me, her eyes finding mine. "And how in the world are two people this fucked up ever supposed to make it?"

"Maybe that's exactly it," I tried. "We're meant for each other."

Belle scoffed, shaking her head and turning away from me as more tears slipped free. "I want you to go."

"Belle, no, please, just listen to me, give me another chance, I swear—"

She ripped away from my grasp, holding up her hand. "Stop. Just stop, Makoa. There's nothing more you can say to change my mind and this," she added, waving her hand between us with a sardonic laugh. "*All* of this is a waste of time."

I swallowed. "You don't mean that."

"Yes," she said, and this time, her gaze met mine, steady and sure. "I think I really do. Now, please, just leave so I can pick up the pieces of the mess you made."

They were the final crack to my heart, those words, and I felt them split open inside my chest. I was bleeding out as I turned, feet heavily carrying me toward her door. It didn't feel real. It didn't feel like this could possibly be happening, like this could really be the end.

I stopped when I had her door open, gripping the edge of it when I turned to face her once more. "You told me the other night that you were falling in love with me."

She squeezed her eyes shut at that, releasing another flood of tears before she turned her back on me so I couldn't see her face anymore.

"Well, I *am* in love with you. I've known it for a while now, and this, tonight, it doesn't change the way I feel. I'm sorry I hurt you. I'm sorry I lied. But I promise you this, it was never my intention to cause you pain, and if you give me the chance, I will never hurt you again. I will earn every ounce of your trust back and I will prove to you that my word is good."

Belle's shoulders shook with sobs, and all I wanted was to run to her, but I knew it was the last thing *she* wanted.

And so, I said my final words. If they were the last I'd ever have with her, I knew I'd never regret them.

"I love you, Belle. So, if you love me, too, then please forgive me. Forgive me, and don't walk away from this. From us. We *are* meant for each other. I think we both stumbled on this dark and twisted road for so long so that when we found each other, we'd know. We'd know this is it. We'd know all of the pain was worth it."

I fought back my own urge to cry, nose flaring with the effort, and then I left her with my last attempt.

"Why else live if not for love?"

She stood ramrod straight in the center of her condo, back to me, not giving me a single clue that she'd even been listening.

So I left her, the sound of the door shutting behind me like that of a jail cell locking me into the new hell I'd created. It was my own doing, and I had to serve the time.

I'd said all I could say.

The rest was up to her.

CHAPTER 20

Makoa

Gerald yelled *hike!*, and I took off, every muscle in my legs engaged in a sprint down field. I ran ten yards before I cut right, looking over my shoulder for the ball. It was a perfect spiral throw from Gerald, and I reached up for it, muscle memory taking over.

Except the ball tipped my fingers, bobbling between my hands before I dropped it altogether.

"Damn it!" I cursed, threading my hands on top of my helmet as I watched the defensive teammates in the practice scrimmage celebrating. I didn't miss the way coach shook his head, muttering something to the staff member next to him before he blew the whistle and told us to line up again.

Gerald slapped my helmet when we were back in the huddle. "Come on, man. Get focused."

I nodded, blowing out a frustrated breath before he made the next call and we clapped for break. I positioned myself on the line, closing my eyes for a brief second to center myself.

Hike!

I took off again, this time running a curl route that had me juking the defensive player on my tail before I made a dash back toward the center field. Gerald launched the ball, and once again, it was a perfect pass.

A perfect pass that I missed.

The ball slipped through my fingers like my gloves were coated in butter, and I growled, picking up the ball and launching it back down field before I thought better of it. It was bad enough to be having an off day, but to show out like that would only add fuel to the fire.

"Kumaka," coach called, and he nodded to the bench, letting me know without a single word that I needed to sit out and cool off.

Gerald tapped my shoulder pads as I ran past. "It's all good, bro. Shake it off."

I flopped down on the bench, ripping my helmet off and letting it fall between my cleats on the ground. Someone handed me a Gatorade bottle with water, and I squirted some in my mouth, swishing it around before I spat it out and then took a real drink.

The longer I sat there, the more my muscles cooled and my breath evened out, the more disappointed I was with myself.

I was completely falling apart.

It was Thursday, four days since the night everything blew to hell.

And I hadn't heard from Belle.

Not once.

I wished I could say it didn't affect me. I wished I could say I'd been focused on football, on the upcoming away pre-season game against the Giants. I wished I could say I'd been able to focus on anything other than the fact that I'd lost the best woman I'd ever had.

But all of that would be a lie.

I'd been helpless since I walked out of her door that night.

I'd gone home to find my family still there, surprised to see me since I told them I wouldn't be back until the morning.

When I told them what happened, they all consoled me, and having them there was a temporary relief for the burn.

But they left the next day, going back to Hawai'i, and once I was alone, it all sank in.

Monday's practice wasn't too bad. We mostly watched tapes and talked about plays that went wrong and ran drills. Tuesday was an off day, and yesterday, I'd managed to keep my shit together.

But today, I was a dumpster fire.

Coach called practice about a half hour later, and I kneeled around him along with the rest of the team, listening numbly as he explained what he'd seen, what was working, what could work better.

And he didn't forget to remind us how important this next game was, to show what we had before the decision on who would be cut was made.

Gerald tried to talk to me after, but I waved him off, jogging into the locker room for a quick shower and change before I hopped in my car and fled the training facility.

As soon as I was out of the parking lot, I dialed Colby.

"Well, if it isn't the future star wide receiver for *Da Bears*," he greeted, making a deep, funny voice when he said the team name.

"Trust me, if I keep playing the way I did in practice today, I'd be lucky to even make it to the official cut date before they booted me."

"Wait, what? You had a killer game Sunday," Colby said, and I heard him tell someone in the background that he'd be right back. I assumed it was Cheyenne. "What happened?"

I sighed, hitting my blinker with more force than necessary as I waited at the light. "I fucked up and lost the best thing to ever happen to me, and now I can't focus on anything but that."

There was a short pause before Colby let out a sigh of his own. "She found out."

"She was at the fucking game."

"*What?*" Colby whistled. "Jesus, man. I thought you said she hated football."

"She does," I affirmed. "But her best friend is a huge Bears fan. She has season tickets and her fiancé couldn't go to the first pre-season game. So..."

"So she took her best friend."

"Yup." The word popped on my lips, and I shook my head, stomach bottoming out like it had done all week whenever I thought about how Belle must have felt, sitting there with Gemma when she realized it was me on that field in front of her. "I went to her right after the game. I explained everything, man, but she didn't want to hear it."

"I mean, can you blame her?"

"No," I said quickly. "But I guess the bigger part of me didn't think it would be this big of a deal. I thought once I explained, she'd understand, and we'd work through it... together." I swallowed. "But she just gave up. The first sign of trouble, and she wanted out."

"I don't think it's that simple, man."

I frowned. "What do you mean?"

"I mean, if this would have been months ago, and you would have gone to her and told her everything, yeah, I think it would have been sort of laughed off and then you both could have moved on. But... you dug a deep hole for yourself the longer you kept the charade up. And *especially* knowing her past, and the way that guy led her on..."

My fists clenched around the steering wheel at the thought of him.

"You hit her soft spot, dude. The one thing that scared her most was that you could possibly lie to her. And then..."

"And then I did."

Silence fell between us, and the light turned green, allowing me the opportunity to take out my frustrations on the gas pedal as I peeled out onto the street.

"I'm losing it, man," I said, eyes blurring a bit with the admission. I sniffed, shaking my head. "I can't eat. I can't sleep. I can't fucking catch a ball or run a route to save my goddamn life."

"You've got to let her go."

I shook my head even more violently. "I *can't*."

"You have to. Look, you poured your heart out that night, right? You told her everything. You explained, you asked for forgiveness, you did everything you could. But, Mak, if she doesn't want to forgive you, if she doesn't want to be with you anymore... you can't force her to."

I scrubbed a hand over my jaw. "I just... there has to be a way."

"Trust me, man. The best thing you can do right now is give her space. If she changes her mind, you'll find out soon enough. But if you go back to her right now, if you blow up her phone or show up on her doorstep, you're only going to remind her of every reason why she's upset, and the more she sees you in that headspace, the more the wedge is going to drive."

My shoulders deflated. I could still remember the look in her eyes that night, the way she watched me like she didn't know who I was at all.

With one stupid omission, I'd lost all her trust.

Colby was right. It wouldn't matter what I said now, because I gave her no reason to believe me.

"I don't know how to just... let her go. How do I pick myself up and move on? How do I just walk away?"

"Don't think about all that. Right now, you've got a game to focus on. Okay? Listen to me," he said, and I could picture the way he used to lean forward, grabbing my shoulder, leaning his helmet against mine when we were down in a game. "You've worked too hard, for too long, for this opportunity. Chicago needs a receiver, and we both know you're the man for the job. So, right now, don't focus on how to get over Belle. Right now, focus on the game." He paused. "Just... put on your pads, lace up your cleats, and pretend like nothing else exists in this world other than that pig skin. You hear me?" He paused again, and when I didn't answer, he said, "Football, Mak. That's where your head needs to be."

I nodded, swallowing down my urge to argue with him as I turned onto my street. "Thanks for picking up, Colby."

"Always, brother. I look forward to watching your game on Sunday."

That makes one of us.

Belle

On Friday night, Gemma swiped at the tear that leaked free from her left eye, doing it as slyly as she could like I wouldn't notice. But her sniff gave her away, and I pegged a Milk Dud at her.

"Are you seriously crying?"

"What?!" She threw her hands up, not bothering to hide the next few tears. "It's *Queer Eye*. How do you *not* cry?"

I smirked, pretending like I was going to throw another Milk Dud at her before I popped it in my mouth instead. "I still can't believe *this* is your bachelorette party," I said, gesturing to my messy condo. It'd been a mess all week, thanks to the disaster state of mind I'd been in. But Gemma had insisted this was what she wanted to do for her bachelorette party — a classic junk food and guilty-pleasure TV night.

She feigned offense, pressing her hand to her chest. "Are you saying this isn't the most glorious bachelorette party you've ever been to? I mean, look at us," she said, waving her hand over herself. "We're in our PJs instead of heels and some obnoxiously tight dress. We're on the couch instead of out at some bar we don't want to be at. We have enough chocolate and pizza to feed a high school, and the wine is *much* cheaper when we buy it from the liquor store than at the bar." She held up her glass to cheers herself on that one, taking a sip before she smiled at me. "Besides, we did the whole pink penis straw night out on the town thing the *first* time I tied the knot, remember?" She wrinkled her nose then. "And that marriage did *not* turn out the best."

I smiled back. "As long as you're happy, that's all that matters to me."

"I am happy. I really am."

"You're getting *married*," I whispered, squealing a little as I tickled her side. "Like... in four weeks!"

Gemma sighed, sinking farther into the couch with a smitten smile. She might as well have had little hearts exploding in her eyes when she looked at me. "Belle, I feel like everything life has put me through was all for this. He's the reason." She shook her head. "I don't care what happens for the rest of my life, as long as I have him."

My throat tightened, because with every word she said, I thought more and more of Makoa. "Well, Zach's not going anywhere," I told her. "He'd never let you go. So just settle in for a lifetime of happiness."

Gemma chuckled, biting her lip. "I have to tell you something."

"Oh, God," I said, stomach dropping at her words. "Please, don't throw anything crazy on me right now. I can't handle much more."

She smiled, but it was a sad smile. "It's nothing bad. I just... I wanted you to be the first person I told. Besides Zach, of course."

I blinked. "Okay..."

Gemma sat up straighter, hugging her knees. "I think... I think I want to have a baby."

My eyes nearly bulged out of my head. "Wait... really?"

She nodded, smile growing. "Yeah. Really. I just... I can't stop thinking about it. Every day that I'm with Zach, I think of how he'd make the best dad. I get butterfly belly just thinking about him holding our little boy, or girl, watching them play in the park, watching him teach them how to ride their bike..."

"And you told Zach?"

She nodded, biting her lip again. "I think we're going to start trying. Like... starting with our wedding night."

I couldn't explain the range of emotions that flooded me in that moment. The first thing I felt was utter joy for my best friend. It'd been a long time since either of us had brought up kids, but I could remember drunken nights in college, laying together in my dorm and staring up at the ceiling talking about how cute our future children would be, how many babies we wanted, what we'd name them. I thought maybe she'd have a baby with Carlo, but she never did, and all my hopes for a baby went out the window when Nathan broke things off.

And that was the second thing I felt.

An empty, hollow longing for the exact same thing Gemma wanted.

I felt that excitement bubbling up in her belly because I could picture the same thing with Makoa. It was absurd. We'd only spent a few months together, and somehow, I'd fallen for him so hard that I could picture my entire life with him. I could see him down on one knee. I could picture walking down the aisle to him. And, just like Gemma, I could see him holding our daughter or son.

But the big difference between our dreams was that Gemma's was in reach.

And mine would never come true.

"Gem, I don't even have words," I said, crawling over to wrap her in a fierce hug. "I'm so, *so* happy for you. And I'm going to spoil the shit out of that little baby."

Gemma laughed in my arms, smacking my ass when we finally broke contact and I crawled back over to my wine. I took a long sip, and I felt her eyes on me the entire time.

"What?" I asked, arching a brow.

"You know, I want you to be happy, too."

I swallowed, tracing the rim of my glass before I shrugged. "I am happy. I made a mistake and fell off the Badass Bitch Wagon for a hot minute, but I'm back now and better than ever."

"Belle," Gemma said, giving me a look — you know the one. *That* look. "You don't have to pretend to be okay right now."

"I'm not pretending."

"Liar."

I huffed. "What do you want from me? What *should* I do? Just... fall apart? Cry over the fact that I believed a liar, yet again, and ended up just as broken as I knew I would be?"

Gemma didn't say a word to that.

"It is what it is, and now it's over, and I've been reminded exactly why I have a three-date rule."

She sighed, long and heavy before putting her wine down and turning to face me on the couch. "Alright. Time for some best friend tough love."

I rolled my eyes. "Gemma, really, I'm—"

"You're not fine, Belle, and you're also being a real stubborn witch about this whole situation."

"Hey!" I said on a pout.

"I'm sorry, but you needed to hear it," she defended, throwing her hands up. "Now, I'll be the first to say that what Makoa did wasn't cool. He shouldn't have lied to you about his really fucking cool job and the fact that he gets to hang out with my favorite players, naked, in the Bears locker room."

I rolled my eyes again.

"But," she continued. "Belle, I *get* why he kept this from you for a while. Don't you? I mean, after everything he confessed to you..." Gemma shook her head. "We all do crazy things to protect ourselves from being hurt again. I mean, look at me. I almost turned my back on the best man to ever walk into my life, all because I was afraid of ending up in the same shit hole Carlo had left me in." She pointed a finger at my chest. "And *you* were the one who talked me out of it."

"Yeah, well, that's you. This is me. And me doesn't get the fairytale happy ending with the wedding and the babies."

"Why not?" Gemma reached for my hands, taking them in hers. "Look, I know Nathan hurt you. But I think somewhere along the way, it's *you* who really did the damage. You're the one who's been pounding it into your own head for years that you're this certain kind of girl, that you're only good for sex and nothing more. But... do you really think that's what Makoa thinks of you?"

My nose flared on my next breath. "I don't know *what* he thinks of me, because he's a liar."

"Well, so are you, after that statement. You know damn well what he thinks of you, how he feels about you, and you're being a stubborn fool trying to push all that aside just because he lied to you about his job."

I pulled my hands from hers, crossing my arms. "Can we just get back to *Queer Eye* and your bachelorette party, please?"

"In a minute, yes, but right now, you're going to talk to me." She shook her head. "Belle, why are you pushing him away right now?"

My eyes found the ceiling, and I forced a breath to ward off the impending tears building. "He lied to me, Gem. Okay?" I looked at her then. "And now, I don't trust him anymore."

"You don't trust him," she deadpanned. "Really?"

I swallowed but didn't answer.

"You know what I think?" she asked, and she didn't wait to hear if I wanted to know or not before she continued. "I think you're scared. I think you've *been* scared, ever since the moment he didn't try to get in your pants the first night you went out. You've known since the first day you met him that he was different, but you've been waiting for the other shoe to drop. You've been waiting for him to do *anything* wrong so you could point your finger at him and go *ah-ha! I knew it!*" Gemma shook her head. "You didn't want him to prove you wrong. You wanted him to prove you *right*. You wanted him to let you down so you could hold your chin high and say you were right about him and every other guy, and the fact that you're not meant to be happy with someone."

Her words felt like fists around my rib cage, each one tightening the grip more.

"And you know what else? I don't think you really give a rat's ass that he lied to you about what he does for a living.

I don't think it changes who he is *at all* in your mind, except that maybe he's even *more* attractive now." She frowned. "But it's easier to be mad. It's easier to say *now I have a reason to walk away before this gets even more serious*."

I tore my gaze from hers, looking at the television, though I couldn't focus on a thing that was happening on it. Her words played on repeat in my mind, and the truth of them cut me like a dull, rusty knife.

"Just a couple years ago, three floors down from where we are now, you called me out on my bullshit. You forced me to stop trying to mask what I was feeling by cleaning my apartment, or working, or whatever else, and really face the truth. And that truth was that I was scared. No," she said quickly. "I was fucking *terrified* of loving Zach, of being loved by him in return. And you know what you said to me?"

I rolled my lips together, eyes blurring with tears again.

"You said, *he's not Carlo, Gemma.* You said that the way he looked at me, the way he cared for me and fought for me, that it was rare. You said that if you were in my shoes, you would chase that boy." She chuckled, though it was anything but funny. "Well, guess what, baby girl? You're wearing the damn shoes right now. And I'm not letting you back out on your word."

I covered my face with both hands just as the first tears broke free, and it didn't matter how I tried to fight against the emotion, I couldn't help but succumb to it.

Gemma rubbed my back, crawling over to take me in her arms. "It's scary. I know it is. But don't sabotage this *incredible* thing you've found just because he made one mistake. And it wasn't even a big one." She waited until I looked at her before she said, "He apologized. He's asking for your forgiveness. And let me tell you, babe... if you give it to him?" She shrugged on a smile. "Then all this pain you're feeling, it will all go away. And if I know anything about that man you've been dating for the last few months, it's that he won't ever hurt you again."

I sniffed. "How can you be so sure?"

At that, Gemma laughed, tapping my nose with her index finger. "Because he *loves you*, dum-dum. And yes, love is messy and flawed and sometimes it can drag us through the wringer. But he's not going to walk out on you, no matter what comes." She paused. "Now, it's up to you, if you can say the same."

Another wave of sobs hit me, and this one was the worst of all. I choked under the strength of it, breaking in my best friend's arms as her words settled in over me like the orange glow of dawn on the heels of the darkest night.

He loved me.

And I loved him, too.

Those were the only things that mattered, and yet Gemma had seen what I never did — that I'd taken the first opportunity I could get to light it all on fire in the name of being right. I wanted to be right, about the way I felt about myself, about the way I felt about men and dating and love, in general.

Because the alternative was to put myself at risk again, the same way everyone who was in love did.

And being the unlovable girl was easier than that.

"I don't know what to do," I confessed, the words mumbled by Gemma's t-shirt.

She rubbed my back, soothing me. "Right now, you don't need to do anything but drink some wine and watch some shows with your best friend. We'll figure everything else out. But... just think about what I said, okay? Ask yourself what you really want." She bent down to look me in the eyes. "And whatever you decide, I'll be there with you. Okay?"

I nodded, wrapping my arms around her neck in a tight hug that we held for the longest time.

"Alright, now, back to Jonathan Van Ness and his angelic hair," she said, kissing my cheek before she released me. But she smiled at me, wiping one of my stray tears before I had the chance. "I love you, bestie."

That made me cry more. "I love you, too."

With one last squeeze of my hand, Gemma handed me my glass of wine, and we settled back into the couch, muting the conversation for the time being.

But my thoughts were on fire, loud and roaring, and with every pop and crackle of embers I heard the same notion growing louder and louder.

Don't let him go.

Don't let him go.

Don't. Let. Him. Go.

CHAPTER 21

Makoa

Sunday came too fast, well before I felt like I truly had a handle on my mental or physical game. I'd spent the last few days trying to get centered and focused, forcing myself to sleep and eat, even when it made me feel sick to do so. Because with football, there was no calling in sick. There were no personal days — especially when you were a free agent trying to secure a spot on the team.

You either showed up and showed out, or you got cut.

Those were the only options.

I was silent in the locker room before the game, listening to coach and the other players with a distant sort of awareness. Today, the veterans would get a little action, and they'd get more and more as we neared the regular season, which meant I needed to buckle down and use the time I'd get on the field today wisely.

Gerald walked by me on his way out to warm up, and he tapped my helmet. "Let's get it."

I nodded, and the look he gave me told me he understood I was going through shit. But it also said, loud and clear, *whatever it is, man, leave it in here.*

Half the team was already out of the locker room when I reached into my duffle bag and pulled out my phone. I swiped to Belle's name, opening a new text message and staring at the blinking cursor.

There were so many things I wanted to say.

I miss you.

I can't stop thinking about you.

I'm miserable without you.

I'll do anything to get you back.

I love you.

I longed to send her a text with one, if not all, of those messages, but I heard Colby's voice in the back of my mind, and I knew he was right.

She'd asked me to leave her alone, and if I really loved her, that was what I needed to do.

So, I closed the text, threw my phone in my bag and pulled on my helmet as I jogged out onto the field to face off against the Giants.

Football, Makoa. That's what matters right now.

If only my heart would listen.

Belle

"We can change this," Gemma said on Sunday, nodding to the television where the Bears and Giants were warming up for the second pre-season game. "I can see the score later."

"No, it's okay," I assured her, wrapping another little ribbon bow around a wedding program. With just three weeks to go, we were finalizing the last touches for the big day. "I know you love this team. I don't want you to miss the game on my account."

"I really don't mind," she said, reaching for the remote.

I clamped my hand down on hers, not taking my eyes off the next program in my hand. "Leave it."

If I'd have looked up at her in that moment, I know I would have seen her smirking all proud of herself. She knew as well as I did that I wanted to see the game, too. It didn't matter that I didn't understand any of it, or care about football in the least.

Makoa was playing.

And despite everything that had happened between us, I wanted him to do well.

I kept my eyes on the task at hand through most of the first quarter, only glancing up at the screen when Gemma made a grunt of despair or clapped in celebration. The two of us were on the floor, and Zach was on the couch behind us, tending to his own duty of writing cards to his groomsmen and family that he'd give them on the big day.

"Mak's in."

Zach said the words casually, as if they wouldn't steal the next breath from my chest and leave me deprived of oxygen. I pretended not to care, still working on the programs, but my eyes flicked to the screen just in time to see him line up.

Even with the helmet and visor on, even with shoulder pads, I'd know that body anywhere. I was thankful Zach had convinced Gemma to get a seventy-five-inch gargantuan television last fall, because I could see every detail — even down to the edge of his turtle tattoo peeking out from under his jersey.

The ball was snapped, and to me it looked like nothing happened but apparently someone ran the ball a few yards. They lined up again, and this time, the quarterback threw the ball to Makoa.

He caught it, though it was bobbled a little, and he didn't make it but a couple feet before he was taken down. I glanced at Gemma, whose little mouth pulled to the side, and she exchanged glances with Zach that told me what he'd done wasn't the best.

I swallowed, cracking my neck before I reached for another string of ribbon and a program. A few more plays happened, earning them a first down, and when I chanced another look, it was just in time to see the quarterback launch a perfect pass to Makoa down field.

The ball bobbled between his hands again, and in what felt like a millisecond, the guy defending him snatched the ball from the air and took off down field in the other direction.

"Fuck!" Zach said, throwing his hands up to lace on top of his head.

Gemma was on her knees now, watching the screen with her hands covering her mouth. When the defender managed to run it all the way back for a touchdown, she closed her eyes on a sigh, cursing under her breath.

"He's off his game," Zach said. "Big time."

Gemma nodded in sad agreement as Makoa jogged back to the bench, and a few players clapped him on the shoulder as if to assure him it was okay.

But when he ripped his helmet off and plopped down on the bench, it was easy to see it wasn't.

The commentator mentioned Makoa's time with the 49ers briefly, listing off some stats before the camera was on the other team about to kick the ball for their extra goal or bonus point or whatever it was that came after the touchdown.

I frowned. "I don't understand. It's just the pre-season game, right? Do these things even really count?"

"Not for the team's record, and not really to the veteran players, but for Makoa..." Zach clucked his tongue. "He signed as a free agent. These pre-season games are kind of like his Super Bowl. They're his only chance to secure his spot on the team."

"What do you mean?" I asked, gesturing toward the TV. "He's already on the team."

"No, remember what I told you last week?" Gemma asked. "They're going to cut a bunch of guys before the regular season kicks off. They only keep a certain number for each position — first, second, third, *maybe* fourth string." She shook her head, eyes finding the screen again. "If Makoa doesn't impress the coaches..."

"Then, he's out," Zach finished for her.

My stomach sank, and as the Bears offense jogged out onto the field after the kick-thing, I noticed that Makoa wasn't with them this round. The screen cut to commercial, and I stood, throwing my hands up.

"Wait, so they're just not going to play him anymore? That's bullshit. It was one mistake!"

"One mistake that cost them a turnover and a touchdown," Zach pointed out.

I frowned. "Whatever. They should put him back in."

"They might later, but... they could also sit him for the rest of the game, if coach thinks he's off." Gemma touched my arm. "It's okay, he'll—"

"This is all my fault," I murmured, shaking my head. "I haven't talked to him all week, and he's probably all up in his head thinking he's lost me, and that I hate him, and he probably can't sleep or eat just like I can't and..."

"*Has* he lost you?" Zach asked.

I rolled my lips together, still shaking my head as my gaze fell to the ribbon in my fingers. "I don't think he ever could."

Gemma and Zach gave each other a knowing look, and Gemma stood to stand beside me. "I knew you'd pull your head out of your ass."

But I couldn't congratulate her on her rightness, because I was too busy fuming at the stupid coach for pulling Makoa out of the game. "I need to get to New York."

"What? Why?" Gemma asked, but I was already across her condo and pulling my shoes on.

"I need to get to this game and tell him I love him so he can play and not fuck this up."

"Whoa, whoa, whoa," Gemma said, pulling me to a stop once my other shoe was on. "First of all, this game is in New Jersey. Secondly, there's no train or bus or plane that can get you there before this game is over."

I swallowed, standing in her grasp for a minute before I reached for my phone. "Fine. I'll just call him."

"Babe," Gemma said, putting her hand over my phone before I could unlock it. "His phone is put away in his locker. He's not going to look at it until this game is over."

My shoulders deflated. "But... I have to get to him. I have to talk to him. I have to turn this around."

"He's going to be okay," Zach assured me. "Even if this isn't his best game, there are still two more to go."

"Exactly. There's nothing to be done right now, okay?" Gemma agreed, but then she smiled, squeezing my hand. "But if you want to go over what you'll say to him when he gets *back*... well..." She glanced at Zach, who smiled at me, too, when Gemma turned back to me. "We're all ears."

My eyes flicked to the screen, heart squeezing at the fact that I couldn't do anything to help Makoa.

"I don't know where to even start," I confessed. "How do I make this right?"

They shared another look — and I was beginning to think those two had their own secret language that never had to be spoken, just like Gemma and I had.

Then, Zach sat back down on the couch, patting the spot next to him. "I think it's time the three of us made a game plan of our own."

CHAPTER 22

Makoa

It was late by the time the team bus pulled up to Halas Hall after our loss to the Giants.

We'd all shuffled out of the stadium in New Jersey with our heads down, and every step of the way home, we'd been silent — from the bus ride to the airport, the flight, and then the bus ride back to our own training facility.

I'd tried to sleep, but found myself unable to, and spent most of the time replaying the horrendous turnover I'd had or staring at past text messages with Belle and wondering if she'd respond should I send her one now.

My bet was that she'd already blocked my number by now.

I knew Colby was right. I knew I had to find a way to let her go — preferably before the next pre-season game so I could save my chance of securing a spot on the team.

But after how I played today?

I wasn't so sure I had a chance at all.

There was a chorus of groans when the bus parked, all of us starting to really feel all those tackles we took on the field. We were slow going, throwing our duffle bags over our shoulders and slugging off the bus one by one. It didn't matter that this loss wouldn't be on our record for the season — *any* loss hurt.

And when you were a contributor to that loss, the way I had been, it hurt even more.

Gerald stopped at my seat on his way off the bus, waving his hand so I could go in front of him. I slipped into the aisle and as soon as we started walking, he leaned forward, nudging my back.

"You've gotta let it go, man," he said. "It's just one bad game. Shake it off and come ready to work tomorrow."

I nodded, but I couldn't find it in me to even verbally thank him. Right now, between the game I'd played in New Jersey and the game I'd played with Belle, I felt like the biggest piece of scum to ever exist on Earth.

Every muscle in my legs ached in protest when I jogged down the few steps and off the bus. I winced against the pain, adjusting the bag on my shoulder and crossing the parking lot with my head down, letting my feet carry me toward where my Lexus was parked on the other side.

It wasn't until I was a few yards away that I finally lifted my gaze, and when I did, I stopped dead in my tracks.

Belle stood next to my car, her hands behind her back, little mouth pulled to the side as she watched me through her lashes. Her auburn hair had faded to more of that strawberry blonde she'd had when I first met her, and in a long, flowy blue dress with thin straps that accented her shoulders and collarbones, she was a sight to behold — like the goddess of summer, come to say goodbye to her season as fall moved in to take her place.

The longer I stood there and watched her, the more she looked like she was about to cry, or like she regretted that she was there at all. So, I made my way to her as quick as I could before she could change her mind and bolt.

The only light was from the parking lot lights above us, and they cast her in a warm, orange glow, covering half her face with shadows. She swallowed when I stood in front of her, chewing her lip for a moment before she spoke.

"I forgot to ask you something last week," she said.

My chest was tight, breath shallow as I took her in, still not believing she was standing there in front of me. I somehow managed to clear my throat and ask, "What's that?"

Belle's eyes searched mine for a moment, and then she pulled her hands from behind her back, holding out a small, rectangular, white piece of cardstock with gold foil letters on it.

"For the wedding," she said. "Do you want chicken or steak?"

She handed the card to me, and I glanced down at the RSVP with both our names on it — *Belle Monroe and Makoa Kumaka*. My stomach somersaulted at the way they looked together, and even more when I saw the checkbox next to our RSVP saying we'd both be attending.

I held onto that piece of cardstock like it was my lifeline, and then my gaze found hers. "You want me to go to the wedding with you?"

Her eyes glossed, and she shrugged, nodding. "If you don't hate me now, yes."

I almost laughed. "Hate you?" I shook my head, tucking the card in the pocket of my duffle bag before I dropped it to the ground beside us. "I *love* you, you stupid girl."

I swept her into my arms in the next instant, half expecting Belle to swat me away or shove space between us, but she wrapped herself around me, too. Her arms draped around my neck, hands threading where they met as I pulled her in even closer. Her warmth and familiar scent wafted over me, and I realized then that it wasn't a dream.

She was here. She was really here.

She shuddered in my grasp, her tears wetting my t-shirt as I kissed her hair and told her it was okay, over and over, holding her tighter to secure that promise.

And with her in my arms again, I actually believed it, too.

Belle sniffed after a long while, pulling back to peer up at me. "I am so sorry. I'm sorry I didn't listen to you when you came to me after the game last week. I'm sorry I got so fixated on the fact that you lied to me that I didn't hear you out when you explained why. I'm sorry that I'm so goddamn stubborn that I dug my heels in as if I was stronger if I turned you away after one mistake..." She shook her head, rolling her lips between her teeth. "I really am a stupid girl."

I chuckled, sweeping her hair back and thumbing her cheek. "You're not. You had every right to be upset with me. It's *me* who should be sorry." My jaw tightened. "I betrayed your trust."

Belle shook her head, leaning into where my hand held her face. "It isn't that big of a deal. I *made* it a big deal because I wanted to be right. I wanted to have proof that no one could really love me or be true to me, that I would always be just the good-time girl, that I'd be the girl who was lied to and traded in time and time again." She chuckled. "You know why? Because it's easier to be that girl. It's easier to shove you away than it is to admit the truth."

"And what's the truth?"

She smiled, and I thumbed away another tear before it could make it past the apple of her cheek. "That I love you," she said, lips trembling with the admission. "And that I forgive you. And that I'd rather take the risk of losing you down the line than to miss out on the possibility of keeping you forever."

I smiled on a shaky breath, emotion strangling me at the throat and cutting off my ability to speak. But I held her gaze, held her cheek, held her in every way that I could.

"The other day Gemma was talking about Zach, about the wedding and how they want to have kids soon," she said.

"And... I don't know much about love. I don't know how to handle anything that is going to be thrown our way. I don't know if we're going to fight and forgive, or if we're never going to fight again. I don't know if you'll be able to put up with me and the scars I've carried with me for years."

I laughed at that, rubbing her cheek to let her know that I loved those scars.

"All I know, is listening to her talk about Zach that way..." Belle smiled, leaning into my hand and closing her eyes to release another flood of tears before she looked at me again. "When I close my eyes and imagine *my* future?" She shrugged. "I see you in it."

I closed my eyes, letting out a slow breath and trying not to cry myself. It was all I could do to pull Belle into my chest, to wrap my arms around her, to run my hands back through her hair and tilt her chin up and claim that perfect mouth of hers as mine forever.

She leaned into the kiss with a relieved sigh, nearly collapsing in my arms, but I held her steady and strong as a promise that I always would. I deepened the kiss with my tongue sweeping over hers, and then I picked her up, spinning her just like they did in the movies to the tune of distant cheers from various ends of the parking lot.

Belle blushed when I put her back on her feet, looking around before she buried her face in my chest. "Oh, God. I'm sorry, I'm embarrassing you in front of your team."

More whistles rang out as I chuckled and kissed her forehead. "Feel free to embarrass me any time you want. These clowns are just jealous you're not theirs."

She shook her head, leaning back to look at me again. "I'm sorry it took me so long to pull my head out of my ass."

"I'm sorry I hurt you," I replied, and I hoped she saw the sincerity in my eyes when I tucked her hair behind her ear. "I can't promise I won't be a pain in your ass sometimes, but I promise to never hurt you again. Not like this."

She nodded, leaning up to kiss my lips briefly before she arched one brow. "So... you'll be my date to the wedding?"

I scoffed. "Like that's even a question. You better wear comfortable shoes, because we're going to be dancing all night."

"I'm a horrible dancer," she confessed.

I smirked, kissing her nose. "You can stand on my feet and I'll do all the work."

"I'm also sorry I didn't do some grand gesture," she added, waving her hand in the air. "I know you love romantic comedies, and I was trying to think of something super cute and clever to do but... well... when it came down to it, I wasn't patient enough to put a plan together like that. All I knew was that I was sorry, and that I wanted you, and that I had to tell you that as soon as I could."

"No grand gesture needed," I said, framing her face. "All I need is you."

I kissed her with my heart pounding hard in my chest, with every new pull of oxygen feeling like my first and my last all at once. I knew in my gut that this was one of those moments I'd never forget. This was the moment my entire life changed. This was the moment I found what I'd always been looking for.

Football, and love.

And now, *finally*, I had both.

"Now, take me back to your place," Belle said, breaking our kiss well before I was ready. "We have some sex to do."

I barked out a laugh at that. "Oh, do we now?"

"Mm-hmm," she said on a nod, already on her way over to the passenger side of my car. "I've been reading up on sports psychology, and there's a link between sex and sports performance. So, I figure, we've got a solid week of boning to do to get you ready for the next game."

I laughed again, tossing my bag in the back seat before I climbed into the driver side, leaning over to kiss my passenger before I started the engine.

"You know that's all a myth, right?" I asked with an arched brow. "There is no scientific evidence to prove that sex has any effect on sports performance — good or bad."

"Well, I think we should experiment, then. In the name of science."

I slid my hand over her knee to grip her thigh, putting the car in reverse. "I've never been so excited for a science project before."

"I really am sorry I didn't do a grand gesture," she said when we pulled out of the parking lot. "Zach even tried to convince me to take his famous hot dog costume, but I refused."

I frowned, trying to put the pieces together with the strange words that had just come out of her mouth. "Uh... famous what?"

She waved me off. "I'll show you the video later. Just know I saved you from an eyesore you'd never be rid of."

I chuckled, taking her word for it as I pulled her hand to my lips, kissing her knuckles as we drove through the streets en route to my condo.

We talked the whole way — her about her week, and me about mine, which really were quite similar when we broke them down to the molecular level. We had both been miserable, barely eating or sleeping, longing to talk to the other but feeling like we couldn't.

By the time I got her home, all I could think about was holding her and never letting her go.

It was dark in my place, the moon covered by a shadow of clouds, but I didn't have time to reach for a light switch before Belle had my hand in hers, tugging me back to my bedroom.

We shed articles of clothing along the way, her slipping her dress overhead and letting it puddle in the hallway floor, me yanking my t-shirt up the same way, her stepping out of her wedges, me nearly falling as I hopped out of my jogger pants. We made it to the bedroom with me in my briefs and her in a strapless bra and silky lace thong, and I stopped her when she reached for it, wanting to do the honors.

I dropped to my knees, kissing my way down her chest, her navel, the inside of her thighs. My thumbs skated between her hips and the fabric, and I peeled it down, cock throbbing at the sight of her bare pussy in my face.

She held onto my shoulders, stepping out of the thong now at her ankles, and then she unsnapped her bra, her beautiful breasts spilling out above me.

I groaned, reaching up to palm her with one hand and grabbing her ass with the other. I yanked her closer, kissing her mound, down, down, down, until my tongue swept over her clit.

Belle leaned into the touch with a moan, her hands fisting in what little hair of mine she could grab. She hiked one leg up onto my shoulder, allowing me better access, and I answered her plea with both hands holding her ass as I buried my face between those perfect legs.

I would have stayed down there all night, if she'd let me. I would have paid my penance in the form of making her come on my tongue time and time again. But I'd just barely gotten started when she pulled at my arms, urging me up, and then we tumbled into my messy bed in a tangle of mouths and limbs, kissing and touching, moaning and shaking like we were being touched for the first time.

"Please, Makoa," she begged when I was between her legs, her heels digging into my ass, nails dragging down my back.

My cock was buried between her lips, coated with her desire, and I flexed my hips, sliding my length up and down to rub her clit while she trembled at the sensation.

"*Please*," she echoed, nails all but drawing blood now.

I reached between us, positioning myself at her entrance, and then with both hands under her shoulders, I pulled her down onto me as I thrust inside, filling her in one long stroke, both of us shuddering in unison at the overwhelming feeling of being connected again.

For a long moment, I stayed there, deep inside her with her pussy tightening around me, our foreheads pressed together. Then, slowly, I began moving, withdrawing my hips only to flex them again, in and out, our hot breaths meeting between us in the sweetest symphony.

And that's when it hit me.

That moment, right there, with Belle moaning in my ear and her legs tightening around my waist, it all hit me.

She was here.

She forgave me.

She *loved* me.

She was mine.

Realization after realization pummeled me like unrelenting waves, and though I tried with all the strength I had left in me, I couldn't stop what happened next.

I tried to hide it, tried to bury my emotion in Belle's shoulder as I kept my pace, but it was no use. She stiffened in my arms, pressing back on my shoulders gently until I had no choice but to face her.

"Are you... are you *crying* right now?"

I tried to hide my face again, but Belle wouldn't let me, and she laughed before kissing all over my jaw and cheeks, her lips erasing my tears as they fell.

"Oh, my God, you are. You're crying."

She barked out a laugh then, and any proud man would have shriveled up and died right there on the spot. As it was, I didn't give a shit about pride, so I just laughed along with her.

"I can't help it," I said, kissing her neck. "I'm just... I'm so fucking happy."

She chuckled, framing my face until I looked at her fully. Her eyes searched mine, and I slowed my rhythm between her legs, soaking up every second of the way she looked underneath me in that moment.

"You really are a big softie, aren't you?" she asked on a smile.

I shrugged. "The biggest. You're going to have to hold me when we watch Hallmark movies."

She snorted.

"Still love me?"

At that, her smile widened, and she shook her head before her lips found mine. "I do. I really do. So fucking much."

I smiled against that kiss, savoring those words like they were the air I needed to survive.

And for the rest of the night, I showed her just how much I felt the same.

CHAPTER 23

Belle

I f I thought Makoa couldn't surprise me more than he already had in the time we'd been dating, I was proven wrong the second we stepped onto the dance floor at Gemma and Zach's wedding.

It was the strangest, most adorable, and most hilarious thing I'd ever seen, to see that six-foot-five mammoth of a man doing the moon walk, lawn mower, running man, floss, and more in a navy blue tuxedo that fit him like a glove. He was the center of attention, everyone gathering around him in a circle, clapping and laughing as he dove down onto the floor and did the worm all the way back to the edge of the dance floor. He hopped up like it was nothing, grooving his way back over to where I stood with my arms crossed shaking my head. But in the next breath, I was launched up into the air in a spin, and he caught me just as easily as he'd tossed me, twirling me around before he took me in his arms.

"You're a freaking nut!" I screamed over the music.

"I'm nuts for you."

He kissed my neck as I rolled my eyes at the cheesy line, but I couldn't even fake that I was annoyed for too long before I was laughing and kissing him back.

The truth was, I was happy to see him letting loose on the dance floor. God knows he needed it, after all the pressure he'd been under the last few weeks. I'd felt more like his coach than his girlfriend recently, helping him get his head right so he could show out in practice and in the final two pre-season games.

And boy, did he show out.

His third game was even more monstrous than his first, and the fact that he had a solid game last Sunday proved to his coach and the rest of his team that he could be depended on. Yes, he'd had a rough week, but he'd snapped out of it and come back with a vengeance.

And now, he was officially a Chicago Bear.

Tonight felt like a celebration of that as much as it did Zach and Gemma's love, especially with everything in the damn place being football themed. There was a Chicago Bears jersey with BOWEN on the back that everyone signed instead of a guest book. The dance floor had been painted like a football field, green with the yard lines, complete with a field goal post at each end that Makoa had swung on before landing in a half split at one point in the night.

From the centerpieces to the flowers, Gemma had found clever ways to weave in her and Zach's mutual love for the game into their big day, and as much as I had thought it was a hideously stupid idea in the beginning... it worked.

It was so beautifully them.

The day had gone off without a hitch, and as much as I'd sworn to keep my shit together, I'd cried a dozen times already — the first time being when I stood opposite Zach and watched his face as Gemma walked down the aisle to him, and the most recent being when Gemma and Zach held onto each other through their first dance. It had started with the soft, slow melody of "Can't Help Falling in Love" by Elvis Presley, which shocked me, honestly, because I never would have guessed that'd be their pick for their first dance. But when the music cut out and "The Final Countdown" came on instead, the two jokesters breaking out into a wild and crazy dance, I wasn't the only guest surprised. We'd all laughed and cheered, and it was Makoa who filled me in that the dance moves they were doing were from the final number in *Silver Linings Playbook*.

Because, of course.

At the base of it all, the only thing that mattered was that Gemma and Zach had permanent smiles on their faces throughout the day and into the night, too. They looked at each other in the way that made you want to both swoon and gag at the same time.

They were in love.

So desperately in love.

Makoa was a sweaty mess when I managed to drag him off the dance floor for a break. I chuckled when he flopped down into his chair, legs sprawled out, hand fanning himself. I grabbed a spare cloth napkin from an unused silverware roll and dabbed his forehead with it, smiling and shaking my head.

"You're going to be more sore from dancing than from practice today."

"No regrets," he said, flashing his signature smile.

He stole a kiss before we were joined by the newlyweds, and Zach flopped down in the seat next to Makoa, while Gemma wrapped her arms around my neck from behind.

"Are you guys having fun?!" she asked excitedly.

I poked her side, pulling her into my lap, big fluffy white dress and all. "Isn't it obvious?" I asked, gesturing to Makoa. "My boyfriend has already sweat himself out of his suit."

"Take the jacket off, man," Zach said, nodding to his own attire — which was the dress pants from his tux and the dress shirt, minus the tie and jacket. "Trust me. Game changer."

Makoa was already stripping out of his jacket when Gemma wrapped her arms around my neck, leaning her head against mine. "This has been the most perfect day," she said. "And to think I actually have a Chicago Bears *player* at my wedding!"

Makoa chuckled, he and Zach exchanging a look that made me curious what they were hiding.

"I mean, I always dreamed I would, but I never thought it would actually happen." She squeezed me a little tighter. "Thanks for making that dream come true, bestie!"

I laughed. "Yep. That's the only reason I'm dating him, to make your dream come true." I looked at Makoa, then. "You're cool with breaking up after tonight, right?"

There wasn't even a hint of a smile on his face when he answered. "We are never breaking up. You're stuck with me."

I sighed. "Fine." But I winked at him in the same breath.

Makoa looked at Zach again before he nodded to Gemma. "You know, it's funny you brought that up. When I was talking about your wedding at practice today, well... it piqued some interest."

Gemma frowned, confused.

"I hope you don't mind, but I invited a few friends to the party," Makoa said, looking behind where Gemma and I were seated.

We both peeked over our shoulders, and where I was still confused, Gemma's eyes bulged out of her head before she jumped out of her seat and covered her mouth, shaking her head as she took in the three new guests.

I was trying to get to know the game better, and the team, for that matter, but I still had a lot to learn. Still, even with my weak knowledge, it wasn't hard to see in that moment that three Chicago Bears football players had just walked into Gemma's wedding reception.

And she was freaking the fuck out.

"Oh my God. Oh my God. Oh my *God*." She sounded like a parrot, still frozen in place. Finally, she pointed a finger at the first one, a tall, lean, blond man in the middle. "You're Brad Thompson," she said, finger moving to the other two next. "And you're... you're William James, and... and..."

She couldn't even speak when she got to the last man, who was shorter than the rest but built like an absolute tank, the light gray tuxedo he was wearing a stark contrast against his black skin. He had a smile that could make panties wet on first sight, and he wore that smile with his hands in his pockets while he waited for Gemma to continue.

When she still didn't speak after a full ten seconds, he stepped forward, extending his hand. "I'm Mike Howard," he said, arching a brow. "And I *believe*, if what Kumaka here was saying earlier is true, that I'm your all-time favorite football player?"

It was a good thing Zach had gotten up out of his chair to stand beside his bride, because she nearly fainted with Mike's hand in hers. Her knees gave way, and she leaned into Zach with her eyes rolling up to the sky. I really thought she was going down, but then she bounced back, squealing with glee and launching herself at the poor guy.

He caught her on a laugh, giving the other players a look like *what the hell did we get ourselves into* before Gemma squirmed out of his grasp.

"I can't believe this!" She bounced on her toes, hands clasped together at her heart as she stared at all of them for a moment longer. She turned to Makoa then, complete shock and awe on her face. "You did this?"

"Hey, it was Zach who told me your favorite players. I just asked for a favor from my new teammates." Makoa winked at the guys, then, who all smiled in return, and then Mike held his hand out for Gemma's.

"If your husband doesn't mind, I think we oughta get out there for a dance or two. What do you say?"

Gemma scoffed, waving her hand over her shoulder. "I say whether my husband wants me to or not, let's dance!"

She was already tugging the guys onto the floor when Zach laughed, looking back at me and Makoa with a shrug. "That one's mine."

We laughed, too, and then Zach followed them out onto the dance floor, and the rest of the guests were pulling out their phones to snap pictures, realizing who the new attendees were.

I smiled at Makoa as he watched the dance floor, sliding into his lap and pressing a kiss to his cheek. "That was really sweet of you."

He shrugged. "It was nothing."

"Can you believe *you're* a Chicago Bear now?"

He chuckled. "Well, it's not my first NFL team, remember? But... I think this will be even better than San Francisco. I've got a chance to get some real playing time, and maybe, one day... I'll be a starter, and everyone will want *my* name on a jersey."

I frowned. "Hey, I'm supposed to be the only girl wearing your jersey."

"Might have to share me with the fans, babe."

I tilted my head to the side. "Hmm... I'll think about it." I smiled, kissing him quickly before I wrapped my arms around his neck with a sigh. "Man, with the season starting, I'm never going to see you, am I?"

"I'll have Tuesdays off... sort of."

I chuckled. "I'll take whatever I can get." I paused then, searching his honey eyes with my own. "I'm really proud of you."

Makoa answered with a deep, breath-stealing kiss, and then the DJ announced that it was time for all "the single ladies" to gather on the dance floor.

I groaned at the prospect, but Makoa shoved me out there, and I stood with my arms crossed in the back of a group of giggling, excited girls waiting for the bouquet.

Except when Gemma stood on the little stage at the front of the dance floor, she didn't have flowers at all.

She had a football.

Because, *of course.*

And I knew when I saw that devilish gleam in her eyes when she turned around that she was launching that sucker straight at me.

It was a flurry of hands and hair and chiffon when that ball was tossed in the air, but the girls had absolutely no chance at catching the ball. Gemma had thrown it high and far to the back where I stood, and I didn't have to move a single inch to reach up and catch it.

She turned, acting like she was surprised when she saw the ball in my hand, and she did a little dance of glee before hopping down off the stage and going back to dancing with the Chicago Bears players.

I made my way over to where Makoa still sat at the table, tossing the football to him when I was close enough.

He caught it easily, laughing and reading the writing on the ball once I was back in his lap.

"*Great catch, you're next!*" he read aloud, tossing the football up and catching it again before he looked at me. "What do you think of that?"

"What do *you* think of that?"

He shrugged, putting the ball aside and holding me in his arms. "I think you'd look pretty damn hot in a white dress."

I smiled. "That so?"

"Mm," he said, pulling me into him for a long, promising kiss. His lips found my ear next. "Belle Kumaka," he whispered. "Kind of has a ring to it, don't you think?"

My stomach filled with butterflies, their wings so powerful that they floated me up to standing, and I tugged on Makoa's hand until he was standing, too.

"Alright, Romeo. Let's just get through our first year of dating, huh? Then we can talk about weddings."

"You'll be lucky if I wait that long," he said as I pulled him out onto the dance floor. When we made it, he swept me up in his arms, pressing a kiss behind my ear. "I've been waiting my whole life for you, Belle Monroe. And I'm never letting you go now."

He kissed me again before I was spun out, twirled back in, and dipped back for a dramatic entry to the dance floor. I shoved him off me when we were standing again, rolling my eyes as he winked and did the cabbage patch over to where the rest of the team was dancing with Gemma and Zach.

For a long while, I stood at the edge of the dance floor, watching all of them. I watched my best friend smile like it was the best day of her life, and I knew without a doubt that it was. I watched her husband, who looked at her like she was his entire world, and I knew without a doubt that she was.

And I watched Makoa Kumaka, who paused mid-dance with furrowed brows like he'd lost something before he turned, finding me, and held his hand open with the most giant, goofy smile I'd ever seen.

He looked at me like I was his everything, like we were stupid in love, like no matter what life handed us from that moment on — we would make it.

And I knew without a doubt that he was right.

EXCLUSIVE CONTENT
Available in print edition only

Belle

The crisp mountain air bit at my cheeks as Makoa and I stepped out of the car and stared up at the luxurious log cabin perched against the snow-dusted Rockies. It was the kind of place you dreamed about but never thought you'd actually stay in — all high-beamed ceilings, stone fireplaces, and walls of glass overlooking a winter wonderland. The interior design nerd inside me was about to burst with the need to get inside and take in all the details.

This was going to be the perfect escape after the chaos of Makoa's football season.

The Chicago Bears had given it a good run, crowning themselves the NFC North champs before taking on some tough opponents in the playoffs. They hadn't made it all the way to the big game, but it had been a great season – one that proved the Bears were a team to watch out for in the coming seasons.

Makoa wrapped an arm around my shoulders, pulling me close. That man was all tattooed, tan muscle, but it was hidden under his thick coat at the moment. "Well? What do you think?"

"I think you've outdone yourself," I teased, tilting my head up to meet his golden-brown gaze. "But don't get too comfortable. I'll expect nothing less than a private island next year."

He threw his head back in a deep laugh, his breath puffing out in white clouds against the cold air. "Deal. But only if you're still putting up with me by then."

"Makoa Kumaka, don't even joke about that," I chided, swatting his chest. "You're stuck with me."

"Good." His voice dropped an octave as he pressed a kiss to my temple, sending warmth spiraling through me despite the chill.

As we moved to unload our bags, the crunch of snow behind us caught my attention. I turned to see a group of teenagers — all bundled up in puffy jackets —hovering nearby. They were whispering and pointing, their eyes locked on Makoa.

"Uh-oh," I muttered under my breath, but it was with a knowing grin.

Makoa followed my gaze, his signature smile spreading across his face. One of the teens finally worked up the courage to approach, clutching a notebook and pen. "Excuse me, Mr. Kumaka? Can I get your autograph? We're huge fans of the Bears."

"*Da* Bears," I corrected with a little smirk and shimmy, knowing that would make Gemma proud.

"Of course," Makoa said warmly, rolling his eyes at me before he crouched slightly to be at the teen's level. The others swarmed closer, and he signed notebooks, hats, and even a stray ski glove while making small talk about the season. His ease with people never ceased to amaze me. I also couldn't get over how lucky the sonofabitch was that he wasn't a known player when we first started dating. I re-membered a few times when fans stopped him and he pretended like they were people in the real estate industry that he'd met at conferences.

Little brat.

But God, I loved that brat.

I stood back, arms crossed, watching him charm everyone around him. Over the past year, I'd learned this was who Makoa was: generous, kind, and utterly magnetic. It didn't hurt that he looked like a walking Greek god, either.

And yet, as much as he belonged to the world, he always made me feel like I was his center.

When the fans finally dispersed, he turned to me with a sheepish grin. "Sorry about that."

"Don't be," I said, slipping my hand into his. "I'm just glad I get you all to myself for the next few days."

The ski lift creaked as it carried us up the mountain the next day. Makoa sat beside me, bundled in layers that made his broad shoulders look even broader. He was holding on to the safety bar like it was his lifeline.

"Remind me again why we're doing this?" he asked, his voice tinged with both amusement and fear.

"Because skiing is fun," I replied, patting his knee. "And because watching my beastly football player boyfriend kind of suck at something athletic is fun."

He groaned. "You're evil."

"You'll survive," I teased, leaning into him. "And besides, you've got the best teacher in the Rockies."

By the time we hit the slopes, Makoa's nerves had turned into full-blown panic. His first attempt down the bunny hill ended with him face-first in the snow. I couldn't help but double over laughing as he groaned and sat up, brushing snow off his goggles.

"This isn't funny, Belle," he grumbled, though the corner of his mouth twitched.

"Oh, it's hilarious," I shot back, reaching out to help him up. "You're like a baby giraffe learning how to walk."

"I'll remember this," he muttered, taking my hand.

The rest of the afternoon went much the same. Makoa fell. I laughed. He fell again. By the end of it, my cheeks hurt from smiling, and his were flushed red from both the cold and exertion.

On our final run, he gained a bit more confidence, gliding down the hill in wobbly but determined strides. Just as I thought he might make it to the bottom unscathed, his skis crossed, and he went down — hard.

Unfortunately, I was right behind him.

Which meant his tumble took me down with him.

We landed in a heap of tangled limbs and laughter, a cloud of snow bursting up around us. Makoa's arms wrapped around me, and I found myself pinned beneath him, our faces inches apart.

"If this was your plan all along," I said breathlessly, "it worked."

"You caught me." He grinned, his lips brushing mine as he spoke. "Anything to get you close."

And then he kissed me, the world around us disappearing in the warmth of his mouth and the way he held me like I was the most precious thing he'd ever known.

Later that night, the hot tub bubbled around us as we soaked under the stars. Snow fell in lazy flakes, catching in my hair and dissolving on Makoa's broad shoulders. He held me in his lap, his arms snug around my waist, my head resting against his chest.

"This is nice," I murmured, trailing my fingers over the ridges of his abs beneath the water.

"Mm-hmm," he agreed, his chin resting on top of my head. "Although, you keep touching me like *that* and we won't be out here much longer."

"Like this?" I teased, trailing a fingernail from hip to hip under the water.

He sucked in a breath, nibbling at my earlobe. "That's it. Inside we go."

Makoa hauled me over his shoulder as I laughed, but the cold air zapped all the jokes right out of me.

"Wait, wait, wait," I cried, poking his ribs. "I really am enjoying this! You can make me scream your name later. Right now, I want hot tub snuggles."

"As you wish, Miss Monroe," he said, and then we were back in the water and I was back on his lap, purring like a kitten as the water and his body warmed me again. "But behave yourself."

"No promises."

Makoa smirked, kissing my wet hair. "We should make this an annual thing."

"Me giving you a hard on in a hot tub?"

He tickled me until I was squirming, which only made his cock harder where I was rubbing against it.

"I meant an epic ski trip in the mountains," he growled against my neck. "But I like your idea, too."

"I'm in," I said. "But next time, I'm not spending half the day on the mountain waiting for you to get off your ass."

"That's a big assumption, considering how good I'll be by then," he shot back. "I'll be a pro, in fact. Did you see my last few runs? I'll be Marcel Hirscher level this time next year."

I laughed, tipping my head up to look at him. "Sure, babe. Whatever you say."

His answering smile was soft, his gaze tracing my features like he was committing them to memory. I could have stayed there forever, wrapped up in him, in the warmth of the water and the quiet of the moment.

But then, the words that had been buzzing in the back of my mind all day slipped out.

"Remember Zach and Gemma's wedding?" I asked, my voice barely above a whisper.

Makoa frowned slightly. "Of course. Why?"

"Because I caught the football," I said, unable to hide my grin. "You know, instead of a bouquet. And it said, *'Great catch. You're next.'*"

He laughed, the sound rich and deep. "I remember. I had to practically shove you out on the dance floor when she was about to throw it."

"That's not the point," I said, swatting his chest. Then, more quietly, I added, "So... what do you think about that?"

His laughter faded, and he went still, his eyes searching mine.

My heart thudded painfully in my chest, and I started to backtrack. "You don't have to answer that. I mean, I was just—"

"Belle," he interrupted, his hands framing my face. "You better be serious if you're saying you want to get married. Because I'll marry you tomorrow."

My breath caught. "What?"

"I'm serious," he said, his voice steady and sure. "I've known since the moment I met you that I wanted to make you my wife. I've just been waiting for you to be ready."

"You... want to marry me?"

"Hold that thought."

Before I could process what was happening, Makoa was climbing out of the hot tub, dripping wet and stark naked as he sprinted inside. I doubled over with laughter, watching him slip and slide on the snowy deck. A moment later, he returned, shivering but grinning as he sank back into the water.

"Close your eyes," he said.

"Makoa..."

"Just do it, Belle."

Rolling my eyes, I complied. When he told me to open them again, he was holding a small velvet box, the kind that held more promises than words ever could.

"I've had this since last February," he admitted, his voice tinged with nerves. "I've been waiting for the right moment, and... well, this feels like it."

Tears blurred my vision as he opened the box to reveal an engagement ring so exquisite it took my breath away. The centerpiece was an elongated oval diamond, its brilliant facets catching the light and scattering it in mesmerizing rainbows. The stone was set in warm rose gold, the metal's soft blush hue adding a romantic touch that felt perfectly me. Surrounding the diamond was a delicate halo of smaller diamonds, enhancing the center stone's sparkle without overwhelming its elegance. The band was slender and paved with even more diamonds, creating a seamless shimmer that caught the light with every movement.

"Belle Monroe," Makoa said, and my eyes flicked from the ring up to his warm eyes. "When we met, we both had rules. Three dates for me until I got intimate, and *only* three dates for you before you kicked me to the curb."

I chuckled a little at the memory. That version of myself seemed so far away now, but I still remembered her – scared, unsure, tired of being hurt.

"As I think we both know, those rules didn't hold true for either of us. And I think I've decided that you're my favorite person to break the rules for. To break rules *with*. And I can't think of anything I want more than to do reckless, stupid, bizarre things with you for the rest of my life."

He pulled my hand from the water, cradling my ring finger as he slid the ring out of the box and slid it over my first knuckle, waiting.

"What do you say, Miss Monroe." He smiled, big and bright and beautiful. "Feel like marrying me?"

I shook my head, eyes watering even though I tried my best to stop them. "I hate this sappy shit," I whispered.

"No, you don't."

"No," I agreed on a breath, sliding my finger inside the ring. "No, I really don't."

He chuckled, slipping the ring all the way on, and then he brough my hand to his mouth and kissed every knuckle.

"That a yes?"

"It's always been a yes," I said.

I kissed him then, fingers curling in his damp hair as he pulled me flush against him.

"Tomorrow?" he breathed between kisses.

I laughed. "Yeah. Sure. Tomorrow."

"I'm dead ass serious."

I blinked, pulling back to look at him. "You don't want a big wedding?"

"Do you?"

"*God*, no." I wrinkled my nose. "I mean, I wouldn't mind wearing a gorgeous dress, but I don't really have a desire to do the whole traditional thing."

"So, let's do something untraditional. Let's get married now. Tomorrow. On the mountain."

"What about your family?"

"Oh, my sisters will never let me live it down," he said with a grin. "But, maybe we can have a little party with family and friends back in Chicago."

"Or Hawaii," I suggested. "Much warmer there."

"A Hawaiian honeymoon *does* sound quite nice..." He paused, tracing the line of my jaw with his wet thumb. "Think Gemma will forgive us?"

"Honestly? She will probably thank us. She's a new mom now, remember? I bet the last thing she wants to do right now is be a maid of honor and try to plan a bachelorette party."

"Do *you* want a bachelorette party?"

"I want you," I said, folding my arms over his shoulders. "Now. Tomorrow. Next week. Next year. Forever."

Makoa shook his head, kissing me long and deep.

"That settles it then," he said, tapping my nose. "How fast do you think we can find a dress, tux, and officiant?"

The next day, we stood on a snow-covered mountaintop, just the two of us and the officiant we'd managed to procure through a local event planner. They'd been thrilled to help us throw everything together last minute, working with us into the night to ensure every detail was perfect. From the simple yet elegant bouquet of winter-white flowers in my hands to the tailored tux Makoa wore and the soft, lace-adorned dress that hugged my body, every piece had fallen into place like it was meant to be. Even the officiant, a woman with a warm smile and eyes as bright as the snowy backdrop, had immediately understood our vision.

Snow fell softly around us, a hushed blanket of magic that seemed to muffle the rest of the world. The only sounds were the occasional crunch of our boots in the snow and the steady cadence of my breath as I tried to calm my racing heart. The air was crisp, the chill biting at my exposed cheeks, but none of it mattered when I looked at Makoa.

He stood there like a vision, his broad shoulders draped in the sharp black of his suit, his honey-brown eyes locked on me with an intensity that left me breathless. His dark hair was dusted with tiny flakes of snow, and the contrast against his sun-kissed skin made my heart ache with how beautiful he was. The look in his eyes was one of unwavering certainty, as though he knew, deep down to his core, that this was exactly where he was meant to be.

"You're my best friend," he said, his deep voice steady despite the visible emotion tightening his throat. "My partner. My home. I promise to love you every day of my life, through every fall and triumph, for as long as I'm breathing."

My throat tightened, and tears spilled over before I could even think about stopping them. I tried to respond, but my voice broke, and I let out a shaky laugh. Makoa squeezed my hands, his thumbs brushing over my knuckles in silent encouragement.

When I finally found my voice, I repeated the vows we'd written together, the words flowing with effortless sincerity. "You're my best friend, my partner, my home. I promise to love you every day of my life, through every fall and triumph, for as long as I'm breathing."

The officiant smiled as she continued, but the words blurred as my focus remained on Makoa. Everything about this moment felt surreal. I couldn't believe this was real life, that I was standing on a mountaintop, marrying the man who had changed my entire world. It didn't seem like long ago that I had given myself the proud title of the girl you *don't* take home to mom, the girl you don't marry.

I was so glad that version of me was in the past.

That Belle ran from love and anything close to it, scared of being hurt again. I beat men to the punchline before they had the chance to say I wasn't what they were looking for because it felt safe.

But I was everything Makoa wanted.

I knew that just by the way he looked at me now.

"By the power vested in me, I now pronounce you husband and wife," the officiant said, her smile growing. "You may kiss your bride."

Makoa didn't hesitate. His hands released mine, moving to cup my face with a tenderness that made my chest ache. The kiss that followed was everything I'd come to expect from him – passionate, consuming, yet grounding all at once. It wasn't just a kiss; it was a promise, one that echoed everything we'd just vowed to each other.

When he finally pulled back, his forehead rested against mine, his warm breath mingling with the cold air. "What was it you said when we got here... that I was stuck with you?" He nuzzled my nose "Well, you're *really* stuck with me now, Mrs. Kumaka."

I laughed, brushing away the tears on my cheeks. "Good. I wouldn't want it any other way."

"I can't believe I got you to cry this much," he mused, thumbing a tear from my chin.

"If you tell anyone, I'll show them all the videos I have of you falling on the bunny hill."

As the officiant congratulated us and stepped back to give us a moment, Makoa grinned mischievously. "Speaking of, how about we make this official on the slopes?"

I barely had time to protest before he stepped into his skis, his movements confident despite the precariousness of the snow. I followed, laughing as I adjusted my gown around me and clipped into my own skis.

But true to form, Makoa's confidence got the best of him. Within seconds, he wobbled, his knees buckling as he attempted to steady himself. "Uh, oh."

"Don't you dare take me down with you—ahh!" I yelped as he toppled sideways, dragging me with him. We landed in a heap, our skis tangled and laughter spilling into the still mountain air. Snow clung to my hair, my dress, and Makoa's suit, but I couldn't bring myself to care. He wrapped his arms around me, pulling me closer as we lay there, surrounded by nothing but white.

"This is all your fault," I said, trying to sound annoyed but failing miserably as a laugh escaped me.

"Oh, absolutely," he agreed, his grin infectious. "But I'll make it up to you."

"Yeah? How?"

He leaned down, capturing my lips in another kiss, this one softer, slower, but no less consuming. When he pulled back, his eyes were warm and full of love. "By making you laugh every day for the rest of our lives."

I shook my head, biting back a smile. "You've got a lot of work ahead of you, Mr. Kumaka."

"I think this will be my favorite job yet."

And he cemented that sentiment with another snowy kiss.

A NOTE TO THE READER

Thank you for reading *The Right Player*! I hope you loved reading Makoa and Belle's story as much as I loved writing it. If you're new to me and my books, I love to keep in touch with my readers. So, if you want to stay in touch, too, you can...

Sign up for my newsletter
www.kandisteiner.com/newsletter
Follow me on Instagram
www.instagram.com/kandisteiner
Join my reader group on Facebook
www.facebook.com/groups/kandilandks

All My Love,
Kandi

If you enjoyed *The Wrong Game* and *The Right Player*, you'll fall in love with *A Love Letter To Whiskey* an angsty, emotional romance between two lovers, B and Jamie, fighting the curse of bad timing.

Read on for a sneak peek of their story.

A LOVE LETTER TO WHISKEY

PROLOGUE

Relapse

I t's crazy how fast the buzz comes back after you've been sober for so long.

I opened my door and felt tipsy just at the sight of him, eyes blurring and legs shaking. It used to take me at least a shot to get to this point, but my tolerance level had been weakened by distance and time, and just seeing him warmed my blood. I gripped the knob tighter, as if that'd help, but it was like trying to chug water after passing the point of no return.

Whiskey stood there, on my doorstep, just like he had one year before. Except this time, there was no rain, no anger, no wedding invitation — it was just us.

It was just him — the old friend, the easy smile, the twisted solace wrapped in a glittering bottle.

It was just me — the alcoholic, pretending like I didn't want to taste him, realizing too quickly that months of being clean didn't make me crave him any less.

But we can't start here.

No, to tell this story right, we need to go back.

Back to the beginning.

Back to the very first drop.

CHAPTER 1

First Taste

The first time I tasted Whiskey, I fell flat on my face. Literally.

I was drunk from the very first sip, and I guess that should have been my sign to stay away.

Jenna and I were running the trail around the lake near her house, sweat dripping into our eyes from the intense South Florida heat. It was early September, but in South Florida, it might as well have been July. There was no "boots and scarves" season, unless you counted the approximately six weeks in January and February where the temperature dropped below eighty degrees.

As it was, we were battling ninety-plus degrees, me trying to be a show off and prove I could keep up with Jenna's cheerleading training program while she laughed at how terrible my cardio was, despite how I claimed surfing was a better workout than running. She had finally made the varsity squad, and with that privilege came a rigorous fitness routine — crafted by her, not the coach — to get her in shape.

I hated running — absolutely *loathed* it. I would much rather have been on my surfboard that day. But fortunately for Jenna, she had a competitive best friend who never turned down a challenge. So, when she asked me to train with her, I'd agreed eagerly, even knowing I'd have screaming ribs and calves by the end of the day.

I saw him first.

I was just a few steps ahead of Jenna, and I'd been staring down at my hot pink sneakers as they hit the concrete. When I looked up, he was about fifty feet away, and even from that distance I could tell I was in trouble. He seemed sort of average at first — white skin, brown hair, lean build, soaked white running shirt — but the closer he got, the more I realized just how edible he was. I noticed the shift in the muscles of his legs as he ran, the way his hair bounced slightly, how he pressed his lips together in concentration as he neared us.

I looked over my shoulder, attempting to waggle my eyebrows at Jenna and give her the secret best friend code for "*hot guy up ahead,*" but she had stopped to tie her shoes.

And when I turned back around, it was too late.

I smacked into him — hard — and fell to the pavement, rolling a bit to soften the fall. He cursed and I groaned, more from embarrassment than pain. I wish I could say I gracefully picked myself up, smiled radiantly, and asked him for his number, but the truth is I lost the ability to do anything the minute I looked up at him.

It was an unfamiliar, warm ache that spread through my chest as I used my hand to shield the sun streaming in behind his silhouette, just how you'd expect the first sip of whiskey to feel. He was bent over, hand outstretched, saying something that wasn't registering because I had somehow managed to slip my hand into his and just that one touch had set my skin on fire.

Handsome wasn't the right word to describe him, but it was all I kept thinking as I traced his features. His hair was a sort of mocha color, damp at the roots, falling onto his forehead just slightly. His eyes were wide — almost too round — and a mixture of gold, green, and the deepest brown. I didn't coin the nickname Whiskey until much later, but it was that moment that I saw it for the first time — those were whiskey eyes. The kind of eyes you get lost in. The kind that drink you in.

He had the longest lashes and a firm, square jaw. It was so hard, the edges so clean that I would have sworn he was angry with me if it weren't for the smile on his face. He was still talking as my eyes fell over his broad chest before snapping back up to his sideways grin.

"Oh my God, are you fucking blind?!" Jenna's voice snapped me from my haze as she shoved Whiskey out of the way and latched onto my hand, ripping me back to standing position. I'd barely caught my balance before she whipped around to continue her scolding. "How about you brush that long ass hair out of your eyes and watch where you're going, huh, champ?"

Oh no.

I didn't even have time to call dibs. I couldn't even *think* the word, let alone say it, before it was too late.

I watched it, in slow motion, as Whiskey fell for my best friend before I had the chance to say a single word to him.

Jenna was standing tall, arms crossed, one hip popped in her usual fashion as she waited for him to defend himself. This was her standard operating procedure — it was one of the reasons we got along. We were both what you'd call "spitfires," but Jenna had the distinct advantage of being cripplingly gorgeous on top of having an attitude. She flipped her long, wavy blonde ponytail behind her and cocked a brow.

And then he did, too.

His smile grew wider as he met her eyes, and it was the same look I'd watched pass over guy after countless guy. Jenna was a unicorn, and men were enamored by her. As they should have been. My best friend was gorgeous. She had platinum blonde hair, crystal blue eyes, legs for days, and a personality to boot.

Now, before you go thinking that I was the insecure best friend — I had it going on, too. I loved my body, athletic and strong. I cherished the features that made me *me* — warm brown skin, gray-blue eyes, black curly hair. I was headstrong, I worked hard, and I was talented.

Just not at the things high school boys valued, it seemed.

But we'll get to that.

"Hi," Whiskey finally said, extending his hand to Jenna this time. His eyes were warm, smile inviting — if I had to pick the right word for him, just one, I'd say charming. He just oozed charm. "I'm Jamie."

"Well, *Jamie*, maybe you should make an appointment with the eye doctor before you run over another innocent jogger. And you owe Brecks an apology." She nodded to me then and I cringed at my name, wondering why she felt the need to spill it at all. She always called me B — everyone did — so why did she choose the moment I was face to face with the first boy to ever make my heart accelerate to use my full name?

Jamie was still grinning, eying Jenna, trying to figure her out, but he turned to me after a moment with that same crooked smile. "I'm sorry, I should have been watching where I was going." He said the words with conviction but lifted his brows on that last line because he and I both knew who wasn't paying attention to the trail, and he wasn't the guilty party.

"It's fine," I murmured, because for some reason I was still having a difficult time finding my voice. Jamie tilted his head just a fraction, his eyes hard on me this time, and I felt naked beneath his gaze. I'd never had anyone look at me that way — completely zeroed in. It was unnerving and exhilarating, too.

But before I could latch onto the feeling, he turned back to Jenna, their eyes meeting as slow smiles spread on both of their faces. I'd seen it a million times, but this was the first time I felt sick watching it happen.

I saw him first, but it didn't matter.

Because he saw her.

• • •

It was just over a week later that Jenna and Jamie put a title on the flirting relationship they'd been having for a solid eight days. That's how it was when we were in high school — there were no games, no "let's just hook up and see where this goes." You were either with someone or you weren't, and they were very together.

I had the privilege of watching them make out between classes, and as much as I wanted to hate them together, I just didn't. In fact, I'd pretty much forgotten that I'd seen Jamie first because they were disgustingly cute together. Jenna was taller than me, but she was just short enough to fit perfectly under Jamie's arm. She was a cheerleader, he was a basketball player — different seasons, but popular and respected at our high school in equal measure. His dark features complimented her light ones, and they had a similar sense of humor.

They even *sounded* good together — Jenna and Jamie.

I mean honestly, how could I be mad at that?

So, I dropped it, dropped the idea of him, and moved easily into the third wheel position I was used to with Jenna and her long list of boyfriends. Jamie was the first of them who seemed to enjoy me there. He was always talking to me, making jokes, bridging the gap between awkward and easy friendship. It was nice, and I was sincerely happy for them.

Still, I had opted out of tricycling that particular afternoon after school. Instead, I swung my JanSport onto my bed and immediately started ruffling through the clothes in my top drawer for my bathing suit, desperate to get some time on the water before the sun set. Daylight Savings hadn't set in yet, but the days were slowly getting shorter, reminding me that summer was far away.

"Hey sweetie," my mom said, knuckles rapping softly on the panel of my door frame. "You hungry? I was thinking we could go out for dinner tonight, maybe to that sushi bar you love so much?"

"I'm not really hungry. Going to go check out the surf," I replied, my smile tight. I didn't even look up from my drawer, just pulled out my favorite white, strappy top and avoided her eyes. I realized I sounded a bit like a dramatic teen who hated her mom in that moment, and I didn't. I loved her, but things were different between us than they had been just two short years before.

Okay, this is the part where I warn you — I had daddy issues. I guess in a way, mommy issues, too.

Let me explain.

Everything in my life was perfect, at least in my eyes, until the summer before my sophomore year of high school. That was the summer I opened my pretty gray eyes and looked around at my life, realizing it wasn't at all what it seemed.

I thought I had it all. My parents weren't married or even together, but then again they never had been. I was used to that. It was our normal. Mom never dated anyone, Dad dated but never remarried, and somehow we still always ended up together — just the three of us — every Christmas.

I'd always lived in my mom's house, but I'd spent equal time at my dad's. My parents never fought, but they never really laughed, either. I assumed they made it work for me, and I was thankful for that.

We were unconventional, me bouncing between houses and them tolerating each other for my sake, but we worked.

They may not have made enough at their respective jobs to shower me with birthday gifts or buy me a shiny new car on my sixteenth birthday, but they worked hard, they paid the bills, and they instilled that mindset in me, too. The Kennedy's may not have been rich in dollars, but we were rich in character.

Still, not everything is as it seems.

I never understood that saying — not really — not until that summer before tenth grade when everything I thought I knew about my life got erased in a violent come-to-Jesus talk. My mom had drunk too much one night, as she often did, and I'd humored her by holding her hair back as she told me how proud she was of me between emptying her stomach into our off-white toilet.

"You are so much more than I ever could have wished for," she kept repeating, over and over. But then the literal vomit turned to word vomit, and she revealed a truth I wasn't prepared for.

You see, the story I'd been told my entire life was that mom and dad were best friends growing up. They were inseparable, and after years of everyone around them making jokes about them dating, they finally conceded, and it turned out they were perfect together. They had a happy relationship for several years, a bouncing baby girl who they both loved very much, but it just didn't work out, so they went back to being friends. The end. Sounds sweet, right?

Except it was a lie.

The truth was much uglier, as it so often is, and so they hid it from me. But mom was tequila drunk that night and apparently had forgotten why she cared so much about lying to me. So, she spilled the truth.

They had been best friends, that much was true, but they had never dated. Instead, my dad had turned jealous, chasing every guy who dared to talk to my mom out of her life. But he didn't stop there. One night, when she was crying over the most recent guy who'd dumped her, my dad had come on to her. And he didn't take no for an answer.

Not the first time she said it.

Not the eleventh.

She counted, by the way.

Mom was seventeen at the time, and I was the product of that night — a baby not meant to be born from a horror not meant to be lived.

I guess this is the part where I should tell you I immediately hated my dad once I found out the truth, and in a way I did, but in another way I still loved him. He was still my dad, the guy who'd called me *baby girl* and fixed me root beer floats when I'd had a bad day. I wondered how the soft-spoken, caring man I'd grown up around could have committed such an act.

For a while, I lived in a broken sort of limbo between those two feelings — love and hate — but when I finally had the nerve to ask him about it, to tell him that I knew what happened, he had nothing to say. He didn't apologize, he didn't try to defend himself, and he didn't seem to hold any emotion other than anger that my mother had told me at all. After that, I slipped farther toward hate, and I stopped talking to him a short five months after the night my mom told me the truth.

And though I shouldn't have resented my mom for not telling me sooner, I did. She didn't deserve me to blame her for letting me think my father was a good person, but I did.

There was a raw wedge between us after that night, an unmovable force, and I felt the jagged splinters of it scrape my chest every time I looked at her.

So, more often than not, I chose not to.

"Okay," she replied, defeated. "Well, I hope you have fun." I was still rummaging, searching for my bottoms, and she turned to leave but paused long enough to call back over her shoulder. "I love you."

I froze, closed my eyes, and let out one long breath. "I love you too, Mom."

I would never not say those words. I loved her fiercely, even if our relationship had changed.

By the time I found my suit, dressed, strapped my board to the top of my beat-up SUV and made it to the beach, the weight of the day was threatening to suffocate me. But as soon as I set my board in the water and slid on, my arms finding their rhythm in the familiar burn that came with paddling out, I began to breathe easier.

The surf in South Florida was far from glorious, but it worked for my purposes. It was one of my favorite ways to waste a day, connected with the water, with myself. It was my alone time, time to think, time to process. I used surfing like most people used fitness or food — to cope, to heal, to work through my issues or ignore them, depending on my mood. It was my solace.

Which is why I nearly fell off my board when Jamie paddled out beside me.

"Fancy meeting you here," he mused, voice low and throaty. He chuckled at my lost balance and I narrowed my eyes, but smiled nonetheless. Everything I thought I knew about his body was erased in that moment and I swallowed, following the cut lines along his arms that led me straight to his abdomen. There was a scar there, just above his right hip, and I stared at it just a second too long before clearing my throat and turning back toward the water.

"Thought you had plans with Jenna."

He shrugged. "I did. But there was a cheerleading crisis, apparently."

We met eyes then, both stifling laughs before letting them tumble out.

"I'll never understand organized sports," I said, shaking my head.

Jamie squinted against the sun as we rode over a small wave, our legs dangling on either side of our boards. "What? You'll never understand having a team who works toward the same goal?"

I scoffed. "Don't be annoying. You know what I meant."

"Oh, so you hate fun?"

"No, but I hate *organized* fun." I glanced sideways at him then, offering a small smirk, and I grinned a little wider when the right side of his mouth quirked up in return. "I didn't know you surfed."

"Yeah," he answered easily. "Believe it or not, us organized-fun people enjoy solo sports, too."

"You're really not going to let this go, are you?"

He laughed, and I relaxed a bit. So what, Jamie was impossibly gorgeous and had the abs of the young Brad Pitt? I could do this, be friends, ignore the little zing in my stomach when he smiled at me. It was nice to have a friend other than Jenna. Where she made friends easily, I tended to push people away — whether by choice or accident. Maybe the Jamie-B-Jenna tricycle wouldn't be so bad, after all.

But when I truly thought about that possibility, of having a guy as a friend, my stomach dropped for a completely different reason. A flash of Mom bent over our toilet hit me quickly, her eyes blood-shot and her truthful words like ice picks in my throat. I swallowed, closing my eyes just a moment before checking the waterproof watch on my wrist.

"We should try to catch this next wave."

I didn't wait for him to answer before I paddled out.

We surfed what we could, but the waves were sad that day, barely offering enough to push our boards back to shore. Eventually, we ended up right back where we started, legs swinging in the salt water beneath us as we stared out at the horizon. The sun was slowly sinking behind us, setting on the West coast and casting the beach in a hazy yellow glow.

"Where do you go when you do that?"

"Do what?" I asked.

"You have this look, this faraway stare sometimes. It's like you're here, but not really."

He was watching me then, the same way he had the first day we met. I smoothed my thumb over one of the black designs on my board and shrugged.

"Just thinking, I guess."

"Sounds dangerous."

He grinned, and I felt my cheeks heat. "Probably is. You should steer clear."

Jamie chewed the inside of his lip, still staring at me, and opened his mouth to say something else, but didn't. He turned, staring in the same direction as me for a few moments before speaking again.

"So, what are you thinking right now?"

I let out a long, slow breath. "Thinking I can't wait to get out of here, move to California, and finally surf a real wave."

"You're moving?"

"Not yet. But hopefully for college."

"Ah," he mused. "I take it you have no interest in going to Palm South University, then?"

I shook my head. "Nah, too much drama. I want a laid-back west coast school. Somewhere with waves that don't suck."

Jamie dipped his hand into the water and lifted it again, letting the water drip from his fingertips to the hot skin on his shoulders. "Me too, Brecks. Me too."

I cringed at the use of my name. "It's just B."

"Just B, huh?"

I nodded. "You want to go to school in California, too?"

"That's the plan. I have an uncle out there who has some connections at a few schools. You have a specific one in mind yet?"

"Not yet. Just somewhere far from here."

He nodded once, thankfully not pushing me to expand on that little dramatic statement. We sat in silence a while longer before paddling back in and hiking our boards up under our arms as we made the trek back to the cars. The sand was a bit course under our feet, but I loved the way it felt. I loved everything about the beach, especially surfing, and I glanced over at Jamie, more thankful than I thought I would have been running into him.

He helped me load up after we rinsed off, strapping my old lime green board to the top of Old Not-So Faithful. And just like the reliable Betty that she was, the 1998 Kia Sportage failed to turn over when I tried to start her up.

"Great," I murmured, my head hitting the top of the steering wheel. Jamie had just finished loading his own board a few cars away, and he made his way back over.

"Not starting?"

"Seems to be my lucky day."

He smiled, tugging the handle on my door to pull it open. "Come on, I'll drive you home."

I didn't know it then, but that one small gesture, those six small words, they would be what changed everything between me and Jamie Shaw.

A LOVE LETTER TO WHISKEY

This paperback will be available from October 2025. Pre-order now to secure the first print deluxe edition featuring new and exclusive content – supplies limited.

MORE FROM KANDI STEINER

THE WRONG GAME

Available now

Gemma's plan is simple: invite a new guy to
each home game using her season tickets for the
Chicago Bears. It's the perfect way to avoid getting
emotionally attached and also get some action.
But after Zach gets his chance to be her practice round,
he decides one game just isn't enough.
A sexy, fun sports romance.

ACKNOWLEDGEMENTS

A book does not get written by just one person. It takes an entire team to bring this sort of magic to life, and I'm so thankful to have the best team by my side. I'll try to keep this brief, but bear with me...

Jack, I'm pretty sure this book would have been a disaster without you. Thank you for letting me talk to you about plot all hours of the night, and for helping me with all my football questions when it came to researching for Makoa, and for always rubbing my shoulders and reminding me I could do it on the days where it felt like I couldn't. Your love and support means the world to me, and I'm lucky to have you in my life.

I'll never be able to write an acknowledgement section without thanking Staci Hart, who is there throughout the daily grind of every book I write. Thank you for sprinting with me, pushing me on the days I was stuck, and reading my book baby when I needed extra eyeballs. As always, your feedback took this book from one level to the next, and I am so thankful. More than tacos, babe. Always.

I want to shout out a group of my friends, who listened to my weird brain dump thoughts about this book before I'd even sat down to plot it. Sasha, Maggie, Hannah, and Angel – thank you for getting as excited as me about Makoa and Belle. Your ideas and enthusiasm helped more than you'll ever know, and I love all of you.

I truly have the most amazing team, when it comes to alpha, beta, and charlie readers. That may sound like a lot of nonsense to most people, but essentially, these are the first brave souls to read my rough draft and help me figure out what's missing, what could be better, and what needs just a little fine tuning. So, thank you SO much Kellee Fabre, Trish QUEEN MINTNESS, Sarah Green, Danielle Lagasse, Carly Wilson, Zainab M., and Sasha Erramouspe. You're all the bees knees, and I hope you'll never ever leave me.

I also want to shout out two lovely humans who hopped on board especially for this project – the lovely K.K. Allen and Nikki Terrill. With Makoa being Polynesian and from Hawai'i, I wanted to make sure I got everything right with the culture, language, and more. Thank you for being amazing sensitivity readers and helping me as I wrote. This book would not have been the same without you!

There are only a few authors lucky enough to have Tina Stokes as their personal assistant, and I'm one of them. Tina, you are not only the most helpful and thoughtful PA to exist, but also one of my dearest friends. I am so happy this book world brought us together. Thank you for always loving my book babies as much as I do.

Elaine York of Allusion Publishing is responsible for polishing up the final rough draft of this bad boy and formatting it into the edition you're reading now. Elaine, we've been working together for years now, and I'm forever thankful for your professionalism, friendship, and willingness to work with me – the scatter-brained PITA I can be. Thank you so much for all your love, time, and attention.

To the lovely ladies of the Valentine PR team, thank you for helping make this release a stellar one. I'm so thrilled to be working with the best of the best.

A heartfelt thank you to my incredible agent, Ariele Fredman. Your belief in this book matched my own, and I'm endlessly grateful for championing it and breathing new life into it with a print publishing deal. Here's to an exciting future ahead!

To Sarah Jane, a brilliant illustrator with the sweetest touches — thank you for capturing Belle and Makoa so beautifully in this stunning new cover. I'm absolutely in love with it and everything you create.

In this updated acknowledgments section, I want to extend my deepest thanks to the incredible team at Keeperton and Arndell for seeing the potential in this story and breathing new life into it with a print deal. The thought of walking into a bookstore and spotting Belle and Makoa on the shelf brings me to tears. Christine and the entire team — thank you for your unwavering support and belief in me. Here's to crafting more unforgettable moments together!

The truth is that hardly ANYONE would be reading this if it weren't for the amazing bloggers we have in the indie romance community. Thank you to everyone who read ARC copies, reviewed, shared, and raved about *The Right Player*. I am beyond thankful for each and every one of you.

I have this small little corner of the interwebs where all my favorite people hang out, and it's called Kandiland (http://www.facebook.com/groups/kandilandks). I remember when that group was just me, a friend who twisted my arm into creating it in the first place, and my mom. Now, we have more than 10,000 members, and every single one of them feel like a close friend of mine. Thank you, Kandiland, for being my cheerleaders, support team, and just the best place online. I love you all.

And finally, to you, the amazing reader who made it ALL THE WAY to the end of the acknowledgements – thank you. Thank you for reading indie. Thank you for reading romance. And more than anything, thank you for picking up MY book when you have so many choices. I am eternally grateful, and I hope you'll stick around for many more books to come.

ABOUT THE AUTHOR

KANDI STEINER is a *USA Today* and #1 Amazon Bestselling Author living in Tennessee. Best known for writing "emotional rollercoaster" stories, she loves bringing flawed characters to life and writing about real, raw romance — in all its forms. No two Kandi Steiner books are the same, and if you're a lover of angsty, emotional, and inspirational reads, she's your gal.

An alumna of the University of Central Florida, Kandi graduated with a double major in Creative Writing and Advertising/PR with a minor in Women's Studies. Her love for writing started at the ripe age of 10, and in 6th grade, she wrote and edited her own newspaper and distributed to her classmates. Eventually, the principal caught on and the newspaper was quickly halted, though Kandi tried fighting for her "freedom of press."

She took particular interest in writing romance after college, as she has always been a hopeless romantic and found herself bursting at the seams with love stories she was eager to tell.

When Kandi isn't writing, you can find her reading books of all kinds, planning her next adventure, or pole dancing (yes, you read that right). She enjoys live music, traveling, hiking, yoga, spending quality time with her family (fur babies included) and soaking up the sweetness of life.

CONNECT WITH KANDI:
NEWSLETTER: kandisteiner.com/newsletter
FACEBOOK: @kandisteiner
FACEBOOK READER GROUP (Kandiland):
facebook.com/groups/kandilandks
INSTAGRAM: @kandisteiner
TIKTOK: @authorkandisteiner
WEBSITE: kandisteiner.com

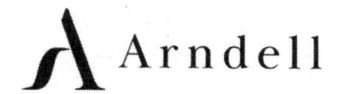

Connect with Arndell
Love this book? Discover your next romance book
obsession and stay up to date with the latest releases,
exclusive content, and behind-the-scenes news!

Explore More Books
Visit our homepage: keeperton.com/arndell

Follow Us on Social Media
Instagram: @arndellbooks
Facebook: Arndell
TikTok: @arndellbooks

Stay in the Loop
Join our newsletter: keeperton.com/subscribe

Join the Conversation
Use **#Arndell** or **#ArndellBooks** to share your thoughts
and connect with fellow romance readers!

Thank you for being part of our book-loving community.
We can't wait to share more unforgettable stories with you!